Now and Then in Tuscany

ANGELA PETCH

For my children: Jonathan, Emily and Rosanna.

"Com'è triste fare una passeggiata in campagna!
La maggior parte è abbandonata.
Non si sente più il chiasso dei contadini, il canto dei pastori, il belare delle pecore, il muggito delle vacche, il tintinnio dei campani ché ogni gregge aveva il suo sonaglio..."

"How sad it is to walk in the countryside now!
Most of it has been abandoned.
You no longer hear the sounds of country folk, the singing of shepherds, the bleating of sheep, the lowing of cattle, the tinkling of bells particular to each flock..."

[From "Sù, Bellarosa...sù, Pastorella!"
Published by "Dina Dini", documentation centre of peasant life,
Pieve Santo Stefano (AR).]

i

Acknowledgments

On a misty Sunday in late September 2012, I joined my local friends from Badia Tedalda on an outing down to the Tuscan coast. *'Si va in Maremma per la festa del ritorno,'* they told me and I was intrigued about this nostalgic pilgrimage. I learned on the long journey how their relatives (and indeed a few of the elderly passengers themselves) used to make this trek on foot at the start of the long mountain winters because they had no choice. Out spilled the stories of hardship, of families separated for five whole months. I heard about bandits, cowboys and malaria infested swamps. My imagination prickled. In the museum of Alberese I discovered old recipes, grainy photos of peasants, antiquated machinery, tools, clothes and accounts of life away from home. And so I began to research further and to write "Now and Then in Tuscany", a sequel to my first novel "Tuscan Roots".

My thanks go to Fulvio Pieghai for persuading me to join in that day and subsequently providing me with encouragement and documents. The Villa Garavelle Folk museum at Città di Castello was a revelation. Maria Assunta Bellucci shared her photographs, Andrea Meschini helped with maps, Pierluigi Ricci let me use his paintings for the cover and Ben Harvey patiently put it together with his talented eye. Thanks also to my Beta readers from Sea Scribes and Arun East U3A, to Maureen Blundell (aka Roz Colyer) for her editing skills and to Alison MacLeod for her timely lecture at Worthing WOW Festival 2016, on "Editing your Novel".

But most of all *grazie infinite* to Maurice, who lets me scribble away in Italy while he hacks at weeds and grows delicious vegetables.

Main characters

NOW

Francesco Starnucci
Anna Starnucci (neé Swilland)
(Parents of: Alba, Davide, Rosanna and Emilia)
Teresa Starnucci – Francesco's sister

Giselda Chiozzi – an elderly descendant of important local landowners

THEN

Vincenza and Olinto Starnucci
(Parents of Giuseppe Starnucci, Francesco Starnucci (d. 1915), Angelo, Maria Rosa and Nadia)

Marisa (neé Bravini) – a herbalist
Dario Starnucci – Giuseppe's son

Luisella Sciotti – a waitress

***

Author's note: In the map, the Via dei Biozzi is the actual route of the *transumanza*. I have changed the family name to Chiozzi.

Many of the illustrations in my book are copies of old, original photographs and as such, the quality is grainy and indistinct. I have chosen to include them as testament to a past way of life.

PROLOGUE - 1957

Old Giuseppe had been in the bar playing cards, making a couple of glasses of wine last three hours. His friend Franco had been grumbling on about his grandson's cushy life, how the spoilt, mollycoddled rascal wouldn't have lasted even one afternoon of what they'd had to endure as youngsters.

'Suffering begins the journey to wisdom,' he'd pronounced, slapping his losing cards on the table. This remark had set Giuseppe's own memories stirring again, like leaves scuttling down dusty cobbled paths.

After the noisy game of *briscola* was over he set off home. In the corner of the piazza, a battered Fiat Topolino was parked alongside a sleek Lancia where, once upon a time, mules and horses had been tethered.

As he made his way down the alley steps to his house, he pondered how different his life would have been if he'd been wise when still green behind the ears. Mistakes in his youth had led him to sleep with the wrong woman in the wrong bed; to live a life he wouldn't have chosen; to travel a long way to eventually find peace. He thought of all the hardships he had endured. Perhaps Franco had a point about the journey to wisdom.

The key was hanging from the latch by its length of string. So engrossed was he in his thoughts that letting himself into the cool shade beyond the sun-blistered door he called out, 'Luisella, I'm back. Put on the pasta.'

But Luisella had been gone for years. His mind was playing tricks again and he wasn't hungry. These days he was never hungry.

The wine had been strong and the August heat had drained him of energy. Leaning his stick against the cherry-wood table and heaving himself onto the bed, he stretched out and within minutes he was asleep, dreaming of his past.

The setting sun spilled orange, pink and red onto a glass-calm sea. Giuseppe swam towards the island: a dark, triangular silhouette looming in front of him. With each stroke he could only tread water, his arms and legs leaden as if in treacle. He had to get there before the sun disappeared and the world turned black. She was waiting.

The sea's mood changed. Waves heaved and crashed into deep valleys, like ravines he'd crossed on journeys from his mountains. Salt spray stung his eyes and each wave swept up a new image. The frothy foam was a flock of sheep, a dozen riderless horses tossed manes in thundering surf and the sun's dying rays were embers from a camp fire. He recognised faces of old shepherds as they stretched hands towards the glow. He thought he heard a bell clanging from a gelder's collar but it might only have been the clink of shells and pebbles tumbling to the shore. Giuseppe was dragged back to the sea's edge where skeleton trees and driftwood were piled like funeral pyres on the sand. In lace-edged shallows, the dwindling tide lapped at his bruised body like the tongue of a cat or the touch of a woman, stroking and caressing him, teasing him.

He grunted, turned over and drifted into deeper sleep.

NOW

Chapter 1

2010 – Francesco, Anna and family

Francesco peered at his son over the top of his newspaper, the *Corriere della Sera*. Davide was flat on his back on the stone floor of their converted stable, La Stalla, bouncing a tennis ball off the beams of the large sitting room.

'Davi, I'm only going to ask you once more to stop that, or there'll be trouble. You're going to break something.'

With an exaggerated sigh, the boy scrambled to his feet and moved over to the window.

Rain poured down the steep banks separating the garden from the meadows. The roar of the swelling river crashing over the weir near the road bridge was loud in the sitting room, despite double glazing and thick, stone walls. Curtains of rain almost obliterated the view of the mill, Il Mulino, which the family rented out to holidaymakers. Davide wondered what the guests were doing to occupy themselves inside. This morning two girls had been sunbathing on the grass at the river's edge. No chance of that now. Only half an hour earlier he and his father had been engrossed in putting finishing touches to a long awaited den up in the walnut tree. In summer its wide branches shaded the mill race which ended up in the former mill pond, now an ornamental garden area.

He would have preferred a den built in one of the oaks nearer La Stalla. He sighed again as he thought of how he'd now have to share the tree house with children staying at the mill.

'It's soooo boring being stuck indoors,' he moaned.

'Careful…you know what happens when I hear that word. I'll find you an *interesting* job,' Francesco said, folding his paper and walking over to his son. 'Boredom is banned in this household. I thought you had some homework to finish anyway. If it's not done when Mamma comes back with the girls, you'll be getting grief from her too.'

'Don't know where to start.' Davide blew onto the window pane, doodling a picture of a pin man with an unhappy mouth. 'Haven't got any grandparents to help me with my homework like others in my class,' he muttered.

'What about some help from your old Dad?'

Davide squinted up at his father through his glasses. 'You're not old, Babbo. At least not very. Your hair's a bit grey and you've got wrinkles round your eyes. But you're not old.'

Francesco chuckled. 'They're laughter lines but thank you for the compliment.'

He swept up the little boy and dangled him upside down, wondering for how much longer he would be allowed to play like this. His ten-year-old son had shot up recently and Anna had taken him down to Sansepolcro on a shopping expedition to buy new clothes. She'd commented afterwards how much easier it was to shop for boys, although their three daughters were not nearly as streetwise and fashion conscious as some of the children who came to stay at Il Mulino during summer.

He set Davide down. 'Very trendy,' he said, ruffling up his son's already unruly hair, sticking up as if gelled into a style. 'What is this awful homework then?'

'Research about relatives who moved away from here. What they did, why, where they went - all that kind of boring stuff.'

'That word again!' Francesco waggled his finger. 'Bored people are boring…'

'But it's soooo unfair. Everybody else has grandparents still alive and they've been able to record what they did and it's easy-peasy for them. I don't know where to start and Signorina Grazia warned us we've got to get good marks and those who don't can't go away for the sports trip in June and I know I'll be one of them…'

He broke off before tears fell. He hated crying, tending to button up his feelings, unlike his twin sisters who chatted away like nightingales. In many ways, Francesco thought, Davide was like his mother. Brought up in England, Anna was not as gregarious or extrovert as many Italians, although she had Italian ancestry. Francesco had helped her in many ways – not least in translating her Italian mother's war diaries and, in so doing, they had discovered her father was not the Englishman she had known but, in fact Danilo, a local Italian who had died seven years ago. Over the ten years of their marriage he had found ways to winkle Anna out of her introspection.

'Right!' Francesco said, clapping his hands together. 'Bring me the biggest piece of paper you can lay your hands on and we'll see if we can put together a family tree.'

Half an hour later, when his younger twin sisters returned from Music Club with Mamma, father and son were kneeling on the floor by the stove and already had a few names written in thick black felt-tip pen on their tree.

'What are you two doing?' Emilia, the slightly taller twin, dark hair plaited to her waist, was the more outgoing. Rosanna, also brunette, but with a pudding basin crop, picked up Emilia's music bag which had been dumped by the door and tidied it away into the basket labelled with her name. Anna had devised this system of individual baskets for her children in an effort to keep the farmhouse-style kitchen tidy. Her brood, ranging from eight-year-old twins to eighteen-year-old Alba (Francesco's daughter from his first marriage), took some organising. Anything to avoid extra stress on chaotic school mornings was a bonus.

'We're building up a family tree,' Davide answered, tongue on his bottom lip as he concentrated on spelling his paternal grandfather's name.

'S- t- a- r- n- u –c- c- i,   D- a- r -i -o. When did you say Nonno was born, Babbo?'

'1923 and his birthday was in May, but we'll check on dates and names at the *Comune* where everything is recorded. Maybe Mamma can take you in after school on Monday?' Francesco looked over to Anna, eyebrows raised in question.

'Did Nonno go abroad?' Davide asked, sitting back on his haunches. 'Gianni's grandfather went to work in France.'

'Your grandfather stayed in Italy. And so did your great-grandfather Giuseppe. But he had to go down to the Maremma every year during winter months.'

'We've learnt about the Maremma area at school. Signorina Grazia told us it was very hard work on the coast because of malaria and that we don't realise how lucky we are that our families don't have to go there anymore.'

'So you've studied about the *transumanza?*'

'Yes, but not that much.'

Rosanna, who had been poring over the names on the family tree, piped up with, 'It's when men took sheep and cows down to graze at the sea-side during winter.'

Emilia added, 'And they stayed away for months and months, because there was no work up here and it was too cold to work because of the snow and everything.'

'Correct!' beamed Francesco.

Anna came over to Davide and ruffled his hair. 'Well, I know very little about it.' She crouched down beside him to look at the chart on the floor.

Francesco looked up from what he was writing. 'I suppose people who've always lived up here take it for granted. It was a given that from October until May there was mass migration of men to the coast. There was no choice and it went on until the 1950's. You remember when we first met and you asked me to help you look into your parents' past in Italy? How difficult it was to get people to talk to us about the war years? They wanted to forget and I suppose it's the same about the *transumanza*. Now they're no longer poor, past hardships are best forgotten in their eyes. But I think it's brilliant children are studying about their heritage at school.'

'Was Nonno like that too?' asked Davide. 'Didn't he want to talk to you about it?'

'He didn't talk about the past much at all. But I do know your great-grandfather Giuseppe was a cobbler and farrier,' Francesco continued. 'Somewhere in the attic there are some old horse shoes he made. He was an expert in forging them for lame animals and won awards in Rome for his work. Maybe you could take some in to show at school?'

'That would be cool,' the little boy said. 'Signorina Grazia's set up a table in the classroom and there's already stuff on there like old tools and a pair of boots that Maria's grandfather wore. They're clumpy and full of holes.'

'I'll see if I can gather more information for you, Davide,' Francesco said. 'I've some books we can look through together.'

'And if you want more details about the English side of the family I could help you fill that in too.' Anna said, picking up a pen to start writing the names of her half-brother and sister, Harry and Jane. But Davide swiped it from her hand.

'No, no – the English side doesn't matter, Mamma. This is just about family in Tuscany.'

'And he doesn't like having English family anyway, do you,

Davide?' Emilia added in a knowing tone.

'Don't you? Why not, sweetheart?' their mother asked, getting up from the floor to start preparations for supper.

Davide shrugged and continued to write on the sheet.

'It's because he gets teased in English lessons,' Rosanna explained. ' They tell him he's showing off because he knows all the answers,' she said, turning a perfect somersault but knocking over the pot of marker pens in the process. 'And they call him Harry Potter 'cos of his glasses and because he's got some *inglesi* relatives.'

'Now look what you've done, you cretin,' Davide shouted at his sister, jumping up and running from the sitting room, pounding up the wooden staircase to his bedroom.

His door slammed and there was silence for a few seconds. Anna put down the knife she was using to chop onions and made to follow him but Francesco persuaded her to leave him to stew for a while. 'Are you worried about him calling his sister a cretin or the fact he's being picked on at school for having English connections?' he asked, rolling up the family tree and securing it with an elastic band.

'Both!'

'Let's deal with it later, darling. Leave him be for a while.'

Anna returned to supper preparations, wondering what on earth she had managed to fill her time with before having children. "B.C", they jokingly described it. She loved all of them to bits. But there were times when she longed to escape from the bedlam of family life. Lately she felt constantly tired. Some mornings she forced herself to put one foot in front of the other to confront the day. And she was putting on weight despite being careful with her diet. She worried there might be something seriously wrong, but it was easier to push nagging thoughts to the back of her mind. She craved one week on her own: one week of blissful quiet without the confusion and togetherness Italians craved. To go to bed late if she wanted without a six a.m. alarm call. Time to read a whole book in one sitting or drink wine in the middle of the day, without the responsibility of being the afternoon chauffeur to one of her children: for swimming lessons, music clubs, gymnastics and now regional tennis coaching, for which Davide had been selected. And a week of sleeping in a bed on her own might be good, she thought - without having to get up to soothe a child's nightmares or being kept awake by Francesco's snores or his hand stroking her thigh, when sex was the very last thing on her mind...

'Penny for them?' Francesco had crept up behind her, folding her in a hug, nuzzling the back of her neck as she tried to concentrate on chopping parsley and celery for a meat sauce.

'You wouldn't want to know,' she said, thinking that he really wouldn't and that she was an ungrateful cow to fantasize about a life without them.

'Mamma, Babbo, stop it!' Rosanna and Emilia were trying to insinuate themselves between their parents to break up their embrace.

'Is supper nearly ready?' Emilia, always hungry, asked.

In bed that evening when the children were asleep, Anna and Francesco talked through their day.

Francesco told her how he'd sat with Davide up in his room, sketching out more ideas for their tree-house. Last month their son had announced he was too old to listen to bedtime stories but they recognised he still needed the same special time they devoted to all their children before lights-out.

'I don't think it's too serious, this teasing,' he told Anna. 'Children don't like being different, that's all.' Francesco said, placing the latest Camilleri detective story on his bedside table.

'Would it help, do you think, if I had a word with Signorina Grazia? Perhaps I could offer to help with English lessons and try and suss what's going on?'

'Maybe wait a while to see if he can sort it out himself? Sometimes it's worse when parents stick their noses in.' Francesco had taught for several years at Bologna University and despite his students being older than Davide, he was a good mentor and had a special sensitivity with youngsters.

Anna yawned, plumping up her pillow before settling down. 'I suppose you're right. But it's a shame if he's being picked on for having English connections.'

Snuggling nearer, Francesco stroked her arm. 'He'll be fine. Don't worry.'

And a little later, 'Are you tired again?' His hand had moved to her breast but she gently removed it.

'I'm sorry, *tesoro*. I'm not in the mood tonight and tomorrow I have to take Davide down first thing for a tennis lesson in Sansepolcro, remember?'

'Maybe you should think about booking an appointment for a check-up?'

'No, no – I'm fine. Just tired. It's to be expected with four children to look after.'

'Plus a demanding husband,' he added.

'Sorry, *tesoro*.'

'Only kidding, my darling.'

Kissing her chastely on her forehead he wished her sweet dreams, wondering if when they were sixty, with no children living at home, there would be more time for each other. They made love far less nowadays and he was worried at Anna's constant fatigue. She was due a break. He thought about asking his sister, Teresa, to take over for a couple of days sometime soon. Then he would whisk Anna away for a weekend.

Upstairs in his attic bedroom, Davide shone his torch on the gap where the poster of Big Ben had been. After Babbo had pulled up his covers and kissed him goodnight, he'd tiptoed from bed and ripped it up, hiding the pieces in his secret box at the back of his clothes cupboard. The picture of the tower of Pisa could definitely stay, he decided, along with the framed photos of Uncle Harry's Labradors. Dogs couldn't help it if they were English and anyway they were really cute.

He felt beneath the quilt where he hid Steggy during the day and, hugging the green velvet dinosaur to his chest, he was soon asleep.

Chapter 2

At the weekend Francesco carried a breakfast tray up to Anna. On it was a pot of tea, brioches warmed in the oven, a bowl of home made plum jam and a single red rose picked from beside the entrance porch. He climbed back into bed, turning to kiss her. But she covered her mouth with her hand, 'Sorry…haven't brushed my teeth yet.'

He laughed, 'Never used to matter.'

'Yes, well, ten years down the line and three children later, lots has changed.'

Nevertheless she reached over to him, planting a kiss on his mouth. 'To what do I owe this lovely treat?'

'No reason and every reason,' he replied, pouring her a cup of tea. His morning drink was always a strong espresso which he had already knocked back in the kitchen.

'Sunday morning. Twins watching cartoons. Alba and Davi dead to the world. I thought we'd have breakfast on our own, for a change.'

'Thank you, *tesoro*.'

As he spooned jam onto her plate, he glanced at her pale face and the bruised shadows under her eyes, even though she had slept ten hours.

'Bad night?' he asked.

'Not particularly,' she yawned. 'I just can't seem to shake off this tiredness.'

'How about we take a long weekend break? There are no guests in the mill at the end of the month. Seems to me you could do with a change.'

'I'm going back to England, remember? "A change is as good as a rest," as they say.'

'It will be tiring.'

She had promised to return to Surrey to help her older half-sister, Jane, move into a bungalow from the big house she had lived in for over thirty years. Although the sisters got on better than they used to, their personalities were very different and Jane could be difficult and touchy.

Francesco helped himself to a second brioche. 'I still don't understand why she can't use professional movers. She has pots of money.'

'She's using a removal company but she still wants me there for moral support. She's family, *tesoro*, and living over here I don't help her as much as I should. I feel guilty. We've discussed this so many times.'

'I know, I know and I'm only thinking of what's best for you.'

She smiled at him. 'What idea have you cooked up for this long weekend, then?'

'I was thinking we could pop down and stay in an *agriturismo* in the Maremma and visit the area for Davide's project.'

'Brilliant idea! Then I can find out more about the *transumanza* myself and get involved.'

He watched her as she removed her nightie to get dressed; still lovely, her breasts firm despite feeding three babies. When she turned and saw him staring at her, she knew he wanted her back in bed – but what was the point of pretending?

'Sorry, Francesco. I can hear the kids are up.'

He got out of bed and went over to search in a bookcase in the alcove.

'You've got to promise me you'll see a doctor, Anna. This tiredness is wrong.'

She came over, turning him round to face her and went into his embrace.

'I don't deserve you,' she said, kissing him briefly on the lips. 'I'll go and see Jane's doctor when I'm in England.'

'Why not go here?'

She shrugged. 'It'll be all round the village. You know what it's like.'

Seeing that he was about to insist, she slipped out of his arms. 'Look, I've said I promise. It's only a few weeks to go.'

At the door she turned, 'Come and help me feed the hungry hordes.'

With the children's breakfast cleared away and the table wiped clean of Nutella and plum jam, Francesco produced his books.

'Davi, come and sit next to me and look at these old photos.'

The twins asked if they could go outside and investigate the new den. Having promised they wouldn't stray far they left, chattering in the secret language known only to themselves. Alba curled up in an armchair near the dining table to read.

Anna sat down next to her son. 'I'd like to find out more about the *transumanza* too, Davide. In England, drovers led sheep to market in London from all over the place but I don't think they stayed away for months and months.'

Francesco pointed to a faded photo of a group of men standing amongst a vast flock of sheep. 'This was taken up at the Viamaggio Pass,' he read from the description underneath, ' from where they started the *transumanza* in our area. Look - the priest's blessing the animals and then they'll be off on their ten-day walk to the coast.'

'*Ten days?*' exclaimed David. 'It only takes a few hours to drive down there now, doesn't it? What a mission!'

Francesco turned another page.

'Look at this group of youngsters. They're about your age.'

Anna peered at the picture thinking how undernourished they were.

'Tell me again who went from your family?' she asked.

'I think Nonno did when he was quite young,' he answered. 'I've read that children as young as eight left on their own for the coast.'

'*Eight?* That's so harsh,' Davide said.

'People were very, very poor back then – it was the only way to survive,' Francesco explained, turning more pages.

'You've heard of Mussolini?' When Davide nodded, his father continued. 'He encouraged large families and sometimes there could be ten children , so in order to put food on the table even the youngest had to pitch in and help.'

Flicking through the book, he found what he was looking for and pointed to another image of a forlorn young boy standing in the middle of a ploughed field. Round his neck, tied on with string like a drum, he wore an empty petrol can. In one hand he brandished a stick. Francesco read out the caption:

"Omero Bravaccini, aged seven, scaring crows from crops."

'I can't believe such young children had to leave their families,' Anna said. She glanced at the poster-sized print of her children on the kitchen wall. Francesco had snapped them playing one hot August afternoon at the waterfall.

'Can you imagine our kids managing that?' she asked her husband.

'But I still don't really understand why they had to,' insisted Davide.

'Life is very different now,' Francesco said, putting his arm round Davide's shoulders. 'If little Omero had stayed up here in the mountains he'd have starved. You know what our winters are like – how the temperatures can plummet below freezing for weeks on end.'

'So?' Davide said. '*We* stay here.'

'Well, their animals needed winter grazing, so they had to be taken to where the grass was - down at the milder coastal area.'

'And they didn't have freezers then – and there was very little food, with snow covering everything,' Anna added.

'Exactly!' Francesco said. 'I think women and children and old people who stayed behind survived on anything they could store from the summer, like chestnuts and maize or fruit they dried.'

Davide was turning the pages now and his father continued, 'Nowadays animals are kept inside huge barns when the snows come, like on Gori's farm up near Montebotolino where he puts his Chianina cattle. But his grandparents used to have to make the annual *transumanza* trek before that.'

'You never talk about your grandmother.' Anna said.

'She died when I was five and Nonno had already passed away. About the only thing I remember about Nonna Marisa was her beautiful smile and her lovely singing voice…'

Alba wandered over to peer at the photos.

'I heard you mention Montebotolino. I'm going up there to do some sketching. Are there any pictures of the village like it used to be?'

'Here's one, I think,' Davide said, pointing to a group of smiling peasants eating on the grass, in front of a line of stone houses.

Francesco reached over to take a better look.

'It must be a harvest time snack,' he said. 'That's in the little square where we go and light the oven for the *Ferragosto* pizzas.

'My goodness, how the place has changed,' said Anna. 'Look at all those chickens scratching about and the haystacks in the background and all the people. It's buzzing! The guests from the Mulino went up there for a walk after their meal at Piero's restaurant last Sunday and they said they didn't like it. They described it as a ghost town.'

'I love it up there,' Alba said. 'I know it's deserted but – it's kind of nice like that. I don't think it's ghostly at all. It's beautiful.'

'Too remote for me to live up there permanently,' Anna said.

'And there've been robberies from those holiday houses too. Anybody wanting to break in can take all the time they want. There's nobody there most of the time.'

'Well, one day I'll earn pots of money from my paintings, 'Alba said, 'and buy up all the empty houses and turn them into an Art School. I'll live up there in splendour and you can all come and visit me! I'm off now. Is there enough petrol in the Vespa, Babbo?'

'I think so. Don't forget your helmet.'

Alba raised her eyes in despair and Anna smiled at her step-daughter.

'Francesco, she's eighteen, not eight,' she said.

'Yes, well Omar's nearly thirty and he's still in hospital.'

'That's entirely different,' responded Alba. 'He swerved on his bike to avoid a porcupine and it was at night. Plus he races round like a crazy thing…the Vespa can't go that fast.' She pulled her sneakers from the shoe-rack and changed from her flip-flops.

'But there are plenty of boar during the day.' Francesco persisted.

'Babbo, I *always* wear my helmet. What *is* this?'

'Sorry, Alba – just being a normal, protective father!'

'Normal, *neurotic* father, more like' she said, going over to hug him. 'What the hell will you be like when I go off to Uni?'

'Neurotic about what colour your hair will be next time we see you and how many tattoos you'll have?'

Alba laughed, touching the streak of blue in her long brown hair. 'How do you know I haven't got tattoos all over my bum already?' she said with a sparkle in her large eyes and she was out of the door before her father could say another thing.

It might feel great not to wear a helmet, Alba thought, as she drove away from La Stalla, and to feel the breeze whipping her hair about. But she'd tried riding without her visor down once and an insect had struck her in the eye. It was painful and she'd had to stop and wait until her blurred vision returned to normal. Anyway, she'd always wear her crash helmet - she wasn't stupid. There were enough gory adverts on TV showing mangled bodies after road accidents.

The road to the little village of Montebotolino took her through the hamlet of Rofelle, past Piero and Manuela's popular restaurant, l'Erbosteria. They were sitting outside and waved as she passed. After the cheese maker's house, tarmac changed to an uneven dirt track and she slowed down. It was overcast today and the view towards the rocky outcrops of Sasso Simone and Simoncello was blurred and murky.

As she turned a bend, thirty metres in front of her an Alsatian walked slowly across the track. The dog stopped, sniffing the air for her scent, it's muzzle contorted with a snarl – or was it a smile… Alba was transfixed by the animal's piercing blue eyes and its erect stance. 'You beauty,' she whispered. Babbo had warned her to be cautious about stray dogs because of rabies but this animal seemed calm. It moved towards the forest and she let the motor die, parking the Vespa at the side of the track before cautiously approaching the forest's edge. 'Good boy!' she called softly, peering into the gloom beneath the canopy of spruce. 'I won't hurt you.'

But it had disappeared into the shadows. She hadn't seen an Alsatian around here before and wondered if somebody had abandoned it. It happened regularly with cats. In early spring she'd found two drowned kittens in the river near La Stalla, below the road bridge. She couldn't understand the mindset of such cruelty.

Kick-starting the scooter she continued along the track. The roofs and bell tower of Montebotolino came into view and she approached the barrier that prevented vehicular access. Ernesto's white Mini Cooper was already parked. It was an eighteenth birthday present from his wealthy father, a shoe factory owner who lived in San Marino. Her best friend, Bruna, had just started going out with Ernesto and the girls hardly saw each other now. Leaving her scooter propped on its stand, she walked a few metres to the tiny village square. They were on the grass, Ernesto's head resting in Bruna's lap, smoke spiraling from their cigarettes into the fresh country air.

'Ciao, Alba,' Bruna called. 'Come and join us. Alfiero will be here soon.'

She chatted to them for a few minutes, refusing their offer of a spliff, telling them about the stray Alsatian she'd seen down the road.

Bruna sat bolt upright. 'My God, Alba. Are you sure it was a dog and not a wolf?'

'Almost certainly a dog,' she replied. 'But - you've got me wondering now.'

There had been recent reports of wolves taking Gori's calves in broad daylight.

'Probably took one look at you and could see you weren't Little Red Riding Hood,' Ernesto said, getting up to brush grass from his white jeans.

'Are you going to be okay on your own?' he asked with a snigger, 'with the big, bad wolf hanging around?'

Bruna laughed too and Alba realised the pair of them were high.

'I'm not worried,' she said, thinking that even if it had been a wolf, it had seemed more scared than aggressive. 'Anyway, Alfi's coming soon. I won't be alone.'

She waved them goodbye, then as an afterthought she ran to their car, tapping on the window.

'Don't breathe a word to my parents. Promise me!' she pleaded. 'If they thought I'd seen a wolf up here they wouldn't let me come on my own anymore.'

Ernesto started the engine and, as if he were taking part in a Formula One race, he let the tyres screech on the stony track. Then with a blast on his horn that ripped into the peace of the isolated village, he zoomed off down the mountain.

Alba sat on the steps to the church leaning her back against the locked doors. She loved this place. Many of the houses were in need of serious restoration but a handful were used as holiday homes. Her favourite, shaded by a gnarled apple tree and the only one possessing a traditional outside oven, was where Anna's father had lived until his death. It had never belonged to him; he'd rented it from the Church. Although she was only eight when he came into their lives, Alba had grown to love Nonno Danilo, as she'd called him. The whole story of her step-mother discovering him to be her real father was amazing – like something from a novel. Alba really missed him. They'd formed a special bond and she'd spent many hours in his company, even staying overnight during school holidays in his tiny house. The wooden bed where she slept was built into an eave in the roof, a round window above framing a view of the church and mountains beyond. She had to climb a ladder to reach her 'nest', as Nonno Danilo used to call it, and he'd stand at the foot holding a candle until he was sure she was safely snuggled down. She remembered how he'd woken her one night and taken her to watch porcupines and badgers in the woods. He was a mushroom expert and locals would ask his advice about a species if they were unsure of its edibility. She'd helped him collect honey from his many hives dotted around the edges of meadows and woodland, and she'd learned respect for his hard-working bees. Nonno Danilo was a man of few words, having spent many years living alone in Montebotolino, but she knew he had adored her and his newly-discovered family and loved to join them for Anna's famous Anglo-Italian Sunday lunches. One subject he refused to talk about was the time he'd spent as a partisan in the war. And she couldn't blame him for that. Why dredge up painful memories? She believed war sucked anyway.

Her thoughts were full of Nonno Danilo while she tried to sketch. The view opposite of the Apennines cloaked in green, where a solitary wind turbine jutted above the peaks, was hazy. She couldn't capture on paper the mood she wanted. And it was obvious Alfiero wasn't coming. She was sure she'd hurt his feelings.

She thought back to the last time they'd been together. It was after the cinema at Pennabilli, where they'd laughed their way through "Scary Movie II" and sat on a wall afterwards drinking cans of Peroni.

'I looked online again about Newcastle University,' she'd told him. 'I might persuade Mamma to let me go with her to England when she helps Aunty Jane move house. Then I can go to the Open Day.'

'My parents are adamant I have to go straight to Bologna at the end of summer. They can't afford for me to have a Gap Year.'

'You could find a holiday job and save to pay your own way.'

'In your dreams, Alba. Where and how? The only work round here is as a waiter and there's only one restaurant open now in Badia. And the pay is so low it would just about cover my petrol. I couldn't save anything.'

They'd thrown their cans in a bin and wandered down from the square to where he'd parked his motor bike, next to a large statue of Padre Pio.

Alba had wrinkled up her nose as she stood in front of the full size image. 'Eww! Weird! Looks as if he's about to come alive and preach to us about drinking Peroni on a Sunday night.'

'My Nonna has three holy pictures of him on her dressing table. She adores him.'

'I think old people turn religious in a panic,' she'd said, swinging her leg over the back pillion, 'as a kind of insurance policy before they die.'

Then he'd gone and ruined their lovely straightforward friendship by saying something stupid like he hoped they could grow old together and he'd turned round and tried to kiss her. She'd laughed.

'Get off me,' she'd said. 'It's like kissing my brother.'

'I don't feel like your brother,' was his reply, and the drive back after that to Badia had been awkward. She'd held onto him gingerly – in case he got the wrong message - and they hadn't seen each other since.

She threw her drawing stuff into her rucksack and decided to call it a day.

Anna escaped for an hour down by the river, leaving Francesco and Davide chatting about the book. She and Alba were similar in many ways despite having no blood ties; they both needed their own space every now and again. Anna had her own favourite spot along the water – further upstream from the mill on the other side of the bridge, a little too far off the path for day trippers to venture.

Willow tendrils brushed against her face, wiping away tears that she seemed to shed too often these days. Her knees felt bee-stung, her eyes red with fatigue and her limbs were treacle.

She arrived at the pool she called her green lagoon. Dark fronds of algae floated beneath the surface like drowned hair and the sound of the river trickling over a series of miniature waterfalls was soothing. She believed her pool to be more beautiful than any landscaped feature in a glossy Garden Design magazine. She watched the ripples as if mesmerised, willing them to carry away her tiredness and scratchiness.

The pictures in Francesco's book were fresh in her mind. She reflected that once upon a time a woman of her age, in her mid-forties, would have had no time to sit by the river at ten in the morning. Instead she would be pummelling clothes on the rocks, gutting trout with work roughened hands, collecting twigs for the fire, gratefully harvesting these gifts carried by the river, tying them in bundles to carry home on her head. Maybe while she worked she would worry that last night's fumble from an insistent husband might result in yet another mouth to feed.

Anna listened to the ghostly whispers of the water. They seemed to murmur to her to stop wallowing in self-pity. But she couldn't remember the last time she hadn't felt tired. In the past, coming to this spot could have washed away her fatigue within minutes. She'd steal a half hour and return home, her soul restored, ready to face the world again. But now, even the river seemed to have lost its restorative powers.

Cancer. The word had crept into her head and the worry was preventing her from sleeping. She lay next to Francesco at night worrying how the family would cope without her. When she returned to England to help Jane with the move, she would definitely arrange to see her sister's doctor and keep her worries from Francesco for now, until she knew the prognosis for certain. There was no need to concern him yet. He'd been a widower once already and even though his first marriage to Letizia had already turned sour by the time of the fatal car crash, it had still been hard for him bringing up Alba alone.

She slipped into the water and lay on her back, willing her body to relax, even if her mind couldn't. The sky was mottled and blotchy, a moody grey. An egret flew overhead. She lay still, floating on the surface, watching the bird flap its wings, its long beak outstretched. Its form against the sullen clouds resembled a nun hurrying along in her white summer habit. The sun remained hidden, erasing shadow patterns from the stones, turning the water bottle green.

Her time up she gathered her thoughts together, although it felt as if she were pushing them into a string bag from where they would come tumbling out again. Slowly she picked her way over the boulders back to La Stalla.

She had a pile of sheets and pillow cases to iron for the next influx of visitors.

THEN

Chapter 3
Giuseppe - 1915

When I was eleven, I became a senior altar boy, serving most Sundays in the little church of San Tommaso in the mountain village of Montebotolino, high up in the Apennines where I was born. Rubbing sleep from my eyes, I would drag myself up fourteen steep steps, push open the heavy wooden door and avert my eyes from the gruesome image of San Tommaso inserting his fingers into Jesus's wounds. I would turn my back on the altar and swing my thurible back and forth, cloaking the odour of unwashed bodies and damp stone in an aromatic haze of incense. With San Tommaso safely behind me, I scrutinized old ladies in black, perched like crows on a fence in the front pews. I counted only three teeth between them and wondered if that was why they were so scrawny – because they couldn't eat their crusts.

Our priest, Don Mario Darrini, was always urging us to be proud of the sixteenth century altar panel sculpted in the della Robbia style, but I couldn't see what all the fuss was about. I liked the words della Robbia, however and began to mutter them over and over under my breath.

After Mass, Don Mario congratulated me for murmuring my prayers. But he was mistaken. To me della Robbia had the sound of dirty words, like the filth shouted by simple Amadeo in our village, with his squint and ragged trousers worn back to front.

The image of the open wound in the side of Jesus and doubting Thomas poking it with his finger made me squeamish. It reminded me of the time my cousin Marco had been gored by a wild boar in the beech woods above our village, when we were out collecting firewood. Marco had squealed like the pig my father and uncles slaughtered each New Year. Fortunately he didn't die like the pig or get strung up to have his bristles burned off by flames. Instead he was sick for weeks and nearly died from his infected wound. Marisa, our village herbalist, came round to poke her fingers into his wound to administer salves and ointments and she cured him.

On special feast days, I served in the bigger, older church of St Michael the Archangel five kilometres down the mountain, in the town of Badia Tedalda. I preferred the shining blue, green and yellow altar panels in this church. As I swung my thurible here, I was almost eye level with the brilliant white feet of a more pleasant St Thomas, kneeling barefoot before the Madonna. None of the saints or Jesus or Mary wore shoes and this made me feel close to them, although their feet were cleaner than mine. I thought they were poor like us, walking barefoot to save shoe leather. If I moved slightly closer to the wall, I could almost tickle San Tommaso's feet. My mother used to do that to me when I was younger until I nearly wet my drawers.

On another panel, a pig peeped out from behind St Anthony Abbot, the patron saint of animals, and there were trees and flowers and a goat or maybe a dog. I felt I could step into the lush green countryside and run free and wild, play hide-and-seek and pick lilies next to the Madonna to take home to my mother, or maybe herbs, like my friend Marisa.

All these thoughts danced around in my head as I swung the incense back and forth. Don Mario told my mother later he sensed a vocation in me, because I always had an innocent, almost angelic look on my face during Mass. Little did he know!

On that last Sunday evening of August, Don Mario knocked at the door of our little house in Montebotolino and invited himself in to take part in our *veglia*. Family and neighbours were gathered round our table, keeping company.

My father had been telling us a grisly ghost story about Enrico Stoppa when he knocked. The women shrieked, thinking the ghost of this wicked brigand was going to steal them away. They soon calmed down when the beaming, dimpled face of Don Mario peeped round our door.

'Come and sit in this chair, *padre*,' my mother said, fussing over him, fetching the best glass from the corner cupboard and filling it to the brim with fortified *vinsanto*.

'Thank you, Vincenza. But first give me a beaker of fresh spring water, I beg you.' He pulled off the beret he always wore at an angle and mopped his brow, fanning his face with a large, linen handkerchief. 'We could do with a night of rain to take away this heat and to water our parched vegetables,' he said.

Everybody loved Don Mario. He visited us often and liked to sit conversing with Nonno. He and grandfather were expert hunters and would discuss the best way to catch boar; which breed of dog was ideal for truffle searches; which bullets to use in which rifle; when the moon was in the best phase for catching hares.

He had a generous appetite. Whenever he came to lunch it was a feast for us too. There would be *crostini* liberally spread with ground chicken livers and sage, ravioli stuffed with greens harvested from the meadows, roast chicken or *rompicollo*, which was a cut of meat from a cow slaughtered due to some injury. The meat was not the best quality because of the bruising, but it was always tasty and flavoured with plenty of garlic and herbs. My mother was an excellent cook and knew how to make meals out of nothing – a necessary skill during our long, harsh winters.

Don Mario himself came from a peasant family on the other side of Pieve Santo Stefano. He didn't have airs and graces like some of the clergy and understood perfectly our way of life and hardships. We would be in stitches when, after three or four glasses of wine, he started to mimic personalities in the parish.

But that evening he was intent on business.

'My friends,' he said to everybody present. 'I need to talk alone with Giuseppe's family, so if you don't mind…?'

Respecting his wishes our friends shuffled from our kitchen, bidding us all goodnight.

It was growing late. I picked up my three year old brother, Angelo, to make my way towards the ladder leading to our bedroom area.

'Stay here,' the priest ordered and turning to mother suggested my little sisters could surely take over my duties for tonight. I could tell Nadia was itching to know what was going on. She was only seven but mother was always saying she had an old head on young shoulders. Scooping Angelo onto her hip and pushing five-year-old Maria Rosa towards the step ladder, my siblings made their exits. Nadia stuck her tongue out at me just before she disappeared through the upstairs hatch and I wrinkled back my nose.

Mamma poured more wine into Don Mario's glass and told my father to lift down the ham hanging from the beam so she could slice some for our visitor.

'Now then,' said the priest. 'I want to discuss Giuseppe's future.'

'Giuseppe's future is already decided,' my father was quick to intervene.

'Since we lost Francesco,' my mother added, pausing to control her emotions, 'we need Giuseppe to help us. The girls and Angelo are too young, not strong enough yet.'

We had all waved goodbye to our eighteen-year-old brother Francesco when he marched away from the square in Badia Tedalda with seventy five local boys, to fight in the north of Italy. A letter had reached us three months later to say he was missing. My parents were brave but there had been a change in both of them. Mother still set his place, sure that one day he would walk into the kitchen, whistling like he always did, his hunting dog snapping at his heels. When the news first filtered through, she'd uttered a scream that could surely have woken the dead, a sound like a wounded animal. Then she plummeted to the floor. We were used to our mother being always in control and it frightened us. Women in the village took turns to cook and do our washing and sat with her, their gentle voices drifting down from upstairs to the kitchen, a cold place without her presence. When she rose from her bed almost two weeks later, she was almost the Mamma we remembered, but not quite.

'Life has to continue,' she announced. 'Jobs won't go away. There is firewood to collect and store, the meadow to be cut, sheep to watch over, family and animals to feed.'

But she'd gone about her chores silently ever since that time, saying she would only sing again when Francesco returned to our hearth. Our friends and neighbours kept vigil with us in the evenings. They were kind but my parents craved more than kindness.

Don Mario continued, 'I'm not intending to take Giuseppe away from you for the whole year, my dear friends. When he returns during the school holidays, he can help you as much as you need.'

'School!' my mother uttered, raising both hands to the ceiling in a gesture that asked the priest if he were mad. 'How can we afford to send Beppe away to school? We have barely enough money to manage as it is.'

'We need Giuseppe here with us, padre,' my father said. 'This idea of yours is impossible.'

'I believe it is God's will that he should enter the seminary in Arezzo. Giuseppe is an intelligent, sensitive young boy. Surely you can see what an honour it would be for your family?'

'But, padre, we can't afford school for him.' Mamma sat down at the table, slicing bread and ham with such vigour, she was in danger of slicing off her fingers.

Don Mario placed his hand over hers to still her. 'You don't need to worry about that side of things, Vincenza. I have funds set by. No need to worry about clothes or books. I even have spare shoes hardly worn and a new warm cloak the boy can have.'

I found out later these items had been given to him by another grieving mother who had lost her son to the Great War. But he was sensitive enough not to elaborate on this.

'And with Giuseppe living in the seminary during school term,' Don Mario added, 'you will have one less mouth to feed.'

So my destiny was decided. My parents agreed to my being sent away for an education I couldn't hope to receive locally. I think Mamma was secretly proud, for I heard her boasting at the village fountain next time she was bent over our laundry, scrubbing dirt from sheets and work clothes with the other women.

'Just imagine, my son might be ordained one fine day,' she said, pushing her hair back with soapy fingers, 'and he won't have to trudge down to the coast with the animals, like everybody else.'

The women agreed how lucky I was, one of them commenting it was rare to see a thin priest, how I would never have to worry about providing for a family.

'We shall miss the boy but maybe it's a blessing in disguise,' I heard Mamma say as she spread washing to dry on juniper bushes near the village fountain.

Chapter 4
Giuseppe

During the evening of September 7th 1916, Mamma sat up late adjusting and lengthening a pair of my brother's cord trousers with a piece of material she had put by. It was a different shade of grey, but it would do. When she had finished her work, she folded the trousers carefully into the cardboard suitcase used to carry her trousseau to her new home in Montebotolino nineteen years earlier. She also packed a scarf she had knitted for Francesco, whispering to me it was best to use it. If my brother returned, I would have to give it back. It was the first time I had heard her use "if" instead of "when". Then she handed me a holy picture of Our Lady, urging me to say my prayers each night. I laughed and reminded her I would be living in a seminary where prayers were bound to be recited until they came out of my ears. She boxed mine playfully, a rare smile on her face. She, Babbo and Nonno always stressed the importance of mixing with good people and they believed their good manners would rub off on me at the seminary. They had made huge sacrifices to send me and hoped one day I would take Holy Orders and become a priest. They showed us love but they were also strict. One of my mother's many sayings was: *'chi va con lo zoppo impara a zoppicare.'* (If you go round with the lame, you will learn to be lame.)

I couldn't sleep that night. Mamma had sprayed petrol on the bedding and walls of our little room with even more care than usual. 'I don't want you turning up at your new school covered in flea bites. They would think we were living in filth,' she said, squirting into every crack in the plaster walls and drenching our bedding with her noxious concoction. If we hadn't hidden under our covers, she would have drenched Angelo and me too. The stench of petrol was nauseating and my mind was spinning with a million worries.

When I was younger I'd been terrified of storms. Lightning would illuminate our room and turn the cape hanging from the nail on the door into a corpse waiting to jump back to life with the next flash. I'd wriggle under the blanket to muffle the din of the thunder, a monster announcing his angry arrival from the next valley. But Francesco held me in his arms and calmed me. 'We'll weather the storm together,' he laughed, tickling me and distracting me with stories. When there'd been a candle stub to spare, he'd light it and put on a shadow show against the plaster wall, shaping his hands into angels' wings or fantastical creatures until the wind and rain subsided. But I knew he wasn't coming back and I had to face my worries on my own. Our room felt cavernous without him and far too tidy. Each night I folded my breeches and shirt onto the wooden chest at the end of the bed and arranged my clogs side by side. But Francesco never bothered. Life was too short, he used to say. And he'd been right.

I sighed as I tossed and turned on the rustling mattress, until little Angelo sat up in the metal bed we shared, '*Uffa!* Bother you,' he said. 'Go outside and sleep with the chickens, Beppe...'

Ten minutes later I gave up, deciding it was going to be a "white night", devoid of sleep. I crept down the ladder to the kitchen. Nonno Piero was there, hunched on his wooden settle in the corner of the hearth, a sheep skin over his knees even though summer had barely passed.

'Can't sleep?' my grandfather asked. He beckoned me to pull up a stool and to sit near him. 'Come and keep your old Nonno company.'

We sat in easy silence. I threw a small log onto the glowing embers. Nonno always felt the cold, even under an August sun. He would laugh his toothless cackle and say his blood had been diluted from drinking too much bad wine. I listened to the flare of flames as the log caught light, watching the changing shapes, wondering if there would be a fire to sit beside at the seminary. I wondered too where I would sleep; if I would like the food and the other students; if I would be clever enough to keep up with lessons. Thoughts buzzed around my head like bees about to swarm from their hive.

'I have something for you,' Nonno said, digging his hand into his pocket. He pulled out his most prized possession, a beautiful fob watch.

As a young man, he had worked as a cowboy, herding cattle with the other *butteri* down to the *Maremma* region each winter, along the Tuscan coast. On one famous occasion he had saved the life of a landowner's young daughter. The men had stopped at the fair in Pugliano to buy new harnesses and bridles for the long journey. Nonno noticed a little girl wander into the enclosure where the huge *Maremmana* cattle with long curved horns were penned for sale. Quicker than you could down a glass of fiery *grappa,* Nonno had leapt on his horse, jumped the enclosure fence and scooped the child up onto his saddle, saving her from certain injury or death. Her parents had been so overcome with gratitude that, at a ceremony on the following day, they had awarded him a gold watch. He was the only peasant for kilometres around Montebotolino to own a timepiece and, whenever he was in the *osteria,* he allowed fellow-drinkers to hold it. They would listen to the *tick-tock, tick-tock* of the mechanism in exchange for a glass or two of strong red wine. I had heard the story over and over but Nonno didn't launch into his favourite account tonight.

'I want you to have this.'

'But, Nonno I couldn't possibly…'

The old man swiped away my protests, thrusting the watch into my hands, raising his voice to me. 'Show me some respect! Let me speak, boy!'

I held the treasure in both my hands. Firelight glinted on the casing, the hands showing eighteen minutes past three. It would be growing light soon and time for me to leave for the seminary in Arezzo.

'I am very proud of you, Giuseppe,' Nonno continued. 'Who would have thought a grandson of mine would be going away to study? *Eeee*! It will be like going to America.' He wiped his eyes with the back of his knobbly fingers, disfigured from a lifetime of labour. 'You won't be back until Christmas. I was going to leave this to you anyway but I have decided to bring the occasion forward.'

It was useless to argue and in any case I could not have found the right words to explain how I felt. In my heart, I understood that by handing me his precious watch, Nonno was bidding me a final goodbye.

Next morning was bright, the sky empty of clouds. I knew Mamma was trying not to cry. It was time to leave and I looked everywhere but in her face: at Maria Rosa's sleep tousled plaits, the patch on Nadia's pinafore, the cat feeding her kittens. Nonno was nowhere to be seen but we had said our goodbyes last night by the fire.

The door burst open and my father entered, breath rasping after his run across from the barn. 'I'm not too late, am I? The calf is sick - you must call the vet, Vincenza.' He pulled off his cap, wiping sweat from his face. 'Best make haste, Beppe, if we are to get down to Sansepolcro by two o'clock.'

I was grateful for brief goodbyes. Mamma cupped my face in her hands and I felt them rough on my cheeks. 'Be good, my son,' she said. 'Work hard at your books and you'll soon be home for Christmas.' Then she turned away from me to stir soup in the black cauldron hanging in the hearth.

My little sisters clung to me and at the last minute, Maria Rosa pushed something into my pocket. 'Look at it later, Beppe, when you're on the train.'

My father took my suitcase and hoisted it onto his shoulders. I followed him down the mule track that led from the village through newly planted pine forests. His feet flew over the stony path and I found it hard to keep up. My heart had no desire to follow my feet and I kept turning round until I could no longer see the roofs of my village outlined against the sky.

'Hurry up, Giuseppe!' Babbo kept saying. 'We'll miss the coach to Arezzo. It won't wait for you, you know.'

An hour and a half later, we had climbed again to 1,000 metres. I had never been beyond the pass of Viamaggio and in front of me spread a view that seemed to extend to infinity. It was nearly nine o'clock and quite warm. In the distance, mountains were hazy blue and purple in the September sunshine. We stopped to eat a late breakfast.

'Those are the Apennines and, far beyond, the mountains of Pratomagno,' my father pointed out. 'Think how vast they are, Beppe, and how small are we. They provide us with a living - but they can be cruel too.'

It was a profound statement for my father and as if to cover his embarrassment, he made a play of cutting me two slices of *pagnotta* which he pulled out of a sack cloth, adding a small hunk of *pecorino* cheese, made from our own sheep's milk.

While we sat on the ridge chewing on hard bread, Babbo touched my arm. 'You are fortunate Don Mario has given you this opportunity. Fortunate not to have to make the journey down to the Maremma to work your guts out this winter for next to nothing. Study hard and maybe one day you will be able to look after all of us.'

Don Mario had told my parents they wouldn't have to worry about paying anything for school, but that was not quite the case. Although heavily subsidised by the Curia, they still had to find one lira per day to send me to the Salesian friars. This meant extra work and great sacrifices for the whole family. Mamma would now have to sell all our eggs at market and there would be no more delicious omelettes dished up at table. And five-year-old Maria Rosa would have to help watch over our neighbour's flock on the meadows. It meant rising at dawn and not attending school. My parents saw no need for her to be schooled anyway. She already knew how to write her name; that was all she needed.

I felt guilty for everything my family were doing for me. I didn't feel like eating my breakfast and I decided to save it for later. In searching in my pocket for a rag to wrap it in, my fingers touched Nonno's watch and my little sister's gift. The weight of responsibility to do my best for my family was overwhelming. I felt like the family *treggia,* the wooden sleigh we used to lift heavy items from place to place: boulders, sacks of grain or loads of firewood. And I wondered if I would be strong enough to bear my burden.

It felt easier once I had said goodbye to Babbo down in Sansepolcro. He shook my hand as if I were already a man and not a boy of eleven. He muttered he had to hurry back up the mountain before darkness fell and then he turned abruptly and left me alone.

I watched him for as long as I could make out the muddy green of his long cloak. Where we lived up in the mountains, it was excellent camouflage in the forest and countryside, excellent disguise for melting into the undergrowth to hunt boar and deer. But Babbo didn't merge into the bright cottons and wools of city people's garments. At the edge of the main square he turned, but when he noticed me watching, he hurried off round a corner and was lost from view.

I had about one hour to wait for the Arezzo coach to come. I sat in a corner of the square near the stop, on top of my suitcase. Mamma had advised me to do this in case somebody should try to steal it. I listened to the chatter and watched the dazzle of movement, so different from our quiet village. A family was seated on the floor not far from me. A well-trussed duck poked its head from a basket and a middle aged woman sat nearby, a baby asleep on her lap. A little boy leant against her, picking his nose. I pulled him a face and stuck out my tongue, whereupon the child buried himself in his mother's skirts. I wondered where they were bound, where they were from. I soon knew the answers to my questions because the mother noticed me and struck up conversation, producing a shiny red apple, urging me to take it.

'We have plenty,' she said, 'it's been a good harvest. Just as well with my daughter's wedding coming up. We need all the extra lire we can find. We're off to Arezzo to celebrate. Where are you going, young man?'

When the coach arrived ten minutes late, I felt I had known this family all my life. The woman had not stopped talking. The driver was all a-fluster, anxious to continue the stretch to Arezzo as soon as possible to make up for lost time. I helped the woman load her bundles and pass them up to the driver who tied them to the roof. She shouted at him not to bruise the fruit intended for the wedding party and the special cake.

We said goodbye at the coach stop opposite Arezzo station. I thought it strange that a woman I had never met before and felt sure would never meet again, seemed more upset at our parting than my own Babbo had been.

From across the square I watched people scurrying in and out of the railway station. Ever since I was tiny I'd dreamt of becoming a train driver in charge of an engine, pulling along carriages like a huge, mechanical caterpillar. Our teacher, Professor Daniele, had shown us pictures of trains and I wanted to see one for myself so I made my way to the wide doors and slipped past the ticket office.

I was in luck. Several uniformed station officials were clustered round a stall selling refreshments. Whilst they were enjoying their coffees and too busy to notice me, I slipped onto the platform. I had never stood next to a train, let alone travelled in one. The enormous, shining steam-engine blew smoke from its funnel like a bull blowing steam from its ringed nostrils on a crisp winter morning. The volume in the station was deafening from the hissing of steam, grinding of shovels on metal and coal being loaded into the furnace, coffee and newspaper vendors shouting their wares and people scurrying about like ants in my mother's larder, so sure of their destinations. Overawed and overwrought, tense and exhausted from lack of sleep, I was all set to turn tail and run away from this new world, back to the bus to climb aboard for the return journey to Sansepolcro. I hurried back to where I had alighted and came face to face with somebody I had hoped never to encounter again.

Chapter 5
Giuseppe

It was Fausto.

I knew him only too well from school in Rofelle; he was a year older than me. His father was the village butcher and I'd often pictured his son as a Chianina bullock; big and beefy, like the carcasses hanging from hooks at the back of his father's shop. He used his size to pick on younger children, hiding their copy books to get them into trouble with Professor Daniele. And he would steal mid-morning snacks from the pockets of coats hanging at the back of the single classroom, where we huddled as near to the stove as possible. These treats were simple: a piece of bread and herring or an apple or pear – some morsel to fill a hole in the stomach after our long, early morning walks to school. Nobody dared report him. I'd watched him mimic Marisa from Montebotolino, as she hobbled across the piazza to his father's shop. Once only had I dared to stand up to Fausto, when he tripped up poor Alessandrino, a sickly child suffering from polio, his right leg encased in a heavy caliper splint.

'Don't you ever, ever talk to me like that again, you little piece of chicken shit,' he whispered, holding a sharpened pencil in his fist, like a dagger, 'or you will feel this go right through your eye-ball.'

And I had no reason to believe he wouldn't do this.

'What brings you down here, clodhopper?' Fausto leered over me, barring my way, hands folded over his chest.

He was flanked by two other boys. I knew one of them: Geremaia, an altar boy, from the village of Colcellalto on the road to Sestino. I'd never had any bother from him. He smiled and raised a hand in greeting. 'Leave him be, Fausto,' said my saviour. Geremaia came and stood next to me so that he and I were facing Fausto and the other boy, very tubby and vaguely familiar. He gestured to my suitcase, 'I reckon you're off to the same place as us, Giuseppe. Did Don Mario manage to convince your folks too?'

I was surprised to learn I wasn't the only new boy and wondered why the priest hadn't arranged for us to travel together. Maybe it had something to do with the times I'd confessed my evil thoughts about Fausto. He probably sensed I would have refused to leave if I'd known of the presence of this loathsome oaf - and he would have been correct.

'Just as he convinced yours,' I replied. 'Do you know how to get there?'

The tubby lad standing next to Fausto responded that he remembered but he was starving and wouldn't go another step until he'd eaten something to give him energy.

'But I gave you some of my food earlier on the train, Agostino,' Fausto said.

'I didn't like the ham,' replied tubby Agostino, wrinkling up his piggy nose, 'I threw it out of the window.'

And then I remembered who he was. A relative of the bishop, Agostino had spent one week up in the mountains a couple of years earlier, eating Don Mario out of his presbytery. He'd found our games too exerting and preferred to remain slumped in the square under the shade of the lime trees.

The four of us trooped to the centre of Arezzo where a market bustled with colour and confusion. Agostino pulled a leather money pouch from his jacket and bought a portion of fried sardines, wrapped in a twist of oily paper. Fausto dipped in his hand and Agostino allowed him to help himself. I wondered what kind of arrangement the pair of them had. No doubt Fausto had ingratiated himself with the promise of protection, in the knowledge that Agostino's purse was full. Later, when we passed by a stall laden with fresh bread, I saw Fausto steal a roll while the baker was busy slicing a loaf for a customer. Geremaia and I exchanged looks and he rolled his eyes.

Agostino led us down a dusty alleyway off the market square. From the windows, grey washing flapped down against grimy walls. At home my mother and sisters always spread laundry on bushes to dry in the fresh mountain air. I wondered how washing could ever come clean in a city. Pigeon droppings lay thick on ledges, window sills and the ground; the musty smell of dirt and decay lingered in the narrow passage way. Agostino stopped to pull on a wire in a niche in the wall beside huge arched wooden doors, taller and wider than any I had ever seen. They creaked open like castle portals in a fairy tale. A fat friar with a shining, beaming face welcomed us in. The door squeaked again as he pushed it to and when he slid the bolt across, the sound echoed within the depths of the building.

All I could think of were lines we had learned at school by heart from Dante's *Inferno*:

"Through me the way into the woeful city,
Through me the way to the eternal pain,
Through me the way among the lost people…
Abandon every hope, ye that enter."
("Per me si va nella città dolente
Per me si va nell'eterno dolore
Per me si va tra la perduta gente…
Lasciate ogni speranza, voi ch'entrate." [Canto III])

It felt like we were passing through prison gates and I stood there, trying not to tremble, wondering if the others felt as nervous as me. By this time I badly needed a pee but didn't dare ask, wishing I'd done it in one of the alleyways that stank of cat piss.

'Come along! Follow me, follow me,' the fat friar intoned in a sing-song voice. He was rotund but he was fast, his bare heels slapping against leather sandals as he hurried down the corridor, past walls decorated with fragments of old frescoes, colours faded, half figures and parts of buildings rendering a ghostly finish. 'You must all be starving after your long journey.'

'Yes, we are,' piped up Agostino. I wondered if he had worms or was just plain greedy.

Pushing open another door, the friar called out, 'More newcomers for you, Fra Domenico.' He half sang, half shouted in an accent I had never heard before. I later learned he was from a village near Turin, close to the French border.

Another friar, as long and thin as the first was short and round, appeared from the far end of the refectory, stooping over a tray piled with food.

The fat friar spoke in couplets, as if chanting verses from a psalm. 'Sit down, sit down.'

The tall one, Fra Domenico, offered us white bread, slices of sausage, a hunk of cheese, and apples bigger than any I'd seen hanging from branches in Nonno's orchard. He set down a pitcher of cool, refreshing lemonade and some tumblers. I began to think this place might not be a prison after all. I'd been told by Don Mario this was a college for poor boys, but if the food was going to be half as good as this first meal, it seemed to me more a college for princes.

'Before you sit down to eat, do you need to visit the bathroom?' Fat friar asked, his moon face cocked to one side.

We all did, so we followed him down yet another long, cool

corridor. A statue of the Madonna stood half-way down in a niche, candles glowing red in the gloom, flickering at her bare, creamy feet. And there were fresh white roses in a vase on the ledge beneath her. I thought of my mother and Nonno and bowed my head as I passed, making the sign of the cross. A smell of polish, candle wax and antiquity lingered everywhere.

We reached another huge door leading to a room with a shining stone floor and a row of six wash basins with taps, like I had seen in the doctor's surgery in Badia where I collected Nonno's medicines.

In one of the cubicles was a large white bowl fixed to the floor, a chain hanging above it. I looked for a hole in the floor, for I badly needed a pee but there wasn't one. Not knowing how to relieve myself, I climbed onto the rim of the big, white bowl to peer over the top of the cubicle where Agostino had disappeared.

'Hey! What are you staring at, pervert?' he squeaked up at me, standing with his legs apart, a stream of piss aimed at his own white bowl.

I got down from my viewing point and I copied him. I pulled the chain as he had instructed and yelped in surprise when water gushed down into the bowl. Agostino sniggered in the cubicle next to me.

At home we 'fertilised' the fields or used a bucket left at the foot of our beds. This new method of relieving oneself was only the first of many new experiences I'd encounter at the Seminary.

On my first night, despite feeling dog tired I took a long time to fall asleep. My mind was brimming with new images from the journey and the many faces and names to be remembered. I worried I would lose my way round the building with its echoing rooms and lofty ceilings. The food was new to my stomach too. White bread never appeared on our table at home and my tummy felt bloated. All around the college was an army of friars and scholars; the friars all dressed the same: sandals and bare toes peeping from beneath chocolate brown habits, jangling rosary beads fastened from cords round their middles. It was hard to tell them apart and I fretted about confusing their saintly names: Ignatius, Francis, Benedict, Aloysius...

When we were shown to our beds in a large room on the top floor which had metal bars at the windows, I was anxious about them too. Twenty-five, identical, single metal beds arranged in rows of five, each bed made up with cotton sheets, a pillow and a blue blanket. How would I possibly remember mine from the others?

We were told to unpack our cases and arrange our possessions in our bed-side cupboards with two shelves and a single drawer each. When I pulled out my little sister's gift, I sat for a while smiling at the tiny rag book she'd sewn for me. On each page she'd drawn simple pictures: our house, our dog Fede, the river Marecchia and the old mill, an image of Nonno sitting by the hearth smoking his clay pipe. I removed his watch from the scrap of linen in which Mamma had wrapped it, fingering the glass, holding it close to my ear to hear its reassuring tick. Then I wrapped it up again and placed it at the back of the cabinet, beneath a pair of red socks Mamma had knitted. Maria Rosa's rag book I placed on top of my cabinet to remind me of home, as well as a way of identifying my bed.

The mattress was harder than mine at home. As I tossed and turned, I missed the rustling sound of the corn husks and sheaths stuffed inside our mattresses. Instead, all around me I heard snuffles and snores from twenty-four other boys. And muffled sobs.

In the early morning the clanging of bells woke us. Bells ruled in the seminary. We washed in cold water, which was nothing new to me, but I heard others complaining. Then we knelt in church for one hour for morning prayers. This was followed by breakfast, also announced by a bell. A bowl of milky coffee and more white bread with jam was set before each place at table. I tried not to be greedy but I was hungry and devoured every last drop and crumb. The coffee was good and strong, made from coffee beans and not roasted barley as at home.

The long French bean of a friar, Fra Domenico, prodded a bony finger into my back, making me jump, 'You and Fausto... you will be *squatteri* for this first week.'

Yet again, my heart fell to my boots. Would I ever escape from my enemy?

'You're both from the same village, I hear. Well, he's older and can explain your duties.'

Squatteri were always selected from amongst the poorest pupils. We were scullery boys, dishwashers and servers at table for the midday meal for one week at a time. It meant no midday recreation when it was our turn.

Fausto sat on a stool near the sink where I was washing up. It was located in a scullery area away from the main part of the kitchen, so we were hidden from view. He leant back against the wall, his stocky legs wound round the stool legs whilst he chewed on a hunk of bread and meat he'd taken from a serving dish earlier. As *squatteri,* we were only permitted to eat once all our jobs had been completed.

'Get a move on, clodhopper,' he said, pointing to a pile of greasy plates. 'You'll have to work twice as fast if we're to be back in class on time, because there's no way I'm helping you. I'm too busy.'

He pulled another slice of roast beef and a chunk of *taleggio* cheese from his pocket and sniggered, 'I hope there'll be something left for you to eat.'

I wanted to kick the stool away from under him and see him sprawl on the kitchen slabs, but I lacked courage. Instead, I embarked, single-handed, on the mammoth task of scrubbing clean eighty or so white soup plates, my stomach rumbling with hunger. The soup had looked delicious when we'd ladled it out for the students: meaty, with plenty of fresh vegetables and pieces of home made pasta. The second course had been slices of roast beef, salad and a spoonful of *cannellini* beans baked with tomatoes. I couldn't wait to enjoy my portion and hoped Fausto hadn't wolfed down the lot. I stacked clean soup plates on the stone draining board and turned to place another dozen in the soapy water, when I heard a crash as my clean plates were pushed to the floor.

Fausto grinned like a mad dog, 'Oh dear, what have you done?' he exclaimed, as Fra Domenico rushed over to investigate.

My punishment was two more weeks of being a *squattero*. I tried to keep out of Fausto's way as much as possible and this was fine during lessons as he was in the year above me, but the friars knew we were from the same village and assumed, incorrectly, we enjoyed each other's company. So, we served together at Mass on Sunday mornings and were selected for the same football team. Fausto never missed a chance to torment me. He tied my shoe laces together so I tripped over on the altar steps before taking the jug of wine from the priest; he removed the clappers from the bells which I was supposed to ring at the most important part of the Mass – the Holy Eucharist. He hid my boots so I had to play football barefoot and took every opportunity to stamp on me during the match.

Fat friar Michele, who had welcomed us on our first terrifying day, was a kindly soul. One day towards the end of our first term, I noticed he was limping and not his usual jolly self.

Once again I was on scullery duty. Fausto had landed me in it again, hiding half a dozen apples in my bedside cupboard and making out he had seen me steal them from the kitchen.

'In here again?' remarked Fra Michele. 'You should move your bed to the kitchen, young man.' He laughed and lowered himself onto a bench at the table I was scrubbing clean. 'Have you had anything to eat yet?'

I shook my head and he went to the larder to cut me slices of home-cured *prosciutto*, slapping them between two generous hunks of fresh bread.

'A body can't be expected to work on an empty stomach,' he said, ruffling my hair. Then he removed his leather sandal from his left foot, rubbing the big toe. 'My feet are playing me up today.'

I picked up the sandal and examined it. 'This thong needs a slight repair,' I said. 'I think I can help you. Will you excuse me for a couple of minutes, Fra Michele?'

Hurrying upstairs to my dormitory, I found the purse sewn by my mother from a scrap of soft goat skin. It was empty and perfect for the repair job I had in mind for Fra Michele's sandal.

He couldn't believe the difference the patch made and walked backwards and forwards across the kitchen several times.

'Miraculous! Where did you learn how to do such a neat job, Giuseppe?'

'My Nonno is a farrier and a cobbler. People come to our village from all around for his work and he's taught me a few tricks.'

'I shall tell Fra Angelico about your skill and maybe you could earn some lire to pay for extra text books.' He stood up rocking backwards and forwards on his new feet and turned a pirouette, his smile making his face appear even rounder.

'One good turn deserves another,' he said, telling me to wait while he fetched something. 'This is for you, Giuseppe. On one condition...' He handed me a copy of Ariosto's *Orlando Furioso* bound in red leather, gold lettering on the spine.'...I was instructed to throw this copy away as there are a few pages missing,' he continued, 'but throwing books away goes against my soul.' He leafed through the mildew-stained volume, stopping at a page with a hole in the middle. It was an illustration of Rinaldo leaning over a cavernous precipice, a deep valley separating him from a castle piercing the clouds.

'Now, Giuseppe,' he said, snapping shut the book so dust flew into the air, 'this volume can be your reward for soothing my poor old feet, IF...' he held up a podgy finger, '... you can recite me the words from the two missing pages of this second canto and write out the lines and insert them - before the end of next week.' He beamed at me before placing the old book high up on a shelf of copper pans, away from view. 'It will be a good exercise for you, my boy. You've been stuck down in this kitchen too often, for my liking.'

I smiled my thanks, knowing the book was mine already. Little did he know that some of these lines were part of one of my party pieces. I was frequently called upon to recite them for my proud mother at *veglie* on winters' nights, as we and other families sat together around our fireside. The descriptions of the knight's six-day journey up and down steep slopes, through isolated countryside unmarked by paths, where there was little sign of other humans, was similar to the journey our shepherds took each year with their livestock on the *transumanza* and therefore very popular. I would only have to brush up on a couple of verses to make my recital word perfect.

So far in my life I had never owned a book of my own and I resolved to give him a perfect recitation. This volume was full of wonderful illustrations by an artist called Gustav Doré, Fra Michele informed me, and I was determined to make it mine.

Nonno's watch had disappeared from my bedside cupboard.

'Have you seen it, Geremia?' I asked. He slept in the bed next to mine and we'd become good friends. He wasn't a quick scholar and I'd discovered a knack of simplifying explanations for him. In fact several students had started to come to me for help with their homework and, in turn, they would warn me whenever Fausto was on the war path. They had invented a warning whistle and would group themselves around me like guards.

'No,' my friend replied. 'Turn out everything from your cupboard onto your bed. Maybe it's hidden inside a sock, or something.'

It was nowhere to be found. The trouble was, I wasn't supposed to have a watch or any valuable item at school. Upon arrival at the seminary I should have handed it in to Fra Angelico, the senior friar. But I had chosen not to. Whenever I felt homesick at night, I would put it to my ear and the rhythmic ticking was a link with my family.

How could I report it missing if I wasn't supposed to have it in the first place?

I stumbled over my recitation of the canticles for Fra Michele. Nevertheless he lifted down the book from behind the pans and placed it in my hands, whereupon I burst into tears.

'Well, I never did,' he said, wringing his hands. 'That's not the reaction I was expecting, dear child.'

The missing watch was the last straw and I found myself telling kindly old Fra Michele all about Fausto and the way he took delight in tormenting me at any opportunity. I also told him about the watch.

He shook his head and tutted. 'I can see why you are so upset - it was after all a gift from your grandfather. But you *do* know you are not supposed to have such things at college, don't you?' He tutted again and rubbed his balding head. 'What to do? What to do?' he repeated, before disappearing into the larder and reappearing with two slices of freshly baked seed cake, one of which he thrust into my hands. 'Eat this up, it'll make you feel better,' and he munched on the second slice. 'Run along now. Leave it to me and the Good Lord, young Beppe.'

Fausto left the seminary on the following day and never returned. In a quiet moment, Fra Michele handed me back Nonno's watch, telling me to take it personally to Fra Angelico's study near the chapel for safekeeping.

I thought my troubles were over.

Chapter 6
Marisa – Easter 1917

Montebotolino

I finished pounding Nonno's darned cotton sheets at the fountain and spread them out to dry. Grandfather's mind and body grew feebler by the day and he soiled himself regularly. I tried to be discreet and choose sunny days so wet laundry wasn't draped around the hearth. But spring had been very wet and there was a basket piled high with a backlog of dirty washing that morning.

Next I proved the dough for our bread. I like this task. My hands are strong, unlike my legs, and I enjoy pummelling and kneading, singing while I work. Nonno joined in occasionally, prompting me when I forgot words. It was strange how he remembered everything from the past but some days forgot to put on his trousers. After shaping loaves and rolls, I put them to rise again inside my wooden *madia*, closing the lid gently so as not to cause a draught.

My last job was to scatter handfuls of corn for our hens where they scratched among stones and scrubby grass. Then calling to our good neighbour, Elena, to keep an eye on Nonno, I escaped for my one hour of freedom before returning to prepare the midday meal. Chicco, my faithful friend ran ahead of me, his shaggy white tail wagging in happiness. A cross between shepherd dog and collie, he'd been destined as a guard dog for grazing sheep but Babbo said I'd spoilt him when he was a puppy, stroking and caressing him too much so he was considered too domesticated, not fierce enough to keep away prowling wolves.

That winter had been harsh, one of the coldest and wettest I could remember. Snow had fallen at the end of February to almost two metres and lingered for weeks in cold corners. Babbo had been forced to tunnel paths from our house to the bread oven and barn where we penned our hens and goats.

So it was wonderful to feel the sun kissing my face. I removed the shawl from my shoulders to tie it round my waist. I needed these walks up the steep path to the mountain ridge not only to ease my stiff legs, but for the freedom I craved. After fifteen minutes we arrived. Clouds had been blown away by yesterday's rainstorm, leaving a sky as blue as wild chicory flowers and a view that spread over three regions, from Tuscany to Romagna and Le Marche. I stood proudly on my hilltop, my face raised to the sky, my shoulders back, queen of all the Earth. All around me the meadows were studded with purple orchids, and thyme-covered rocks attracted bees foraging for pollen. I stepped onto a large flat rock and slowly turned full circle, balancing my arms like wings. Chicco bounced around me barking and I laughed, breathing in hungry gulps of fresh mountain air as if it were medicine. My very own "Elixir".

I'd read that word on an advert pinned to the wall of Doctor

Negrini's surgery in Arezzo where father had taken me the previous year. He'd saved hard to pay for his consultation fee by trapping skylarks for the butcher in the square in Badia Tedalda. And he'd collected frogs to sell for a few cents whenever showers brought them hopping from their ditches. He'd worked as a contractor, breaking up rocks with a hammer for the new road snaking its way down to Sansepolcro. He'd chopped and bundled up dried juniper branches to take to the *osteria* up in Rofelle to burn in the bread oven. All this he'd done over more than eighteen months, only to hear Dottor Negrini pronounce there was nothing to be done for my rickety legs and I would have to continue to hobble about as best I could.

Deep down I'd sensed this would be the verdict. But even if I'd voiced that to Babbo, he would still have persisted in his belief in a cure. That's where my stubborn streak comes from too. Mamma died eleven years ago and maybe Babbo was concerned about how to cope with elderly parents and a crippled daughter. But I preferred to believe his concern was because he loved me. Even if I never heard him say as much.

I untied my pouch of coarse cotton from the cord round my waist and began to hunt for herbs for my salves and cures. Chicco kept running back to me, making sure I was safe. I needed chamomile flowers for stomach ache and insomnia, mint for wounds and grazes, salvia for tooth ache. The juniper berries I needed for inhalants were still too green to harvest so I left them for later in the season. Instead I planned to crush linseed flowers already stored in a jar on the kitchen shelf. Later on I would boil a measure or two in water and wrap them in a warm cloth to place as a poultice on Nonna's chest. It would ease her wheezing and coughing at night.

The pouch was full, so I lay down on the coarse grass and lifted my skirts from my shrivelled legs to let spring sunshine seep into my bones. A buzzard coiled high above me and I shaded my eyes to squint at its flight, listening to its mewing call. A second buzzard swooped into view and the pair danced in the thermals vying for each other's attention. At primary school I'd written a poem describing how it might feel to fly - weightless as a floating feather, spinning, circling, detached from a world of pain. To my embarrassment, Professor Daniele had read it aloud to the class and I was so ashamed that, later at home, I ripped the page from my exercise book and threw it on the fire, watching the flames gobble up my silly thoughts.

Two early swallowtail butterflies hovered in a flirtations dance over a clump of clover. I wondered what it would feel like to be courted by a mate, knowing it was something I was unlikely to experience. Who would fall in love with a girl with such an ugly, crippled body? Most of the young men had gone off to fight in the war anyway, up in the mountains of northern Italy. The only boy who ever paid me the slightest attention was thirteen-year-old Giuseppe who lived behind the church of San Tommaso. And that was because from time to time I helped him with homework when he was back from seminary. He was always grateful, bless him. Together we'd work on the old fashioned text of Dante's *Divina Commedia*, putting it into simpler words. But he was ten years younger than me. A gangly young boy, with a head full of dark curls and kind eyes - sensitive eyes that would charm some lucky girl in the future. Thank Heavens he was too young to go off and fight in the Great War.

Lying there on the ridge I thought back to our talks together. One afternoon we'd discussed the circles of hell in Dante's *Inferno*, where thieves and the slothful suffered the torture of permanent fire.

'I don't believe in all that.' I'd said. 'It's hogwash.'

His beautiful eyes widened in a mixture of awe and amusement. 'If I dared say anything like that,' he said, 'the friars would send me home immediately.'

'That's why I can't believe in it. They say such things to make you toe the line, to be meek and mild,' I replied.

'Do you mean you don't believe in God?'

'I didn't say that. I believe in a God but I don't believe in everything I'm told.' I closed *The Divine Comedy* and pushed it across the table. 'Have you ever thought why people believe the way they do, Giuseppe? Think about it. Have a mind of your own!'

'What do you mean?'

'How can I explain?' I collected my thoughts for a moment. 'I'm not talking just about religion and accepting what priests tell us is right and wrong. Take for example the stories of so-called brigands who roam the forests down in the Maremma. You've heard of Tiburzi, no doubt?'

'Of course I have,' he replied. 'I may spend much of my time cooped up in a seminary, but we're allowed to talk. Of course I know about Domenico Tiburzi. *Everybody* knows how evil he was - even my little sisters!'

'Exactly my point! You say he's evil but you don't really know what he was like. You think you know all about him because you're repeating what people tell you.'

Everybody knew something about Domenico Tiburzi. He was the stuff of legends, a famous brigand from the last century with a reputation grown distorted with each tale narrated around the hearth. The poor wretch had stolen a couple of bunches of grass for his cow so she could provide milk for his starving baby. His emaciated wife's milk had dried up and, despite working from morning until night for his greedy landowner, he could never make enough money to live on. Eventually he was arrested for the theft and sent to Tarquinia to work in the salt mines. But he escaped and hid in caves near Farnese, ending up helping the poor and downtrodden.

'Next time you hear somebody tell this or that frightening tale about him,' I said, clenching my fist, 'stop and ask yourself why Tiburzi became a brigand in the first place. Certainly not for the fun of it, Giuseppe.'

He shrugged his shoulders and that made me angry, so I shouted at him. 'He was poor and hungry and no matter how hard he worked for those landowners, he still ended up with nothing. Stealing from the rich *latifundista* was the only way to survive...'

I leant back against my chair, my outburst over. My cheeks felt flushed and my heart pounded at the injustice. 'Sorry,' I mumbled, 'but it makes me so angry.'

'I can see that,' Giuseppe said and he laughed. 'You should be a teacher, Marisa. You make all subjects come alive.'

I laughed too but it came out more of a bark than a laugh.

'How could I possibly become a teacher?' I said. 'There was no chance for me to go to high school, like you. I loved my school days, Beppe, but when Mamma died I had to look after the family.'

"*La scuola non da pane,*" they used to say to me. School doesn't give you bread.

'You're so lucky, Giuseppe,' I sighed. 'Seize every opportunity to learn. And use this...' I said, tapping my forehead. 'I've been taught to read and write but I use my brain too, to think in my own way.'

I always enjoyed these conversations with Giuseppe.

For a while I dozed on the grass but fat splashes of rain on my legs and face roused me. The breeze tugged at my skirt and shawl as I struggled to my feet. I should have known the warmth of April would tease. It was too good to be true but winter had kept me away from my ridge for too long.

A huge clap of thunder took me by surprise and I jumped, losing my balance, a sharp pain jarring through my hip which made me cry out. Chicco came padding across to investigate, fussing at my feet with his wet muzzle.

From tall beeches at the edge of the ridge, birds exploded into the sky. The day had turned gloomy and forks of light split through sullen clouds. I held my breath, listening out for the rumbling and grumbling, counting for the noise of thunder to crash into the waiting silence. I loved its hollow sound, caught in the valleys, echoing and magnifying as if straining to escape its rocky prison. Everybody else in the village was terrified of these storms but as each tumultuous thunderclap cracked in the ravines and gorges and rumbled along the river valley, a shudder of joy passed through my body in this circle of noise. And then the rain arrived – hesitant at first - then pouring down as if emptying from huge pails. This sound was almost as loud as the thunder itself.

By the time I arrived, soaked through, back in Montebotolino, women and children were banging pans together, upturned buckets were beaten with broom stick handles or anything metal they could lay hands on in an effort to ward off the storm. Church bells in the tower of San Tommaso rang their warning to villages along the river Marecchia, babies were crying and a dozen barking dogs added to the bedlam.

I hurried indoors to check on my grandparents. They were clinging together in fear, Nonna wailing and clutching her rosary beads. Nonno thrust a cow bell into my hands shouting at me to go outside and make as much noise as possible to avert the storm devils. 'They've come to ruin our vegetable plots and maize fields with their evil hail stones,' he shouted at me.

'Nonno, no amount of noise will stop what will be,' I told him for the umpteenth time. 'It's only weather; it's just a storm…'

I tried to calm them down but Nonno and Nonna had been brought up to believe these superstitions. They were too old now to think otherwise.

I believed in many of our traditions but I've always known that a belief in storm devils was ridiculous.

Chapter 7
Giuseppe 1917

With Fausto off the scene, I settled down and by the end of my second year at the *Seminario Vescovile* I was third in the class. In exchange for simple shoe repairs for the Salesian friars, I had been able to acquire a few old text books. I felt like a prince.

All the same it was good to return for the summer holidays to Montebotolino, to spend time with family and friends who had known me all my life. I felt at ease with myself. More than ever I appreciated the beauty of my mountains, with their springs and waterfalls to plunge into on balmy days.

The downside to my time at home was that, with Nonno gone, I was expected to take on his work, repairing boots and clogs. Sometimes I had to forge shoes for mules and horses that had gone lame.

I had started helping my grandfather when I was eight years old. At that stage he used to give me simple tasks: straightening nails so he could use them again, putting studs onto old shoes to make them last a little longer and helping him with cutting out new soles to reinforce boots worn thin. When I was older I progressed with work of my own, sitting on a little three-legged stool. I worked with alder wood. It was ideal as it was dry and light and the longer the strip of wood, the more pairs we could make. After cutting strips into seven or eight centimetre lengths, I would trace around the shepherd's foot to make a template of card. And then I checked the length of his sole. This was crucial, for each clog was different.

Then with my *pialletto*, a knife with two handles, I cut out the shape and finally sand papered it to smooth the inside.

In winter, as I grew stronger and older, I helped Nonno at the forge with metalwork. When it was so cold that the landscape froze and ice would cut our breath in two, Nonno's workshop became an unofficial *osteria*. Nobody could carry out their outside tasks and folk – even strangers we didn't know – came to sit in the fuggy warmth of the stone building next to our house. Nonno hammered on pieces of metal – braces for wheels or farm implements that needed to be repaired in time for spring, iron buckets and tin baths with holes. Somebody would produce a bottle of wine to help keep winter at bay. Nonno even acted as a dentist occasionally. He would use his pincers and remove an offending tooth in one fast movement, before the suffering patient had a chance to cry out. But he didn't like doing it and refused payment of any kind, which made people reluctant to take advantage of him. I always enjoyed watching these gory extractions.

If I was honest, the work of a cobbler was purgatory to me. I preferred to be out on the hillside, watching over sheep in the fresh air. Most of Nonno's customers were old shepherds and their feet smelt like ripe cheese. Their work made them walk for kilometres and they seldom had a chance to wash. More often than not, the shepherds' shoes and feet would be caked in manure and even though Nonno had taught me to wash their footwear three or four times in cold water before working on it, the strong odours still clung. It was a ready made business for me to take on, but I was reluctant.

Marisa was one of the few fellow villagers who understood my dilemma.

One baking day in the middle of July, when the potent aroma of newly-harvested hay permeated the village and fields, she and I sat and chatted after our work. It was the custom for everybody to turn out to help each other at these times. After the harvest was completed, the whole village stopped to enjoy a three o'clock *merenda.*

In the field known as Fountain Meadow, on account of a stream trickling through that never ran dry, the women had laid out a welcome snack of fresh bread, slices of cucumber, tomatoes and dried herrings. Flasks of *vinello* rested in the shade of a willow and the stream provided drinking water to quench any thirst. After the *capoccia* had said an Ave Maria and made the sign of the cross over the meal, Marisa and I moved to a large rock to escape a file of ants attracted to the crumbs.

'To me it doesn't make any sense,' I grumbled. 'What is the point of attending the seminary all the way down in Arezzo when my family really want me to work as a cobbler? And now that my father is so sick, I feel I should be at home to help Mamma. I don't think Babbo is going to get better, Marisa. He's aged so much while I've been away.'

I plucked a loose strand of hay from the ground and chewed on it, enjoying its honeyed taste.

Marisa leant back against the rock, arranging her patched skirt over her legs and pulling down the sleeves of her blouse. Her arms were a golden brown and I thought she looked healthier than the last time I had seen her. For a while we were quiet, listening to the sound of crickets and the murmur of other people's conversations.

A group of younger children were playing with a puppy, trying to tie a headscarf round its head. Their laughter and antics made me wistful. It seemed my carefree days were over.

'What do *you* want to do, Giuseppe?' she asked me eventually. 'It's no good protesting unless you have some kind of alternative plan in your head.'

'If I had my way, I'd be a teacher. And I'd come back here to teach,' I said without a moment's hesitation, for it was something I'd thought about often in college whilst helping my fellow students. I looked at her. 'Do you think I'm mad?'

'Why would I think that? You're clever. You're in a place where you can study and you hate working as a cobbler. What's the problem?'

'I can see myself leaving that place as a priest.'

She made a noise of disgust, wrinkling her nose and blowing air through her teeth, she spat out, 'Giuseppe, you disappoint me. What rubbish you talk sometimes.' She rose from her place by the rock. 'Actually you infuriate me! You have the chance to study down there. If you really want to become a teacher, there's nothing stopping you.'

She hobbled over to where her neighbours were sitting on the ground and arranged herself next to them, her back to me.

I began the following term at the seminary resolved to fulfil my ambition of becoming a teacher. As well as following day time lessons which would enable me to take end of school *Maturità* examinations in four years' time when I would be almost eighteen, I continued my duties as a *squattero*. And whilst my companions slept at night, I sneaked into the toilet to study for another couple of hours. My day was long but if my parents were making sacrifices to scrape together one lire a day for my schooling, then I must do my bit too. Marisa had been right to be angry with me.

Two weeks into term, I was summoned to Fra Angelico's study. I wondered if I had done something wrong but the expression on his face wasn't one of anger.

'Sit down, Giuseppe.' The elderly friar gestured to a bench and came to sit beside me. He pulled back his hood from his silver hair and sighed.

'I have sad news, my child.'

In my heart I knew what he was going to tell me but until I heard the words, I hoped for the best.

'Word has come to us from the mountains that your father was buried two days ago. Your mother asked us not to send you home, but to keep you here until the end of term. She wants you to immerse yourself in your studies and make your father proud.' He handed me a holy picture and I read the inscription: "Walk with your feet on earth but in your heart, be in heaven."

I didn't want my father in heaven – I wanted him forever at home in Montebotolino, hoeing in our *orto*, telling us tales by the fireside, guiding us with his quiet wisdom.

The screeching of swallows outside distracted me from reading the rest of the pious words. I pictured the fleet birds soaring and swooping about the monastery walls, preparing for their long winter flight and I wanted to join them.

Fra Angelico's voice brought me back to the austere seminary.

'I've relieved you of your *squattero* duties for the next few weeks, Giuseppe, and we will pray for your father in chapel tonight…and for you.'

And with that I was dismissed.

I went to the kitchen to seek homely Fra Michele. He embraced me as my tears fell and said nothing. And when my tears were spent, he handed me a damp cloth to wash my face and disappeared into the larder to fetch a freshly baked cake.

**

I sat with Fra Michele frequently in those first raw days and he encouraged me to pursue my dream of passing the Maturità exams.

He helped me by finding extra textbooks and scrap paper to write my notes. And he put by extra food, telling me my brain needed sustaining as well as my stomach. There was no difficulty for me in arts subjects and I was doing well in Italian, especially literature, but geometry was my weak point.

'Fra Domenico is gifted in mathematics,' Fra Michele told me when I reported back about another mediocre grade in that subject. 'Why don't you ask him for help? You could offer to do jobs in exchange.'

Fra Domenico looked to me like an exclamation mark, his scrawny neck supporting a small round head, his limbs spindly and long. I had never seen him smile or heard him laugh. If he was so good at mathematics, I wondered why he wasn't teaching this subject instead of working in the kitchen. His sickly, pallid skin would have benefited from working outside in the cloister vegetable gardens too, but I had never once seen him outside helping his fellow friars.

He told me to bring my books to him in the kitchen on Saturday afternoon. It meant I couldn't play in the football match scheduled against the boys from Città di Castello. I reminded myself nothing was gained without sacrifice and another boy took my place on the team.

Fra Domenico, myself and another elderly sickly priest too poorly to leave his bed, were the only souls inside the college building that afternoon. Everybody else was out on the field supporting the most important match of the school year. Whoever won today would win the coveted *Coppa*. The College was intent on winning it back – 'To honour the memory of our many boys who died in the Great War' – Fra Angelico had said at the end of his homily at Sunday Mass. I tried to blot out the shouts drifting indoors from the watching crowd, the *ooooh's* and the *aaaah's* as they followed the match's progress..

I only had one ear tuned to Fra Domenico's explanation of the importance of plane geometry. He sat close to me, his breath sour, pointing at my copy book with bony fingers, asking me how on earth I couldn't see why my answers were wrong.

'It's so obvious, boy, that even a toddler could do this. You have confused adjacents and opposites. Haven't you been taught that tan is opposite over adjacent?' He prodded my back as he spoke. 'And sine is opposite over hypotenuse?'

If it had been obvious to me, then I wouldn't have needed help in the first place, I wanted to retort. I was beginning to understand why his mathematical skills were only used for weighing out ingredients in the kitchen. He had no patience as a teacher. But I said nothing.

Then, just as if a coin had been flipped, he began to explain again in precise, clear terms, his voice patient and calm. 'Mathematics is fun, Giuseppe. If you like drawing, you should be good at geometry. I know you're clever at cutting out shapes for your shoe repairs - I've watched you at work - so you should be able to grasp these rules…'

He set me half a dozen further questions and sat close to me, his hand on my shoulder while I worked them out. They were all correct and his hand strayed to my cheek, stroking it while he talked, 'See, you are a clever boy after all, Giuseppe.'

Then he stood up and went over to the sink to scrub his hands, telling me to return the following Saturday for a further lesson on trigonometry.

I wanted to play football but I also wanted to succeed in my dream of becoming a teacher, to escape the drudgery of work as a cobbler and blacksmith. Not to mention the annual trek down to the Maremma with the shepherds and villagers looking for work. So I gave up any idea of playing football and spent an hour for several Saturday afternoons in the company of Fra Domenico.

On the last Saturday of term, he told me he wanted to show me something special that would illustrate the importance of perfecting my skills in geometry.

'Come with me, Giuseppe. What I want to show you is in the library.'

'But isn't the library closed on Saturdays, Fra Domenico?'

'Yes, but I have special permission to use it.' He felt about in the pocket of his habit and produced an old key, a smile quivering on his thin lips.

The college library was housed in its own building, at the end of the loggia that ran along the front of the chapel. The stained glass windows were patterned like the bases of dark green wine bottles and set high up in the walls. They were small in comparison with the scale of the room, so the space was gloomy. We had been told the purpose was to prevent bright sunlight from ageing precious books arranged on library shelves around the walls.

'Over here is where we need to be,' whispered Fra Domenico, pointing to an arched wooden door, around which shelves had been built.

He opened it and when we were inside he shut it again. I looked round at the room lined with wooden panels, each one inlaid with delicate marquetry displaying intricate images. Fields, mountains, a river, a market place with stalls piled high with fruit and vegetables, figures dancing at a village *festa*. There was a school scene, a view of workers scything hay in the fields below a mountain village, another showing a priest preaching from a church pulpit, an artistic picture book of everyday life. Fra Domenico guided me round the octagonal room pointing out details, his arm round my shoulder. 'Look at these perfect shapes! Look at the artistry - all calculated to within a millimetre.'

Finally, he pushed an oak chest away from the wall. It had been covering the only panel we had not examined and he knelt down in front of it.

'And take a look at this, my boy.'

I knelt near him and he caught hold of my arm. His breathing was shallow and I wondered if the walk over from the library had been too taxing.

The picture on this panel was of a garden peopled with men and women wearing few clothes. Snakes coiled around fruit trees and a large lizard type creature sat atop a rock, its long tongue suckling from a girl's breasts. Fra Domenico pointed to an image near the entrance to a cave. It was of a man and small boy. With horror, I saw they were both naked, the boy kneeling, holding the man's erect penis in his hands.

'That is you and me, Giuseppe.' The friar said and grasped me tightly so I couldn't move. With his other hand he felt inside my trousers and fondled me between my legs, eyes closed and muttering the Latin *Pater Noster*. I struggled to free myself but his grip was tight.

Still holding me, he lifted his habit and began to pleasure himself, his mouth open, tongue lolling on his bottom lip. Too traumatized to move, I could hardly believe what was happening. Then he shuddered and let go of me abruptly, making the sign of the cross repeatedly across his chest as I ran to the door to escape.

'It is locked, Giuseppe.' He held up the key. 'Before I turn this, you must promise me on your mother's life not to report to a living soul of what we did together. God will forgive you,' he said, his eyes closed, 'but Fra Angelico will not. If he hears about your lewd behaviour, you will be expelled.'

'But I didn't do anything…' I stammered. All I wanted to do was escape from him and the ghastly panelled room.

'Nobody will believe that for one second.' Fra Domenico gave me a small, twisted smile. 'And, anyway, you owe me so much more than you can ever repay for all the lessons we've had over the past weeks.' He walked over to the door and turned the key in the lock, whispering just before he let me out, 'Remember, this is *our* secret, yours and mine.'

I watched him as he hurried away down the loggia and when he was no longer in view, I vomited and kept heaving until I thought I would sick up my insides.

The sinful secret would remain locked inside my mind for many years. I felt I was to blame in some way for what had taken place within that panelled octagonal room.

Chapter 8

Giuseppe and the *malocchio*

'I don't care what work you make me do – I'll muck out everybody's stables in Montebotolino, the whole region even. I'll do Nonno's cobbler work…I'll do *anything* you ask…I'll even go down to the Maremma at the end of this month and be the *meo* for everybody, forever… But I'm not going back to the seminary in Arezzo and you won't make me!'

'Why would a clever student like you want to work as a dogsbody *meo*,' my mother kept asking, ' at the beck and call of everybody, when we've worked ourselves to the bone saving money, sacrificing so much for you to study? You should be ashamed of yourself, Giuseppe. I can't believe what I'm hearing.'

Every household in the village could hear the crying and shouting issuing nightly from our house and all the women listened daily at the fountain to my mother lamenting about the grief I was causing.

'I'm at my wit's end,' I heard her grumble from my hiding place within the stable. Peeping from behind the manger, I watched her scrub the life from an already worn-out cotton sheet.

'Every night for the last week,' she was telling her friends, 'we have sat together and recited the rosary, beseeching Our Lady to help, but he refuses to return to school. Such a waste of good money and time! He was all but promised a place to study to become a teacher for elementary school. Just one set of exams and he would have been a qualified *maestro*.'

Our neighbour Elena wiped soapy fingers on her apron and shrugged her shoulders, 'You can lead a horse to water,' she said, 'but you can't make him drink. He's a country boy at heart, Vincenza. If he's happier staying here with you, then let him be. I remember lighting a fire under a mule we used to own. The lazy creature refused to budge even when his belly was singed. There was nothing we could do.'

Elena's husband had been found hanging from a tree in the woods behind the cemetery six years earlier. 'Just remember what happened to my Ernesto,' she made the sign of the cross. 'A person can go mad if he's forced to go against his mindset.'

Mamma apologised briefly to Elena for her lack of tact but persisted in her complaining. 'But he's not a lazy boy and I know in my heart he's not going to be happier staying here in the village. Don't you see?' She continued to pummel her washing. 'If only Nonno Piero were still alive. He would have talked sense into him.'

I couldn't help thinking how difficult it would have been to experience Nonno's disappointment in me. There was no way I could have revealed to him the reason behind my decision; I would have died of shame. It was better that he lay in the cemetery oblivious to the upset I was causing.

Maria, the wife of the carpenter, intervened. 'Aren't you pleased he wants to stay near you? You've lost one son to the war, your father's passed on and now your husband – God rest their souls. You should be pleased, Vincenza. If only our sons had been woodcutters, then they would have been excused from fighting in the war.'

Maria had lost her only son, Armando, in the campaign at Asiago too, but she never spoke directly of her own loss and refused to wear black. She believed reports of his death were a big mistake and my own mother had said more than once that Maria would lose her mind completely if she were to accept he was dead.

'I know for certain there's something wrong with Giuseppe, something has happened' my mother said as she spread wet laundry onto thorny sloe bushes to dry in the sun.

'Then, there's nothing to do but take him to see Nanni,' Elena concluded. 'When our cow stopped giving us milk, it was because Gildo's wife walked past our house and cast a spell. She's always been jealous of what we have. Nanni sorted it out in one afternoon.'

'Or you could make him immerse his whole body in the spring below Fresciano,' chipped in Maria. 'When Giuseppina's daughter had an attack of nerves before her marriage to Alfredo, they made her strip off and wash in its cold water. She was cured almost immediately.'

'Anybody would have an attack of nerves at the mere thought of marrying Alfredo,' laughed Elena. 'He's so tiny. Do you think she has to lift him up into her arms every time he wants to give her a kiss and a cuddle? Just imagine!'

'Height is of no importance in bed, silly' chortled Maria, 'only length.'

There were cackles of laughter from the pair and I saw my mother smile. I suspect she was grateful for her friends who were trying to take her mind off the problems I was causing.

After our supper of potato-stuffed pasta, Mamma asked me to come and sit beside her on the stone bench outside the house. We sat in silence for some minutes with the sun sinking behind the peak of Montebotolino. She finished a row of knitting and stuck her needles into the skeins of wool in her basket before turning to me. 'You said you would do anything, my son, rather than go back to the seminary.'

A glimmer of hope stole into my heart but when she told me she had arranged for an appointment with Nanni in two days' time, I knew she was still determined I should continue my studies. She was banking on his skills to reverse my decision.

Nanni lived in an isolated house on the road between Montebotolino and Fresciano, in a spot notorious for vipers lurking beneath stones and brambles. By trade he was a woodcutter and lived alone, having lost his wife and infant son to an outbreak of typhus just before the war. People had always consulted him in times of trouble and bad health for his skills as a *medicone,* for he was reputed to have great powers of healing and magic.

Mamma sat next to me in the gloom of his small stone outbuilding. There were no windows and the only entrance for light came through a hole in the roof which was charred and tarry from years of wood smoke. No fire was burning that afternoon and as my eyes became accustomed to the darkness, I could make out twisted roots of dried plants hanging from hooks on a beam high up in the roof. In a large niche within the side wall, bottles of all shapes, sizes and colours were arranged: some contained liquids, others powders and what looked like dried leaves. Leaning against one wall was a thick stick. Paolo, in our village, owned one and it was known as *il bastone del febbricone,* I knew that in order for it to work successfully to cure fever in sheep, it would have first been used to kill a snake carrying a toad in its mouth. I couldn't take my eyes off it and wondered what other magical possessions Nanni had in his hut.

He mumbled an incantation after ordering me to hold a saucer over a burning candle stub. He poured water into the saucer, announcing it was pure and uncontaminated and that he had collected it from a special spring in the woods, its whereabouts a secret. He knelt down, made the sign of the cross and recited three Ave Marias, followed by two invocations to Jesus.

'Oh blessed Lord, help me rid this boy of the devil within,' he intoned, followed by, 'sweet Jesus, may the wicked spell cast over this boy's spirit be driven out and crushed forever. As you rose from the dead, let him rise and be free of Satan's wishes.'

Then he ordered me to dip my finger into the water and added three drops of oil.

The oil separated and my mother cried out in dismay, covering her mouth with her hand

'Don't worry, signora,' Nanni said. 'It didn't work that time but I shall repeat it once more and the evil eye will surely be dispelled for good. Have faith and patience.'

The next time the oil drops stayed together on the surface of the water and I was pronounced cured. Nanni then asked my mother for two plucked hens and one dozen eggs by way of payment.

'Giuseppe will bring them up to you first thing tomorrow,' my mother told him.

But I had other plans.

Chapter 9
Giuseppe

Mornings were steel edged now, water on the village font ice-crisp. Instead of clear blue skies, tatters of cloud stuck fast between firs on the mountain slopes and leaves on the beech trees dropped yellow and rust to the forest floor. Some days our village floated upon a sea of clouds, forming an island, heralding the separation from the rest of the world that winter would bring.

Before I drifted into sleep, I lay on my sack mattress stuffed with dried corn-cob sheaths and contemplated the stars. I wondered if the sky would look the same down on the Maremma plains. It was time to leave.

Tomorrow the men and older boys would be setting off. Boots had been mended; in fact I had lost count of how many old shoes I had studded with nails to help them last the eight-day journey down mule tracks and dusty mountain roads. Paolo, our other neighbour, had a new pair of goatskin breeches and had proudly shown me his stick, whittled from chestnut wood in the evenings by his fireside. On one end he had skilfully worked a hook to yank necks of wayward sheep. Rossella, his wife, had wrapped chunks of pancetta in cloth and he had bought himself a sturdy green umbrella from the fair at Ranco.

I believed Mamma had no inkling I would soon be gone. Part of me felt bad; she wanted me near her now she understood

Francesco was never coming back from the battle of Asiago. One of the shepherds who had come to have his clogs repaired told us the newspapers had reported the deaths of 147,000 men. And all for what? At the seminary, during a geography lesson, Fra Alonso had shown us the range of mountains called Altopiano where the battle had been fought. I remember hoping, for my brother's sake, that those mountains were as beautiful as the Apennines he had left behind here. On the newly-erected monument in the square in Badia Tedalda and when everybody had disappeared after the commemoration service, I had crouched down and run my fingers over the raised letters of my older brother's name: Francesco Tommaso Starnucci. I wanted to feel close to him, have some sort of connection. But instead all I felt were twenty five cold, metal shapes.

Since the end of the episode with Fra Domenico, I vowed never to return to the seminary in Arezzo and I'd been making secret preparations. I removed Nonno's moth-eaten wool cloak from the wooden trunk at the end of my parents' high matrimonial bed. I'd been squirreling away morsels of pecorino cheese and wild boar sausage whilst Mamma wasn't looking and wrapping them in a rag in readiness for my departure. And nothing was going to stop me.

That time had finally come. Angelo lay on his back fast asleep, his mouth wide open. I timed my getting up from the rustling mattress to coincide with my little brother's whistling snores. Down the ladder to the kitchen I crept, where ashes glowed in the wide fireplace still holding enough heat for Mamma to blow life into and boil up chicory coffee for breakfast. Bunches of newly-stripped corn cobs hung from hooks in the beams, casting ghostly finger-shapes on the plaster walls. As my head brushed against them, they swung to and fro, the shadows seeming to wave a farewell. With care I lifted the latch just far enough to avoid the squeak and then I was out into what was left of the night. The light was eerie; neither night nor day. The huddle of houses of my village seemed to press towards me and everyday objects assumed spectral shapes. A broom leaning against Paolo's house was a spindly old witch. Moonlight glinting off a scythe hanging near his doorway was the open eye of a corpse. A cat hunting for an early breakfast pounced on its prey in long grass at the edge of our yard and my heart wanted to leap from within my ribcage. The cold took my breath away and I pulled Nonno's long cloak tighter, hitching it up to stop it dragging in the dew. Despite being tall for my fourteen years, Nonno Piero had been considerably taller in his younger days. They still talked about him, referring to him as Pierone (Piero, the big one), despite having died a tiny wizened little man more than a year ago.

Creeping along in the lee of shadowy stone houses, I stopped to remove my clogs, muttering a prayer that the dogs wouldn't hear me and set up alarm with their barking. Twenty metres further and I was at the start of a footpath. Milk white in the moonlight it wound its way up and down the river valley. Once I was sure I would no longer be heard, I slipped numb feet back into my wooden shoes.

Within an hour I reached the main square of Badia Tedalda. I hung back, pushing myself into a doorway, waiting for the right moment to blend with the noise and activity. I counted more than fifty men and youths busily tending animals and lifting bags onto carts, whilst a group of older shepherds stood arguing over some detail. Every now and again one of them would pull his pipe from his mouth and brandish it to reinforce what he was saying. Horses stamped their hooves on the cobbles, their harnesses jangling and clinking as they tossed their heads, snorting out their breath mingling with mist curling round the porticoes and steam rising from fresh droppings. The tell-tale clanging of sheep bells in the near distance – *tin, tin, tin*, like part of the Sunday Mass liturgy - told me a flock must be herded in the meadow beneath the square where fairs were held. I knew more animals and men would join in with the caravan along the route and by the time they reached the sea, the numbers of beasts and men would swell to several hundred, together with cattle already driven down by herdsmen.

Parked away from the bustle, I noticed Paolo's two-wheeled cart or *barroccio,* his mule tethered to a metal ring fixed to the wall next to the butcher's. The idea came to me to slip onto the back and hide amongst the load until the caravan was safely on its way. Then, at an opportune moment, I could slip out and merge into the crowd of shepherds and young apprentices. I would certainly not be allowed out of this square, as I hadn't been included on the chief shepherd's contract list, but I was banking they would not send me back once we were at some distance. I waited for the moment when Padre Mario began his ritual blessing of men and animals, sprinkling holy water on their heads and, whilst they were bowed in prayer, I climbed onto the cart and wriggled under the cover.

I remembered Nonno telling me that for the long months away between September and May, shepherds became like snails – carrying their homes upon their backs. It felt as if all of the homes had landed up on my particular cart. There was a huge pile of umbrellas, for autumn always brought rain and mist and it was better to travel dry. I wriggled free of the sharp spokes only to find myself face to face with a caged broody hen which set up such a squawking, I was certain of being discovered. But I needn't have worried: the cacophony of clanking buckets, copper pots, colanders and ladles banging against an iron cooking stove drowned the bird's indignation.

It was an uncomfortable bumpy ride but having lain awake most of the previous night, anxious not to oversleep and miss the three chimes of the church clock, I was now extremely sleepy. Manoeuvring closer to an inviting pile of sacks, it was not long before I nodded off to the rhythm of the rocking, laden cart.

'What in the devil's name and all the saints are you doing here?' Paolo had ripped the cover back from his cart and I blinked up at his frowning face, silhouetted against a sullen sky.

The caravan had stopped a couple of kilometres before the Viamaggio Pass, in front of the church next to landowner Chiozzi's large stone house, to wait for the arrival of the Pratieghi flocks. They were late and with rain falling steadily, Paolo was anxious to hand out umbrellas. Putting a finger to his lips, he yanked me from my comfy nest, shouting, 'Lazybones thought you could get away with it, did you? Now get back to work...'

Under his breath he muttered to me we should talk later, but at the top of his voice he ordered me to hand out all the umbrellas and to be sharp about it or else I would be going without my supper.

I recognised most of the shepherds, including the tall, forbidding figure of Severo, the *vergaio* or leading shepherd, who was reputed to know the way down to the Maremma coast like the insides of his pockets. He tutted and scowled from beneath splendidly frizzy eyebrows when I handed him the wrong umbrella, pointing impatiently at the largest and strongest at the top of the pile. From beneath the generous shelter of his umbrella, while drips sploshed down onto my bare head, Severo yelled commands to all the shepherds, urging them to hurry up now the Pratieghi group had deigned to put in an appearance. Turning on his heels, his long cloak swirling around him like a thunder cloud, he strode to the front of his troop. He thwacked his staff on the rump of the leading gelding and the band of animals and men moved forward as one. The flock meekly followed their leader, packed tightly together like an army, heads low as if wanting to hide amongst each other, some bleating for their newborn lambs slung like soft white scarves around the necks of a few of the shepherds.

'Tell me what to do,' I muttered to Paolo. We were positioned towards the back, Paolo's old mule struggling to pull his load. Four mules tied to each other with a thick rope trotted behind it, bearing baskets full of winter supplies, whilst the final mule carried a young boy called Tullio who, Paolo told me later, had tripped and hurt his ankle not long after leaving Badia Tedalda. He bounced up and down as the animal trotted to keep up, wincing with pain at each jolt.

'Watch the other *garzoni,* the young apprentices, and copy them,' whispered Paolo.

Chapter 10
Giuseppe joins the *transumanza*

At the Viamaggio Pass, the view I'd gazed on two years earlier on my journey down to Arezzo, was now obscured by thick mist. The flocks began to spread out from their tight pack, tempted by grass on the wider verges of each side of the track. Shepherd dogs, their dirty cream coats matted with dung and burrs, pricked up their ears, listening to the shepherds' whistled instructions to round up wandering sheep. I watched a boy not much older than myself leap over the ditch to chase two sheep away from a field of newly planted fennel, its first feathery shoots poking up deliciously green. There would be fines to pay to landowners if the animals spoiled crops and one of the main tasks of the *garzoni* was to make sure this didn't happen. I followed him, waving my hands about in an effort to help, but the sheep were scared of me and scampered deeper into the field.

'For fuck's sake, go back to your nice warm seminary where you belong,' one of the *garzoni* shouted at me. It was Antonio from Badia who used to serve on the altar with me. For a fleeting moment I was tempted.

By noon we had crossed meadows cropped and meagre from summer grazing and descended stony paths past the hermitage of Saint Francis. It clung to the massive round rocks of Cerbaiolo and once again I was teased by a couple of apprentices walking near me. Word had obviously got round.

'Stop off here, why don't you?' they jeered. 'A nice warm cell and dry sackcloth to wear would suit you down to the ground. What are you doing here, anyway?'

I ignored them and instead gazed at the view. Pieve Santo Stefano lay in the valley below. Stone houses straggled along the River Tiber that snaked through the little town. The cupola on the church of Madonna dei Lumi glinted in the autumn sunshine. I could make out women pounding clothes on flat rocks edging the water and one looked up as we approached, the sheep pushing their way across the narrow bridge. One of them shaded her eyes with her hands and then waved vigorously as our caravan drew near.

'That's my aunt,' cried Luciano, one of the *garzoni* who so far hadn't dealt me any insults, 'and she makes the *best* chestnut cake in the world.' He dashed down the bank, slithering as he went and fell into her arms. He returned with a brown paper parcel dangling from his hand and a smile that stretched from ear to ear. I hoped he might share some with me later.

At Sigliano, after another hour's climb up the other side of the valley, we stopped to rest the animals in the shade of a beech forest. The sun was high now, warm for early October. The ground was dry and it seemed we mountain folk were the only ones who had had rain in the past weeks.

Paolo gestured to me to come and sit next to him and I waited for another earful of reprimands. But he must have noticed the strain on my face, for he broke off a piece of his loaf and handed it to me before passing over a generous slice of mature pecorino cheese.

'I don't know why you've run away and I don't want to know,' he said, 'but your mother would never forgive me if I didn't keep an eye on you.'

We ate our simple meal together, to the sound of a gentle breeze rustling through the trees and the bleating of sheep. Crisp, golden leaves spun and fell and occasionally an acorn thudded to the ground. Paolo packed away his knife and the rest of his bread and cheese into a leather saddle bag, talking to me as he prepared for the next stage of our journey.

'As it happens, Giuseppe, you're in luck. They're sending Tullio back to Badia tomorrow morning. He's no use to us with his sprained ankle, so I've persuaded Severo you can take his place. You'll have to pull your weight, mind.' He glanced at my hands, soft and white, more suited to work with pen and ink than manual labour.

'Thank you, Paolo. I won't let you down. I promise.'

'Well, we'll see about that. Stick close by me this afternoon. The paths are very steep and I'll need help with the cart.'

It took over three hours to reach the top of Poggio Rosso. On the way, Paolo pointed out a huddle of houses perched on the mountains on the right hand side of the valley. 'That's Caprese,' he said, 'where the great master Michelangelo was born.'

I'd seen pictures of the Sistine Chapel in a book in the seminary library but I could hardly believe such a famous artist could come from a tiny village lost in our mountains. I stumbled over a stone as I craned my neck, trying to keep the houses in sight for as long as I could and Paolo clipped me round the ear for making his cart wobble precariously as I grasped hold of it, trying to stop myself from falling. 'Wake up, Giuseppe Starnucci,' he shouted, 'you'll be the ruin of me before the end of this journey. I can see trouble ahead.'

That evening when Severo called for us to stop and prepare for camp, I would have bent down and kissed his feet if I'd had enough strength in my body. I was exhausted. But there was still work to be done before any rest. I helped Paolo drag the portable fencing, the *addiaccio,* from the cart, to build a pen for the sheep. Together with two other lads we lifted a heavy stove off the cart and helped the cook who was nicknamed Cipolla, because he loved onions and ate them raw, his eyes watering when he peeled them. We hefted a sack of *polenta* over to the fire for the evening meal. I was ravenous and when it was ready, filled my belly with piping hot corn meal. Cipolla had flavoured it with wild mushrooms foraged from the roadside during the day's trek. It was not as tasty as Mamma's recipe, but welcome all the same to my grumbling stomach. The *polenta* was poured onto a shepherd's cloak on the ground and everybody sliced off their portion with a pocket knife. Paolo lent me his. And all the while I was realising how ill equipped I was for this journey down to the sea.

After supper I sat next to him by the fire but he whispered I should move further back. It was only the more experienced older shepherds and workers who took up positions nearest the brazier. I was quite content to lie further back in the shadows that first evening. My body and mind were shattered and I wondered how I'd manage on the following day. The night chill was a surprise to me after the day's sweaty toil. I had thought that nearer the plains the temperature wouldn't drop quite as low in as in our mountains. I wrapped Nonno's cloak round me like swaddling clothes and lay down near the dogs, trying to put names to the men resting in front of me.

One of the older shepherds, a white-haired man called Ulisse, started to sing. His voice was strong, melodic. I recognised the tune. *"Dove tu te ne vai?."* Where are you off to? The words were those of a young girl asking her lover if she could come along with him. "I'm off to the Maremma, my pretty Rosina, and you can't come with me," was the reply.

My own mother used to sing this tune as she went about her tasks in happier days, before my brother was lost to us. My eyes moistened as I thought of what I'd left behind. A tear escaped down my sun-stung cheeks and I brushed it away, glad of the darkness. I screwed my eyes shut, willing myself to stop.

'Hey, Rofelle boy! Fetch me some water.'

I couldn't believe my ears. It was Fausto's voice and he was poking me in the ribs with something hard. I opened my eyes to make sure it was him and tried to get up, but Nonno's cloak was wound fast around me. Fausto put his crook between my legs and tripped me back to the ground. His guffaws and jeers caused Ulisse to stop his song and glare. His listeners muttered and swore at the noise we were creating.

'Show some respect, you youngsters...'

'Get some rest...we'll be up at four...'

'If you're not tired enough, we'll find you harder work in the morning...'

I ripped off my tangled cloak, spitting dust from my mouth.

'What do you want from me, Fausto?'

I tried to sound big and brave but I was ready to piss in my clogs. I wondered what I had done to deserve bumping into my loathsome enemy once again.

He swayed closer to me. I could smell wine on his breath.

'What do I want?' he slurred. 'First off I want to settle a score with you - for getting me expelled from that cosy seminary. And then what else do I want?'

He ran his tongue around his lips, sucking in air through the gap in his front teeth and scratching his balls.

'I wouldn't say no to those pretty little sisters of yours. That's what else I want. But give them a year or two, they're not ripe enough yet...' He held his hands like cups in front of his chest and grinned.

I head-butted him, knocking him backwards to the ground. He fell on a sheep dog and it started to bark and snarl. Then I jumped on top of him, every blow rained down on his ugly face delivered with expletives, each one filthier than the last. The flames from the fire were red in my head and I'm certain I would have killed him but, mercifully for me, I felt myself hoisted away. As I dangled from somebody's strong grip, I sensed I was in trouble.

The man with the strong grip was Matteo, a farrier and friend of Paolo. He chuckled as he carried me away. 'You look puny, lad, but you've some strength in you, I'll grant you that.'

I struggled and kicked and shouted for him to let me go as he walked towards his hut, whereupon he tossed me into an animal trough filled with icy water. It took my breath away. I coughed and spluttered and Matteo told me to stop behaving like a toddler. Then he roared with laughter and fetched a rough woollen blanket to wrap myself in, telling me to sit near his brazier. A pair of tongs protruded from the flames. Shivering, I watched as he pulled out a metal shoe with the implement and start to hammer it into shape on his anvil, one hard blow followed by a lighter touch, sparks dancing from the iron U-shape as he worked. His touch was firm yet delicate.

'I don't usually work this late,' he shouted between strikes, 'but one of Paolo's mules is in danger of going lame and I owe him a few favours.'

I stopped shivering. My knuckles smarted from the pelting I'd dealt Fausto. I wanted to crawl away somewhere and sleep but Matteo was having none of that. He tossed me a hunk of bread and then, unwrapping a cured leg of pork from a piece of sacking, he cut a thick slice and threw it on top of a griddle to the side of the brazier.

'Even though you don't deserve this, lad, get it down you and then tell me what was going on between you and that half-wit. Then I'll see to your hands - they'll go septic if we don't bathe them.'

I munched the delicious meat. Blacksmiths had a reputation for eating lots of good food; they had to build stamina and strong muscles for their work and Matteo was the chief camp farrier. I watched his right forearm bulging as he hammered the shoe to the desired thickness. He wore a thick leather belt round his middle and a piece of cow hide hung down his front, like an apron. He stopped working when I told him about the theft of Nonno's watch and gave a low whistle.

'He's a little shit and no mistake,' he said.

I felt at ease with him and this was work I'd watched many times in the little stone forge where Nonno worked. I got up to stoke the charcoal and he grunted his approval.

'You're Pierone's grandson, aren't you?' he asked me.

'How did you know?'

'Word gets round here faster than a buzzard swooping on its prey. Anyway, Paolo already told me. He's a good man. Like a brother to me.'

I shrugged my shoulders. 'Well, if you knew who I was, why did you ask?'

He stopped mid-strike, eyebrows raised. 'You're too cheeky for your own good, lad.'

He stuck the tongs back into the hot embers and walked over, his big body looming over me. 'Look, Giuseppe,' he said, 'you'll do yourself no favours if you carry on like this. Whatever has gone on between the pair of you in the past, you need to sort it out. Or else you'll not last another day in this outfit.'

I mumbled an apology.

He pulled out the red hot tongs and horse-shoe and plunged them in a bucket of cold water. A hiss of steam blew up into the night. Then he started to form nail holes around the middle of the shoe, bending closer as he concentrated on piercing the red hot metal.

'We all have to rub along together, no matter what. Otherwise, it doesn't work. There's no time or place for disagreements.' He smiled and held up the finished article. 'This'll see the old mule right for another few months. Quite lame she was, but this will sort the poor old girl.'

The shoe was thicker at the back than normal, like a wedge. I was impressed with the workmanship and said as much. 'The *butteri* herdsmen used to come to Nonno with their lame horses. He was famous for the way he could improvise,' I said.

'Where do you think I learned my craft?' Matteo sat down next to me. 'I was apprenticed to him for a while but you won't remember me. I was a skinny little runt in those days.' He got up to cut another two hunks of bread and pork, offering me one.

'No thanks. I'm stuffed,' I said, patting my belly and yawning.

'Come and see me tomorrow and we'll talk about taking you on.'

'I'm already helping Paolo.'

'Paolo and I work together. Go and get some sleep now.'

I found a spot behind the sheep pen to settle down for the night and curled up under Matteo's blanket. My clothes, hanging next to his fire, would be dry by morning. For a while my head was full of Fausto. I wondered what else he might have in store for me. If I'd known he was going to be part of the *transumanza* caravan, guiding the same flocks, sleeping by the same camp fire, I would have fled away from the square in Badia Tedalda. It would have been as easy as spitting into the river to have backed away from the horses stamping their hooves on the cobbles and to have slipped back home up the mule track through the early morning shadows. But I hadn't and it was a waste of time to dwell on pointless thoughts.

I wondered what on earth Fausto was doing here? Why leave his feather bed and roast meat from his father's shop for five months of hardship? I muttered a filthy oath and turned over. Tiredness closed my eyes and I slept.

On the following day we passed through Ponte alla Piera, the caravan funneling over a narrow humpbacked bridge and along an equally tight track between houses, the noise like fine drizzle as the sheep squeezed against stone. Paolo instructed me to make sure his precious cart didn't scrape against the walls. A few inhabitants stood on their front steps or at gate-ways to neatly tended vegetable plots. He explained the town was notorious for making claims for damage against shepherds. In the middle of the tiny village stood a fountain, with a couple of guards on each side.

'They're making sure we don't take their water to dilute the milk we sell to them,' Paolo explained. 'It happened once in the past and they've never forgotten. And watch out later when we pass through the orchards,' he added. 'Don't even think about picking an apple for yourself, boy. They've got shot guns too, some of them.'

It was just as well my mind was full of concern about Fausto, for descending from Scheggia towards Chiassa, we were nearing Arezzo and the seminary. Any thoughts of Fra Domenico and his perversions I forced to the back of my mind, concentrating instead on placing one foot in front of the other, occasionally turning round to make sure Fausto was not about to pounce on me. After we'd made camp for the night I found it hard to sleep. I stayed by the fire, leaning against the trunk of a willow long after the others had turned in, believing I was hidden by the curtain of leaves trailing to the ground. But Paolo came to fetch and rebuke me, warning I would be no good for next day's long walk if I didn't bed down.

At Pieve al Toppo on the following day we entered a wide valley along a straight road with cabbages and cauliflowers planted on each side. It felt as if our mountains now belonged to another world and, as we passed through a scattering of houses, I smiled at the name of the hamlet: Albergo.

I'm visiting a hotel, I thought to myself. Just like rich people do. I fantasised about the cotton sheets and wool covers I would be sleeping under and a delicious medium-rare *fiorentina* steak I would dine on before retiring. I would send a post card to my family from my '*albergo*' and...

My daydreaming was interrupted as the few sheep I'd meant to be guarding had strayed onto a patch of cabbages. A toothless old woman hobbled out of her house, brandishing a walking stick, shouting obscenities at me, threatening to cut off my balls and fry them for her lunch if I didn't move my sheep fast. 'It's always the same,' she screeched, 'every year without fail you mountain peasants cause us grief. It'll be my son's gun I'll point at you when you return and not this...' She waved her stick in the air before poking me in the backside as I bent to pull the horns of a ram, trying to yank him back onto the track.

I was given a scolding from Severo the *vergaio,* who threatened to leave me behind at the next town of Ciggiano if I didn't sharpen up my act.

'The women there will finish off what that woman started,' he said, spitting tobacco onto the ground at my feet.

This was followed by titters from the other *garzoni* in earshot, including Fausto, who sported the widest smirk of all.

After crossing the river Leprone, the track became steeper. This next stage was a more familiar, hilly landscape to me, like the Apennines. The sun shone warm and I removed Nonno's cape and rolled it up as we climbed towards the castle of Gargonza and Monte San Savino. This was the first of about three fortifications we were to pass on our journey. In history lessons at the seminary and from reading Dante's *Divina Commedia* I'd learnt about the Guelphs and Ghibellines and their continual feuds in the Middle

Ages. Now their castles had turned into villages housing landowners and workers, with their own schools and chapels. I thought to myself that these places were now like barricades against nature and its hardships, instead of marauding armies. The road was lined with olive trees and vines, the fruits waiting to be harvested and several villagers stood guard along this stretch in case we should be the first gleaners. They looked hostile and surly and I began to understand how much suspicion our caravan aroused when I saw two more guards armed with rifles by the mill ponds of Molino del Calcione.

It had been another long day. We washed our faces and hands as best we could in the river Foenna. The animals had drunk thirstily and stirred the waters to mud. That night I slept soundly which was just as well, for another arduous climb beckoned the next day.

The caravan slowed right down as we trudged up a narrow, wooded track. This time, instead of guarding against the sheep straying onto crops, we *garzoni* had to take care they didn't topple down the steep sides and break their legs. Another ancient castle from the 11th century – San Gemignanello - stood on top of this next rise.

The trees thinned and we entered a new world, parched and arid, like a lunar landscape. Soon we were covered in dust stirred up in clouds by the sheep. We crossed an unfinished railway track at Montalceto. Dozens of men were toiling on its construction, lifting heavy sleepers, breaking up stones to make gravel. They waved at shepherds they knew. I recognised one or two faces from Badia Tedalda. Not everybody who travelled down from the mountains worked as shepherds. They came down to do piecework, grabbing anything they could do. Paolo explained that some workers who could afford the fare would one day in the future be able to travel to the Maremma by steam train from Arezzo or Palazzo del Pero along these new tracks. I thought they might have an easier time than we were having, their feet would not be blistered and sore; they would not have to sleep on the hard ground or be covered in dust and sheep dirt for days on end.

As the caravan wended its way around another bend in the dusty, stony road, I glimpsed a hill town in the distance, its houses built on the edge of a gentle escarpment. It seemed like a miniature, tamer version of Montebotolino but set in a more undulating countryside.

'That's San Giovanni d'Asso,' Paolo said, 'we'll be stopping there tonight. It's not such a bad place.'

Instead of erecting shelters, the men who could afford to, slept at "Da Cecco" that night, a local hostelry. We apprentices were to put our heads down on sweet-smelling hay in a barn belonging to Innocenzo. Originally from the village of Fresciano, just below Montebotolino, this kindly, middle-aged man had married a local girl on his journey down with the sheep. He opted to stay and had fared well from the *transumanza* ever since.

That night Cipolla the cook did us proud, shaving a black

truffle or two from the woods back home into our *polenta.*

Innocenzo had set up a challenge.

'The white truffles found here in the clay hills of the Crete Senesi are famous,' he said, lowering his voice to his audience of friends from the past, 'or so they claim,' he added, winking and tapping his long nose. 'So, we'll see who's right and who can tell the difference between the two. And there's to be no cheating!'

Paolo and some of the older shepherds had brought along flagons of Chianti for this occasion in expectation of the contest, and they added these to the generous supply of the local, very potent Val d'Arbia and Orcia. Supper developed into a lively feast. It also marked the halfway point of our journey down to the sea and everybody relaxed a little. After noisy arguments the contest was declared a draw and, in the absence of winners, the prize of a huge flagon of wine was shared out.

Afterwards, in the corner of the main square of Vittorio Emanuele II, I sat next to Luciano and a couple of other *garzoni*. We leant our backs against the bell tower of the little church and chatted about the journey so far. I was beginning to enjoy a feeling of camaraderie with them and Paolo had been a big help to me. Despite my aches and pains, I was growing used to the walking. The only blight was Fausto. In one way or another I knew I had to sort him out.

Perched on the edge of a rocky outcrop, San Giovanni d'Asso did not have as commanding a view as from Montebotolino but it was the closest similarity to home since the start of the journey. I felt happy for the first time since I'd sneaked away from my village and family.

'Like to try my chestnut cake?' A girl with a pretty smile stopped in from of me, carrying a basket of home-baked *cantuccini* and cakes. Luciano whispered to me he bet they would not be as good as his aunt's.

Innocenzo shouted over from his group of fellow-drinkers, 'Careful what you take from her, young man,' he said, 'or you'll end up having to stay here, like I did.'

This was followed by rude laughter and comments along the lines of '*meglio un uovo oggi che una gallina domani*' - (better an egg today than an old hen tomorrow.)

I must have blushed the colour of the kerchief round my neck and of course Fausto joined in loudest with the jesting, bawling out that I wouldn't know which end of the hen to start with anyway. If Paolo hadn't sent me a warning glare, I would have jumped on Fausto and pushed him over the edge of the wall by the church and into the ditch twenty metres below.

Next morning a lot of the men complained of smarting heads but Severo hurried us on our way, accepting no excuses from anybody. We still had another four days or more before we reached our destination.

The broad spaces of the Val d'Orcia countryside changed by the hour. Cypress trees lined twisting white ribbon roads up hills towards impressive stone buildings, larger than any farmhouse I knew. Tall and slender, the trees seemed like stakes holding down the land. Hundreds of olive trees silvered the slopes, their leaves trembling in the breeze on their gnarly trunks. In Montebotolino, nine hundred metres above sea level, these types of plants could not survive in winter. I tried to calculate how much olive oil they would produce and how wealthy the landowners in these parts might be.

As we drew nearer the coast, the valleys were far wider than the ravines cutting through the landscape of our Upper Tiber Valleys. Here, the wind blew over ash-coloured undulating hills. The light was blinding and the earth barren. Yellow dust clouds churned up by the animals' hooves clogged our eyes and nostrils. My mountains so huge and blue in the far, far distance seemed a million kilometres away. It was still very warm, despite it being autumn and I swatted away bothersome insects, pulling the sleeves of my shirt down to cover my wrists. By late afternoon I was covered in sores from scratching bites.

'Bloody mosquitoes,' muttered Paolo, slapping at one settling on the back of his hand and wiping away a smear of blood. 'If I bloody catch malaria again, it will be the last time I trek down to the Maremma… Family or no family to support.'

Malaria was rife on the marshy Maremma plains. In winter when the men were away, those of us left behind to endure mountain winters recited the rosary by the fire each night after supper. We prayed for the safekeeping of our families on the malaria-infested coast. Conditions had improved slightly since Unification fifty or so years earlier. At the seminary we had been shown a film clip of how the landowners – the *latifondisti* – had drained marshes and built large farms for workers – *case coloniche* – and introduced fish to the waterways to eat mosquito larvae. But in summer the plains were still a place of malaria and death. Everybody knew this. We sang songs about it. One of many my mother sang in her fine voice expressed the wishes of so many:

> *"Siamo tornati con l'aguzzo ingegno*
> *Sui nostri monti pronti a lavorare*
> *In ogni cosa noi mettiam l'impegno*
> *Per vivere quassu' senza zanzare…"*

They wanted never to have to live with mosquitoes again and to be able to live and work hard in their mountains instead.

For the last nights of the journey the fire was still lit, although the temperature was warmer. Our staple supper of *polenta* still needed to be stirred in the black cauldron on top of the brazier. Paolo sat next to me and told me of the ordeal he had suffered during the months of last summer. 'I swear to Our Lady and all the saints I wouldn't still be here today if it hadn't been for the feast of St George and what my dear friends did for me,' he said.

He told of how on the 23rd of April his herdsmen friends had captured a foal, taken it to the town of San Giorgio, near Grosseto, and sold it to buy medicines for malaria. Every shepherd knew the story of how St George had slain a dragon and they believed this saint had the power to cure malaria.

'My fever lasted for forty days,' Paolo said 'and I can't remember much about that time. My friends saved my life and I can never show them enough thanks, but I know if I catch the fever again…' He made the sign of the cross on his chest and shovelled the last of his *polenta* into his mouth as if to build up strength.

I decided there and then I would stick close to my neighbour and travelling companion and keep an eye on him. It was a way to repay him for his kindness over the last eight days.

At the end of the tenth day, on a sultry evening, our caravan of exhausted men, boys and sheep arrived at Alberese on the Maremma coast, a flat, desolate spot without a mountain in sight. Paolo pointed wearily at a low ridge a few kilometres away.

'The sea lies over there, Giuseppe. The first chance we have, I promise to take you there. But we've a few days hard work ahead of us and first off we need to set up camp.'

Chapter 11
Giuseppe's new friends

All I wanted to do was lay my head down and sleep forever. I longed for my mattress and woollen blankets back home and vowed that never again would I complain of little Angelo's snoring. I tried not to think of Mamma preparing tasty soup and home made *focaccia* bread over the fire and busied myself tying up my boots in case Fausto or any of the other apprentices might notice the tears in my eyes.

The first task was to set up more secure pens for the sheep. Severo strode about, his long cloak no longer draped around his tall figure. It was too warm for such a heavy garment down here. Instead he rolled up his shirt sleeves and I looked in awe at his swelling muscles, wondering if I would ever be as strong.

'You, boy! Stop gawping and help tie these sticks together,' he shouted, startling me from my daydreams.

Two older shepherds were constructing a hut from robust sticks tied together at the top to form a wigwam known as "A Gesù", similar to the traditional stable in nativity scenes displayed in church at Christmas.

One of them handed me a shovel and ordered me to cut sods of earth to arrange over the sticks. More pieces of wood were set on top to provide extra protection from the rain. The older men had brought simple truckle beds down with them but I only had Nonno's cloak to lie down on in the open air until I and the other *garzoni* could construct our own dwelling. Paolo had described how eventually there would be a whole village of huts clustered together, known as *vergherie*. They would all be sited on slopes above the pastures to allow for drainage and so the shepherds could watch over their flocks.

Fausto beckoned me over to a vacant hut. There were one or two gaps here and there which would need to be repaired to stop water entering, but it looked good enough to me and would save me from building from scratch. 'This will be a fine hut for you tonight,' he told me. 'You can patch it up when you have more time.'

I wondered at his unaccustomed kindness but was grateful not to have to sleep another night in the open, for grey clouds and sultry heat threatened storms. I laid my cloak on the earth floor inside the hut and set down my bag before going to help Paolo finish unload his cart.

Cipolla and the men on kitchen shift had arrived earlier than the rest of the caravan to prepare supper. That night we ate *acquacotta* – a watery soup consisting mostly of beans and bread. This was followed by salad prepared from wild herbs and plants. We finished our simple feast with slices of cheese and a dried pear each. I ate like a hungry wolf and afterwards, my belly full, I found my second wind. I no longer felt so tired and didn't want to turn in straightaway. Paolo had warned me we would be starting work at four the following morning – there was still a lot to do – but I wanted to savour every part of my new adventure and, anyway, nobody else seemed to be turning in yet.

Once again, Ulisse and the older shepherds were singing by the brazier. I went to fetch my cloak from the hut because with darkness the temperature had fallen. I joined my new *garzoni* friends. The words drifted over to us:

O mamma mia non piangere se devo andar' in Maremma
Vedrai che la Madonna non ci abbandonerà...

(Mother dearest, don't cry for me if I have to leave for Maremma, Be sure Our Lady will take good care of us...)

I should have said this to my own mother before sneaking away from Montebotolino. I should have prepared her for the departure of another of her sons. How was she, I wondered. Was she angry with me? Was she crying? Were my sisters looking after her?

All at once my body was on fire and I jumped up, scratching my belly, my chest, neck, hopping from one foot to another at the tormenting irritation. Fausto approached with two of his cronies.

'Oh look, if it isn't little San Giuseppe from Montebotolino wriggling like a piglet! Have you got worms or ants in your pants - or maybe the pox from going with that *puttana* at San Giovanni d'Asso?'

Their laughter and lewd remarks caused Ulisse to once again stop his singing mid-verse. Having already been the centre of disturbance a few nights ago, and with Matteo and Paolo's warnings in my head, I hurried away from the camp fire to my hut, Fausto's taunts ringing in my ears. As I ran I stripped off my clothes until I was down to my breeches, but I could still not stop scratching.

Paolo caught up with me. 'Don't go in that hut, Giuseppe! The mules will be put in there tomorrow!' He explained that over the summer months, the huts used the previous winter were always infested with fleas and lice left from the last occupants. Tomorrow, three or four mules would be locked in for about fifteen minutes so the fleas would jump on them and leave the hut ready for use by shepherds. The mules would then be let out to roll about in a specially designated sandy spot to rid themselves of the parasites.

I should have known better than to trust in any act of kindness from Fausto. Despite Paolo's warnings while he was tending to my bites with soothing chamomile to leave him well alone, it wasn't in my nature to let Fausto believe he had the better of me. I needed to retaliate in some way that wouldn't arouse suspicion.

The weeks passed and I settled into a pattern of work, helping Matteo or Paolo according to whoever needed me more. Slowly my narrow world opened up as a result of joining the *transumanza*. It was hard work but I was enjoying a completely new way of life, new surroundings and, best of all, new friends.

There were four of us in our little band – Luciano, Settimio, Nello and me. We had drifted together and begun to bond like a family – maybe because we were all young and far away from our own loved ones. But we all had different tasks, talents and personalities.

Luciano was my closest friend. He had been the first *garzone* to approach me on the walk down, sharing his aunt's chestnut cake on that first terrifying day, and ever since he had been there to help me. Small, wiry and very strong, he was working as a *stalliere*.

'I'm like the cook and waiter for the animals,' he told me.

I had been lucky to bump into him for he would normally have travelled a few days earlier than the shepherds, with the *butteri*, horses and cattle. But his departure had been delayed as his mother was ill and he'd been needed at home to look after his ten brothers and sisters.

His duties included mucking out stables and replacing fresh hay. In addition he had to comb and groom the horses and he slept with them in the stable. Sometimes when it rained he would let me bed down with him on sweet-smelling straw and we would talk about our families and the lives we had left behind in our mountains. I told him about Fausto but I didn't tell him of my experience in the seminary library. I was ashamed and kept it locked within me.

'I don't always want to do this job,' Luciano told me one night. 'I'm grateful, don't get me wrong, but one day I shall be a *buttero,* riding on my own horse, rounding up the *Maremmana* cattle. I'll wear a big hat and a *cosciale* of goat skin as protection against their long horns. And I'll have a pipe in my mouth all day long, whether it's lit or not.'

The cattle down here were dark grey with black faces, quite different from our white Chianine. Their horns were longer and I was full of admiration for how the *butteri,* with their long, hooked *cerratini* sticks, herded these formidable beasts.

'My ambition is to be a famous herdsman like Nicola Regi,' he continued.

We never tired of discussing every detail about Regi's story. I suppose because he was only fifteen years of age in 1875 when he had left from Motolano, a village not far from Badia Tedalda. We saw something of ourselves in him. He too had suddenly decided to leave the tedium and hardship of life in the mountains and ended up further along the coast from where we were, working on a big farm at Rispescia, south of Grosseto, with his uncle. This was where he learned the skills of a *buttero.*

'His saddle became his home and work place,' said Luciano.

'And he worked his way up until he was head *buttero*,' I added. 'And built up a reputation for keeping bandits like Tiburzi away from stealing the herds…'

We knew the stories off pat and never tired of them. Regi was often the subject of discussion at *veglie* and I'd heard my own Nonno tell of his adventures round our own fire.

Stumbling over the foreign words Luciano said, 'And when Buffalo Bill came to Italy in 1906 with his Indians and Wild West Show…'

…'whose real name was William Frederick Cody,' I interrupted, equally unsure of how to pronounce the name.

'…Regi beat him at his own game…'

'and lassoed more horses in a faster time than Buffalo Bill at a secret contest in Rome…'

'…and at the end, Buffalo Bill presented his own lasso to Regi, in recognition of his masterful victory!' Luciano finished off.

We lay quiet for a while before falling asleep. The fact that a young boy from our own mountains could have led such an eventful life and become so famous was very motivating for us. I shared Luciano's enthusiasm for his hero.

It was good to have dreams. My ambition to become a primary school teacher was gone now. My days of study were over and so I would never gain the qualifications I needed. For the time being it was enough to be away from the seminary, helping Matteo and Paolo. Most likely I would end up continuing in my grandfather's footsteps as a cobbler and farrier once I returned to Montebotolino.

One warm evening at the beginning of November, when all our chores were done, Luciano and I were joined by Settimio and Nello on our way to the beach. Paolo had never found the time to take me but I'd crept away from the camp on my own and been transfixed ever since. The sea intrigued me, the way it pulled and sucked at the shore, scraping the sand clean and leaving treasures in its wake. I'd collected shells to take back to my sisters and on this occasion I picked up a strange little sea horse, wrapping it carefully in my kerchief. Settimio laughed at me but he was used to the ocean, having grown up a little further along the coast.

'That will stink before too long,' he said. 'Best to dry it in the sun tomorrow and then pack it away. What do you want it for, Giuseppe? You can't eat it!'

He was from Orbetello. The seventh son of a very poor family, he was whippet thin and ugly, his face pock marked and scabby. But he was full of spirit and had us in stitches with his stories: how he'd stolen his mother's petticoat to sell at market, swigged wine from his father's beaker while he wasn't looking and topped it up with his own pee. He was resourceful, having learnt the hard way that if he wanted to eat he had to learn to snare all manner of things himself. He knew how to trap frogs from the swamps and in fact they were quite tasty on bread. He showed us how to spear them onto sticks and roast them over a fire. They made a change from our staple *polenta* and pork fat.

'There was never enough food at home,' he said, 'and if anything appeared on the table you had to grab it or it would be gone before you could open your mouth. That's why I left.' He patted his stomach.

The four of us split up and collected driftwood from the beach and made a fire to cook the frogs. Sometimes Settimio would provide an eel, which also made a delicious snack. Poaching was severely punished in the Maremma but his special skill was to trap skylarks and we skewered half a dozen on a thin branch of driftwood to roast over our fire. He also caught leeches and sold them to the chemist in Alberese who used them in his cure for pneumonia. Settimio loved hearing about our lives up in the Apennines. He was fascinated when we told him about our snowy winters. 'What does snow taste like?' he asked, 'is it like ice cream?'

When we laughed he didn't take offence but said he was sure he could make something out of snow. That was Settimio all over – seeing the use in everything.

But I never met a more contented person than Nello, the fourth member of our group. He was plump, generous and extremely smelly. Apprenticed to be a cheese maker, a *caciere*, we always knew when he was approaching. A recognisably strong whiff of sheep, sour milk and ripe cheese would waft before him.

'You're only jealous, you lot,' he would say, a grin on his round face. 'What does it matter if I pong? At least I'll never starve in my job.'

To our feast on the beach he contributed portions of ricotta, which he had carried along in a reed container. I'd watched him make them by the camp fire from reeds gathered from the swamp, cutting them to size and tying them together into cylindrical shapes with hemp. As he dished the fresh cheese out he told us, 'All a cheese maker needs is salt, container, ladle and straw. For the rest, he can get his milk from the sheep, a cloak from their wool and heat from the animals' bodies. What more could a fellow want?'

'I can think of something,' piped up Settimio, 'a nice plump girl to cuddle up to would be just fine.'

We laughed, saying Nello would have to have a good scrub first before any cuddles came his way.

'You should have been born thousands of years ago,' I added, 'the ancient Romans used to bathe in milk. I bet they smelled just like you!' I had read this fact in my history book in my other life at the seminary.

The following day, Paolo and Matteo told me I could have a day off as neither of them needed me. Instead, I offered to help Nello. He thought his job was the most perfect in the world and I wanted to understand why. It meant getting up to start at four o'clock but I didn't mind. Splashing my face with cold water I emerged to a magical morning, mist from the sea making the shepherds' huts look as if they were floating in mid-air.

The cheesemakers worked next to the large hut where we all ate. Inside, the middle of the floor had been hollowed out and a fire was permanently burning there. A huge black cauldron, known as a *fornacetta*, hung above the flames, the smoke escaping slowly through the highest point in the roof. A lamb's stomach dangled from a hook. Nello explained it would be used later to extract rennet.

I helped him milk the twenty sheep he had been allocated. This was a job I had done often at home. Leaning into the warmth of the sheep's belly on cold mornings, working to the rhythm of milk squirting into the metal bucket were all sensations belonging to my early childhood.

We filtered the milk and then poured it into a huge pot, a *caldaia*, and Nello made the sign of the cross over the mixture, before carefully measuring out rennet, explaining this was the most crucial part - getting the dosage just right.

After stirring it for a while, the mixture separated and I watched Nello whisk it, breaking up the curds. I helped him lift the heavy pot back onto the fire to heat up again and when the mix had thickened, I helped him again as he lifted the paste out and pressed it into balls, pushing each into their own wooden mould, known as *cascine*. The liquid was then filtered of all lumps and poured into a bucket. Salt was added to the little cheeses and then they were put into a cheese cupboard, its doors consisting of mesh to let in air and keep out flies. Nello made ricotta out of the remaining paste and we smeared it on hunks of bread for our breakfast. It had been hard work but there was a good atmosphere in the cheesemakers' hut; a lot of laughter, singing and banter. Nello was rebuked when he stole a lump of the soft cheese into his mouth but it wasn't harsh.

'You'll soon go off it, lad,' one of them said, 'when you have to do it day in, day out. All you'll think about eventually is eating a juicy steak.'

'I'll never grow tired of eating it,' he whispered to me. 'It's so good…' and he patted his fat tummy. 'I wish I could eat it all the time!'

A plan was forming in my head. A way to get back at Fausto. I knew he enjoyed ricotta and as Nello had access to this, I decided some of it should end up in Fausto's stomach. But not before I had "doctored" it with a hefty dose of laurel. I had helped Mamma collect these leaves to make a mixture for Nonno, who, towards the end of his days, suffered from chronic constipation. Too many leaves and the laxative effect was almost immediate. As in all home cures the amounts had to be carefully measured out for the cure to take proper effect.

But there was no reason why I should be careful with Fausto. If not packed into reed containers, the cheese was wrapped in fern leaves and often tinged green. So, Fausto would have no cause to question the colour of my fern-wrapped gift of freshly made ricotta. My friends knew all about his bullying ways and I could not wait to sound my idea out on them.

Chapter 12

Giuseppe and the *abbacchiatura* (slaughter of the lambs)

A few weeks passed and in the camp there was an atmosphere of festivity, for this was the day when we would fill our stomachs with meat for the first time in weeks. Even the dogs were livelier, their tails wagging, tongues hanging out in anticipation of scraps flung their way. They could smell meat in the air and it was the task of us *garzoni* to keep them away from the buckets spilling over with blood from the lambs Severo had selected for slaughter. It wasn't easy and dogs that were usually docile and obedient bared their fangs when we tried to restrain them.

Most of the carcasses could be skinned, so the shearers were kept busy. But a few were set aside for sale in Rome for the Christmas market, where butchers preferred the pelts to be left on. Apart from some *lire* from cheeses sold along our trek down from the hills, these lambs provided the first source of income. And tonight, my friends informed me, there would be a *festa* with plenty of wine to be downed and *budelluzzi* to savour - a sausage-like dish made from lambs' blood and offal.

'Wait until you try the liver and onions,' Luciano told me licking his lips, 'once tasted, never forgotten.'

Tonight was also when I'd planned to at last avenge Fausto. Nello had helped me pour ricotta into a small mould carefully lined with fern leaves. The laurel laxative I'd prepared had been added in generous quantities and I couldn't wait to witness my enemy's discomfort.

'Stop sniggering, Nello,' I had to say more than once, 'you'll give the game away.'

We'd planned to wait until Fausto had swallowed a good few tumblers of Chianti. Then Nello would be the one to approach him with the gift; it would be more natural for him, the cheese-maker, to do this and would arouse less suspicion. Fausto was already in his cups before all the offal had been dished out. His laughter and slurred swearing could be heard above the chatter, even though he sat at least six metres from us on the other side of the camp fire. I watched him helping himself from the pitchers of red wine, encouraging his mates to join in. Occasionally he shouted my name, followed by an obscene sexual gesture, bending his arm and striking his elbow joint with his other fist.

Just you wait, you bastard, I thought. The laughs will be on you soon.

Luciano was on edge, proud to be taking part in his first *Gioco della Rosa* later that evening with the *butteri*. He had been chosen by the yellow rose team of herdsmen. His original task had been to groom their horses so their coats gleamed and to tie his team's yellow rosettes to their arms before the tournament. But one of their young riders had been injured at practice and Luciano had been selected to replace him.

'It's my big chance to show I am a good *buttero* in the making,' he told us, hopping from one foot to the other in excitement.

I'd saved him a portion of liver and onions but he was too nervous to swallow, so I enjoyed delicious double rations.

I'd heard about this famous tournament from shepherds who'd brought their repairs to Nonno's workshop and I'd imagined how exciting it would be to watch. But seeing the game unfold before my eyes was a different matter altogether. The brilliance of red, green, yellow and blue rosettes flashing on the riders' arms; the dexterity of the herdsmen in the dusty ring as they leant forwards in their saddles, attempting and usually succeeding in plucking

them from their opponents' arms; shouts of encouragement to their team, yells and screams from supporters and whinnying of handsome animals as they tossed their proud heads, their hooves stirring and scouring the ground; the clinking of harnesses; the dust and swirl and skill; all these made it the most exciting spectacle I had ever watched in my life. We cheered on Luciano's team until we were hoarse but they came second to the blue team who had secured the most rosettes. Their leader was a strong man with long whiskers and I was not surprised when Luciano told me afterwards he was the nephew of Nicola Regi, the famous *buttero* who had beaten Buffalo Bill at his game.

And in all the excitement, we lost sight of Fausto. The special ricotta had been gobbled up by an unfortunate shepherd dog while we had been engrossed in the tournament. I had missed my opportunity to get my own back and revenge would have to wait for another occasion.

A search party was organised on the following evening when Fausto had failed to turn up. When he hadn't put in an appearance for work in the morning, nobody was surprised. He'd drunk more than his fair share of alcohol.

'Probably asleep in a ditch,' Severo said, when his absence was reported. 'He'll turn up with a sore head and he'll have an even sorer head when I've finished with the scallywag. And I'll dock three days' wages too.'

Our group was sent to the beach to search. I couldn't be bothered to exert any energy in looking for him. Fausto had caused me enough trouble and if he wanted to lie low with a sore head, then he could turn up and face Severo when he was ready. 'When we get to the beach let's just light a fire and relax,' I suggested. 'Fausto can piss off, for all I care.'

My friends agreed and we set about searching for driftwood. It was a still evening, the sun descending behind the sea's edge in a splash of orange and pink, the island of *Isola del Giglio* a black triangle across the water.

'*Bella di sera, bel tempo si spera,*' I said, quoting one of Nonno's sayings. Red sky at night, shepherd's delight.

It was good sitting close to our own fire listening to the crackling of twigs and enjoying the warmth. Winter was nipping at the heels of autumn. We lay on our backs, gazing up at the star pierced sky, talking through our dreams for the future. Luciano was still brimming over with excitement about his part in the tournament.

'They said I had talent, that they'd use me again in their team,' he told us again. We let him repeat the details of his adventure, although we'd heard them already half a dozen times.

'One day I'll have a market stall in Orbetello, in the big square next to the cathedral,' said Nello, 'and I'll sell my cheeses to rich people and tourists on their travels and they'll talk about my products when they go back to America and invite me over there.'

I laughed at him but Settimio was full of enthusiasm. 'I could be your assistant, Nello,' he said. 'If you gave me some space on your stall, I could sell my frogs to the French tourists. I've heard they love them.'

The wind picked up, stirring the waves. The tide was coming in and our fire would soon be engulfed in water.

'What's that?' Nello said, pointing to the sea's edge where a large black mass had been washed up.

'It's driftwood, a tree trunk,' I said, 'let's drag it up for next time we come to the beach.'

His hand floating, white in the moonlight, fingers spread as if he'd just cast something away, that was what I noticed first. Then his mouth wide open, as if half way through a blasphemous story. His eyes closed, as if asleep.

'It's Fausto,' whispered Settimio. 'Pull him out. Maybe he's still alive.'

He'd lost his trousers to the sea and the sea had uncovered a secret. Where his genitals should have been, there was only a scar. For some reason we would never know, he had suffered a terrible deformity that he had tried to compensate for by bullying and blustering.

We turned him over on the sand and Settimio worked frantically to bring him back to life, pressing hard on his chest in an effort to expel the sea from his lungs. We all took turns. We did our best but Fausto was gone.

Before we left him alone on the beach to fetch help, I took off my trousers and put them on him. His legs were wet and heavy and I struggled, but it felt the right thing to do.

And we attended his funeral the next day in the little chapel with the statue of St Anthony Abbot bending over his crook. Severo had urged everybody to attend. 'We are a family, we mountain people. In work and rest and death,' he had said.

We learned later from Fausto's friends that, full of wine, he had joked about being able to walk on water. They'd watched him stumble off down the lane towards the sea but thought nothing of it.

But I thought about it a lot, about how a single day or moment can change our lives for ever, how our destiny is shaped. I was grateful he hadn't consumed my ricotta recipe before he died. It would have only added to his misery. His death has weighed upon my conscience ever since.

NOW

Chapter 13
2010 - Davide

Every minute in the gym, where they had to change into their costumes before the *Palio* procession, had been awful. Several of Davide's classmates whispered about him behind their hands, loud enough for him to hear what they were saying.

'What's an English boy doing dressed as an Italian page? He doesn't even look Italian with his Harry Potter glasses and blue eyes.'

The fact that his mother spoke Italian with an English accent and dressed in a different way from their own mothers was enough for them to bully him unmercifully.

He couldn't find the brown tights he was supposed to put on and Signorina Grazia only had a pink pair left. He told her they were too small but she snapped, telling him he was holding everybody up and to stop making a fuss. Later on, while he and the others baked in their tights and heavy velvet cloaks as they processed to the field where the mediaeval jousting took place, he was tripped up. He didn't see who it was, but he had a good idea. It was most likely Loredano, who was probably also guilty of hiding the brown tights. Davide was playing the role of page to the Lord of Montebotolino, holding up his long cloak. He stumbled as he was pushed and then tripped, yanking the heavy cloak from his

Lord's shoulders and receiving a glare and later on a sound telling off, but he couldn't explain he hadn't done it on purpose. Nobody liked a snitch and it would only cause more trouble in the end. At the end of the embarrassing three-hour ordeal when he was changing back into his own clothes in the gym, his foot made painful contact with a drawing pin that somebody, probably Loredano again, had left in his trainers.

He'd had enough. If Davide heard one more stupid remark about Mamma being the sister of Camilla Parker-Bowles, he swore he would borrow a gun from Mirko the gamekeeper, and shoot his classmates – just like the teenager in Minneapolis he'd seen on the news last week. He wouldn't kill them all. On the whole the girls in his class were fine – especially Celeste, the daughter of the bee-keeper in Rofelle. But he could do without Loredano. He was the pits and next to be in the firing line was his stupid, weedy friend, Gianfranco, who tagged along behind him doing everything Loredano ordered.

It was all bravado, of course, this desire to kill. Davide couldn't even bear to kill a scorpion. He'd scoop one off the wall in the house and take it outside sooner than swat it to death.

'So it can come back in again tomorrow,' Mamma would say, laughing. She hated them; there were no scorpions in England apparently and she couldn't rid herself of the notion of horror movie scorpions.

Of course he wouldn't murder his classmates but he was fed up. He had to get away. Not for ever. He couldn't imagine running away for ever, or for more than a couple of nights. It would take real courage to do that. He just needed a little space to sort stuff out in his head. And he didn't want to go back to school next term. Not to his stupid school in Badia Tedalda, at any rate.

He stuffed a fleece and a pair of ski socks into his sports bag.

Although it was summer, where he was planning to go to was 1,000 metres above sea level and cool at night. Mamma was busy over at Il Mulino chatting to holiday makers from stupid England, as usual, so she didn't notice him taking the end of a loaf, a hunk of cheese and a packet of chocolate biscuits from the pantry cupboard. Feeling virtuous, he also took an apple and two bananas from the fruit bowl as he went past. He shouted over to her from the terrace, 'See you later, Mamma,' and made up a story about his tennis coach picking him up at the end of the lane for extra practice. Occasionally this happened – especially if a regional tournament was coming up. There was an old court in the grounds of the Guest House up at Cocchiola, on the way to Viamaggio. The owner let them use it whenever they wanted and made jokes about free tickets for Wimbledon in the future when Davide was a famous champion.

That was another thing that was getting to him. He wasn't at all sure anymore how much he wanted to play tennis but Mamma and Babbo kept saying what a shame it would be to give up now. 'You're so talented, Davi. Wait another year and then see.'

But it was hard entering tournaments twice a month. *They* should try getting up extra early at weekends, he thought. How would *they* like to miss out on other stuff they'd prefer to do? Like nothing in particular. It would be so wicked to do nothing much at weekends for a change.

He started to walk up the hill to Badia. His rucksack was heavier than he'd thought and the apple he'd stuffed in at the last minute dug into his back. He should have packed more carefully instead of shoving everything in any old how.

With perfect timing, Lorenzo came by with his tractor full of sheep manure and Davide stuck out a thumb to hitch a lift. Another fib came easily to his lips.

'My coach has forgotten to pick me up and I need to get to Cocchiola,' he lied.

'No problem. I'm going right past the entrance, as it happens.'

Lorenzo glanced at the boy and asked how he was going to play without a racket.

'Oh, it's just fitness training this afternoon. You know - speed training, upper body strength exercises. All that stuff.'

He was amazed how easily he could make up stories when necessary.

At the end of the drive leading to Cocchiola Guest House, Davide waved goodbye to Lorenzo and, after the tractor had disappeared round the bend towards Caprile, he turned in the opposite direction to make his way up a steep, stony track leading to Viamaggio Pass. He knew the path well as it was a favourite destination for his father's mushroom forages. There was a spot where they had been together in early August after rain to find *porcini* mushrooms, which Mamma adored. Davide had been sworn to secrecy about the location. But this was the first time he had been here on his own.

He stopped to catch his breath after a steep climb and sat down on a boulder. A large Western Green lizard, a *ramarra*, scuttled off into the undergrowth, making a lot of noise as it ran over dried beech leaves. Davide jumped but he wasn't scared. His father had taught him lizards were noisy but it was vipers he had to be wary of. If he were to step on one, its bite could be fatal. The two of them always wore thick socks and walking boots when they went mushroom collecting. He only had on his tennis trainers and thin socks this afternoon, so he rummaged in his bag for his ski socks. As he was already starving, he ate six chocolate biscuits as well.

It was cooler in the woods and gloomy. Wind wooshed through the pines making a noise like the sea down at Rimini, where his family sometimes went for days out in summer. The hut he was making for was about one kilometre further up the track and he needed to arrive before dark because he'd forgotten to pack a torch.

An owl hooted and he called back, trying to imitate its cry. He loved Harry Potter stories, even though he was teased for looking like him. And owls, like Hedwig, were friendly creatures and not to be feared. Further up on the wooded slopes of Viamaggio, a chitter-chattering started up in the trees. He knew this would be *glis glis* calling to each other. In English they were called edible dormice and looked more like black squirrels than mice. They made him laugh. One evening last summer, two of them had kept the family entertained, dashing to and fro along a power line connecting Il mulino with La Stalla. They were like noisy trapeze artists, keeping up a grumbling and a wittering as they crisscrossed each other on the cable. It was as if they were complaining about the presence of humans in their space.

Davide wasn't scared of animals or birds or reptiles. He hated when hunting season began. Big men dressed in camouflage congregating in their 4 x 4's in the parking space near Il Mulino; the howls and shrieks of the beaters as they drove boar out into the open; the eerie silence before the volley of gunfire and then, a frenzied barking of hunting dogs as they chased the outnumbered prey. He couldn't understand how grown men could enjoy being so cruel and he'd asked Mamma to stop serving him meat at meal times. He wasn't frightened of animals but certain people and schoolmates bothered him a lot.

The hut he was making for was in the woods near the peak of Viamaggio. He had only ever passed it with Babbo. His father wasn't sure what it was used for, but told him it belonged to the elderly lady who lived nearby in an enormous house on the road to Sansepolcro.

To pass through its open door, he had to bend down like Alice in Wonderland when she grew tall but, once through, he could straighten up to his full height. His head brushed against something spiky and, startled, he backed off and immediately fell over a metal bucket which made such a clatter he was sure he must have alerted the whole valley of his presence. As his eyes adjusted to the shadows, he made out bundles of plants hanging from hooks in the ceiling and containers on the floor holding seeds and stones. The bucket he had knocked over had spilled acorns all over the tiled floor and he collected a few by hand, before noticing a broom leaning against the fireplace. It was exactly like the twiggy type ridden by old Befana across the skies after Christmas to catch up the Three Wise Men. Or like Harry Potter's broom in the Quidditch game.

A fire had been laid with pine cones and sticks, a pile of logs stacked neatly to one side. On the hearth a box of matches on a metal plate invited Davide to set fire to the kindling. After lighting the twigs, he shut the little wooden door and sat down to watch the blaze while he munched on the remains of his picnic. In the light cast by the fire, the hut grew cosier, less of a place of sorcery and spells. It was like being invited into a story. Pulling a piece of sacking over his body, he lay down and was soon fast asleep in the warmth.

The windows of the old lady's sitting room in the big house looked out over the ridge. She liked to sit in her sagging armchair every evening after dinner to sip black coffee with a dash of aniseed liqueur, her daily tipple. She saw light flicker at the window of her hut down below and, grabbing her thick green Loden cape and stout walking stick, went to investigate.

A young boy was fast asleep by the hearth. He was wearing glasses and she tiptoed over to him and gently removed them. She gazed at his long eyelashes and curly hair. He looked like one of Raffaelo's angels in the museum in Urbino. After placing another couple of logs on the fire she watched him for a while before returning to her house.

At six o'clock the following morning she took him breakfast. A thermos of hot chocolate, a handful of *cantuccini* biscuits and a slab of sticky *Torrone* left over from Christmas. It was a little stale but she imagined a small boy would enjoy it.

Pushing open the little door, she sang out, 'Breakfast's ready!'

Davide sat up, terrified. An old lady, as thin as a strand of spaghetti, grey hair in two long plaits falling below the waistband of her baggy trousers, was looking at him from the doorway. She was carrying a tray of food.

'Relax! I won't eat you,' she said. 'Get this down you and then you can tell me what you're doing in my workshop. Did you sleep well?'

He was hungry but, remembering his manners, offered her a biscuit first.

'No thank you. Very kind but I'm on a diet,' she said.

To Davide she looked like a stringy scarecrow already.

As if reading his mind she laughed a high, tinny sound. 'Not the faddy, slimming kind. I'm on a medical diet, my dear. I have to avoid sugar at all costs.'

He dunked biscuits in the scrumptious hot chocolate and watched her as she moved about the hut fingering plants, stirring seeds laid out on a tray to dry, tutting as she threw a handful of roots onto the ashes in the fireplace.

'Mouldy. No good for anything,' she muttered. Then, sitting down on a bench made from a large, flat stone, she said, 'Well I can see you're not going to enlighten me as to why you've decided to squat in my little hut, so I'll do the talking first.'

She extended her bird-like hand to his grubby one. 'My name is Giselda and I'm very old. I live in that big house on the hill all by myself except for seventeen cats and a very rude parrot called Pasquale. When you meet him, don't be shocked at his language. One of the builders who constructed this marvellous hut for me suffered from Tourette's Syndrome and he couldn't help uttering swear words from time to time, poor chap. Well, I'm afraid Pasquale picked up some of the filthiest words.'

Davide laughed.

'That's better,' she said, clapping her hands together. 'I thought you were going to turn out to be one of those tragic children too traumatised to smile.'

She continued her introduction. 'I'm the last of the Chiozzi family. You're probably too young to know who we were but my grandfather was the richest landowner of this area. Unfortunately my father was only interested in playing cards and drinking red wine and everything has gone downhill since then. He's dead now. I'm not boring you, am I? It's no use talking to Pasquale or the cats about these things, so it's nice to be able to chat with you. I don't see many people nowadays, except for the tiresome doctor.'

Davide liked her. She was different from other adults he knew. He pointed with a half-eaten biscuit to the plants hanging from the hooks and asked, 'Are you a witch? Are these all for your spells?'

'Not a witch exactly – although some might have described me as a white witch in the past. No, dear boy, I'm what is known as a plantswoman.'

She wandered round her hut, touching everything. 'This is all part of my research. I'm carrying out experiments for Aboca, the cosmetic company near Sansepolcro. They use plants to make medicines, creams, shampoos, that kind of thing…'

'…I know where you mean,' he said. 'We drive past it when we go down to the big supermarket.'

'In the past,' she continued, 'people who lived and worked up in these mountains couldn't afford to visit the doctor. When they went on the annual trek to the coast, they had to take their own remedies and cures along with them. I've come across some really interesting papers in grandfather's desk and I've been studying them carefully and even trying out some of his recipes.'

She picked up a withered piece of what looked like dried wood. 'This, for example, is known in our dialect as *erba nocca*.

Do you know any Latin? Do children study Latin at your school?'

He shook his head and said, 'Not yet. We will in a couple of years.'

'No matter. Anyway, *helleborus viridis*, as it is known by botanists, is quite, quite poisonous and when I was a little girl I was always warned not to pick it up in case all my teeth fell out.' She grinned, showing gaps where some of her front teeth were missing.

Davide thought she looked like a mischievous pixie from the pages of one of the Enid Blyton books Mamma had brought back from England.

'Losing these, however,' she said, 'has nothing whatsoever to do with this special plant. *Erba nocca* was used by shepherds who went down with the *transumanza* to cure their sheep from fevers. They inserted a piece of this in the animal's skin.'

Davide's eyes widened as he picked up the word *transumanza*. 'I've been trying to do a project for school about that.'

'Splendid!' she said. 'I shall help you and you'll get top marks.' She clapped her hands again then sat down, flicking her plaits behind her shoulders. 'Your turn now. Tell me, what are you doing here?'

It was easy to pour out his troubles to Giselda. He told her how unhappy he was at school, about the bullying and tormenting by his classmates. He told her he didn't want to go to his school anymore and that if his parents made him he would run away again. They wanted him to be a famous tennis player but he hated all the training and he much preferred the idea of working with animals and becoming a vet when he was older. She listened without interrupting once, sitting still on her stone bench, hands clasped in her lap, her head inclined to one side like a little bird.

When he had finished and brushed away his tears with his sleeve, she stood up and together they tidied the remains of his breakfast into a basket.

'Come and meet Pasquale,' she said. 'He'll cheer you up, but he'll probably tell you to fuck off.'

Davide grinned. He was absolutely forbidden to use that expression and had only heard Babbo say it once, when a man came down to the river to wash his hair with shampoo under the waterfall. He was very impressed that the old lady hadn't even hesitated or apologised before saying it.

As they wandered over to her large house, she told him it would be best if they phoned his parents, for by now they would be frantic with worry. She turned to face him, tilting his face up, one hand under his chin.

'Listen, dear child. Be proud of who you are,' she said. 'Be yourself. When I was a young lady – and I know you probably can't imagine me young – I went against who I was and instead went along with what everybody else wanted me to be.'

Seeing his puzzlement, she explained. 'I was in love with a young man from the village, you see. A special man. Strong and beautiful, inside and out. He adored animals and plants, like me, and used to wander about the countryside with his pockets full of chestnuts and walnuts to push into the ground wherever he thought there should be a tree growing.'

She pointed to the woods on the slopes above her house. 'Next time you go for a walk up there, take a good look around you. Many of those trees were planted by him. My parents didn't think he was good enough and forbade me to marry him. They wanted me to find somebody suitable and boring, like a doctor or a high flying civil servant and I was obedient to their wishes. Life was different in those days.'

She shook her head before continuing. 'But look at me now, Davide. All alone, with no children to take all this on.' She gestured to the land around them. 'It's just me and my cats and a blasphemous parrot. I've always been different but my beautiful young man understood me and accepted me for myself. We were kindred spirits and I should have followed my heart and married him.'

She sighed as they made their way into her house. 'What I'm trying to tell you is, concentrate on being yourself and don't worry what others think or say about you.'

She tugged on her stringy plaits. 'Here's another silly example. The hairdresser in Badia – lovely as she is – is always going on at me to cut these off and to dye my hair and have a nice perm.' She laughed. 'I think I continue to wear my plaits to prove a point. To say – this is me and take me as I am.'

He smiled at her and she continued, 'You tell me your mother was brought up in England. Well, ask her about Shakespeare's *Hamlet*. I studied that play at school, so she's bound to have as well. Polonius tells us something you should take heed of.'

Giselda closed her eyes, clasped her hands together and recited in English: ' "This above all, to thine own self be true, And it must follow, as the night the day, Thou canst not then be false to any man."

Now, isn't that just so clever?' she asked, opening her eyes and peering at him.

Davide couldn't quite understand all the words, which didn't make much sense to him and the way she pronounced English in a funny way made it even harder. And he couldn't imagine her without her plaits either.

Chapter 14
Inside Giselda's house

'Let's go inside now and contact your parents. I don't possess a mobile phone or computer. Just an old-fashioned telephone.'

Davide followed Giselda down a short path through beech woods to her large house. At one stage she bent to pick up a *porcini* mushroom, brushing aside the leaves around it and leaving a smaller one to grow.

'This will do perfectly for my lunch,' she said, 'sliced up in an omelette. By the way, young man. Never put your gathered mushrooms into horrid plastic bags...'

'Why not?'

'You should always use a basket so the mushroom spores fall through the wicker and allow for more mushrooms to grow for another day.'

He resolved to tell this to Babbo. They usually took a plastic bag on their hunts but he didn't want to admit that.

'When we go inside, remind me to show you my special mushroom knife,' she added. 'It has a brush on one end to clean off soil and spores.'

They entered through a wooden door set into an arched stone framework with her surname,"Chiozzi", chiseled between intricate patterns of cows and sheep.

'That was done for me by a clever young man called Valentino. He used to be the chief stonemason for San Marino but he was rather too fond of red wine and he died young. Such a waste!'

He followed her up a stone spiral staircase, the first ten steps holding huge baskets filled with pine cones, interesting shaped stones and large seed heads. Half way up she paused at a long thin window. She was out of breath and he waited politely until she was able to speak.

'I think my architect was very clever, don't you?' she said, pointing to the window. 'Take a look and tell me it's the ideal view to help you pause while you get your second wind…'

He stood on tip toe to look out. The panes were grubby and a cobweb hung across one corner like a tattered net curtain, blocking the view. He lifted his hand to brush it away.

'Don't!' she shouted. 'How would you like it if a great giant hand swooped away hours and hours of your work in one careless movement?'

'But you asked me to look at the view and I can't see a thing!'

'Oh, never mind, you weren't to know. But a cobweb is a thing of beauty to me. One of the joys in my life is to go for a walk after it's rained and the sun comes out. Spiders' webs are like diamond catchers – with raindrops glistening like tiny precious stones inside the most complex patterns. Spiders are *so* clever, don't you agree?'

Davide hadn't really thought about spiders being intelligent and he knew Mamma had a thing about cleaning webs away from the beams wherever she saw one. Giselda was quite different from anybody he'd ever met.

At the top of the stairs was another arched door. All round the handle and on the frame were scratch marks which she told him her cats had made. 'They want to come in and be with me when I sit in here and I do let them sometimes but I have so many precious documents and there are so many cats and kittens. I have to say 'no' sometimes.'

She opened the door to her study. There were books and papers everywhere. The shelves were spilling over with them and on one armchair books were piled so high on the seat, it was impossible to sit anywhere. A precarious pile of encyclopaedias propped up a chair with three legs and not a single surface of any piece of furniture was clutter-free.

A loud squawk made Davide jump and when this was followed by, 'Good afternoon, what time of day do you call this, you wanker?' He burst out laughing.

'Be quiet, Pasquale. You're only showing off because I have a visitor,' Giselda wagged her fingers at a green and red parrot in a cage hanging by the window.

'Willy, shit, fart, arse,' answered Pasquale, much to Davide's delight.

'He'll be quiet in a minute. I'll just let him get it out of his system. Try to ignore him, please,' Giselda said, turning her back on the bird.

'Bossy old cow, shut the fuck up, shut up...'

Giselda put a finger to her mouth, warning Davide not to say anything. She pulled a stone from a shelf which held a variety of objects including a cracked coffee cup, the tail of a squirrel and a piece of tree trunk shaped like a bent old woman.

'I found this stone down by the river Marecchia. Just look at how marvellous nature is.' She thrust it into his hands. 'It's a false fossil. You can see why. It looks like a pressed flower but those patterns have been created by water seeping into the rock.'

Another stone had outlines over its smooth surface resembling the outlines of an ancient city. The sort of background found on a Christmas card, Davide thought, depicting the houses in Bethlehem.

'Wow, that's really cool,' he said, returning it carefully to the shelf.

One wall of the sitting room was completely covered with photographs.

'Let me introduce you to my family,' she said, her arms open as if to embrace the black-and-white framed figures. She pointed to one of the larger pictures. 'This is my grandfather – Nonno Ubaldo. Isn't he the most handsome man you've ever seen?'

She leaned towards a fuzzy, sepia photo of a middle-aged man sporting a battered felt hat and thick cords, a pointer curled at his feet. She blew the image a kiss.

'He was famous for refusing to hunt because he loved animals, but he also knew everything there was to know about hunting in these parts. Just look at his wonderful moustache. Men don't seem to like growing them like that anymore, do they?'

The moustache was very long and droopy, giving Ubaldo the look of a melancholy hound. Davide understood perfectly why this fashion was no longer popular. It would get in the way – dip into food, get caught in zips and all manner of things – but, once again, he didn't have the heart to say this to Giselda. He guessed she was happier living with the ways of the past.

'Wanker, wanker, silly old wanker,' squawked Pasquale and Davide tried not to giggle.

Giselda threw a cloth over his cage. 'It would take all day to tell you the names of my whole family,' she said, moving as far away from Pasquale as possible, 'so I'll leave that to another time. First we have to find my telephone. It's in this room somewhere. Let's start our hunt now.'

Davide made for an occasional table at the side of the book-laden settee, moving aside a shoe box to see if the phone might be underneath.

'Careful, do be careful…that box contains one of my most treasured possessions,' Giselda said, taking the box from him. She held up a crude necklace threaded with lumpy brown beads. 'Guess what this is.'

Davide had absolutely no idea but took a guess. 'Something a child made for you?'

'No, try again.'

'Something made in Africa or India, given to you as a present from somebody who went there on holiday?'

She laughed. 'No. I never get presents. I can see I shall have to enlighten you.' She held the unusual piece of jewellery close to her heart while she told him she had made it herself as a young woman when she had had to go away to Florence for two years to work as a teacher.

'I didn't want to go one little bit. I'd qualified as a primary school teacher and hoped to find a job locally. But no such luck! I *hate* big cities. How can one begin to compare living in a polluted city to breathing this wonderful mountain air of ours?'

She sat down on a pile of books while she talked. 'I made this to remind myself of home. In moments when I longed to be back here at Viamaggio, I would get out my necklace and hold on to it and then I could pretend I was back in my beloved home, surrounded by nature and far away from filthy cars and motor bikes - and filthy people.' She paused. 'I moulded the beads from rabbit droppings and soil, Davide, from my land.'

She laughed at his bemused expression. 'In that way,' she explained, 'I had my very own unique talisman created from mountain earth, plants and animal.'

She returned her unusual jewellery to its shoe box and pushed it under the settee. 'Even though I'm safe now back here, I keep it to remind me how lucky I am.'

Davide didn't know what to say. He thought she was dotty but he liked her and he wasn't frightened of her. 'Where do you suggest I should look for the phone?' he asked instead.

'Well, that's a very daft question. If I knew where to look, then we wouldn't be searching, would we?'

They continued to move papers and books about. Davide lifted the lid from a tall basket and yelped when he saw its contents.

'Ah, you've found Pinocchio the pine marten,' Giselda said, lifting a stuffed animal into her arms. 'He was such a good friend,

God rest his little soul.'

Davide peered at the cat-like mammal, its glass eyes shining too brightly for a dead creature and put out his hand to touch it. A whiff of decomposition lingered in the room.

'I stuffed him myself...I wouldn't trust him to the taxidermist in Arezzo but it was rather more difficult that I imagined. Do you know, he used to play with my cats? He was very tame, you see. I found him when he was tiny; his mother had been killed by a wild boar and I fed him up with cat food and milk from a bottle and one of my cats eventually adopted him into her litter. You've never seen anything like it: a row of kittens and then, Pinocchio suckling in amongst them all. Of course I couldn't let him go free again. He'd grown too used to human contact and wouldn't have survived long on the mountain. A viper got him in the end. He was too nosy for his own good, really, and this viper had made a home in my log pile and I'm afraid he was bitten on the nose by her...'

She smiled and dropped a kiss on the stuffed animal's head before replacing him in his basket.

They hunted some more for the telephone until Giselda, with a cry of "Eureka!" moved a pile of cushions and rugs from a corner and held up the missing object.

'Phone your parents now and I'll go and make another cup of chocolate for you and a coffee for me. Don't know about you, but all this investigation has made me quite exhausted.'

In the car on the way back home, he found it hard to explain to his parents why he had run away and he yawned a couple of times from the back seat.

It was even harder to begin to describe eccentric Giselda and her house crammed with strange possessions. 'I think she's lonely,' he said. 'Can we invite her over one day and maybe adopt her as an extra Nonna?'

He didn't want to talk about her too much as he felt his parents might not approve and possibly stop him from seeing her again.

And he had a sense that too much discussion of her might somehow make some of her magic disappear.

So he closed his eyes and pretended to fall fast asleep on the fifteen minute journey home, trying not to chuckle as he remembered Pasquale's "Willy, shit, fart, arse" outbursts and wondering if Mamma and Babbo would let him keep a parrot as a pet.

Chapter 15
Francesco and Davide

Davide was grounded for a week after running away but he didn't mind. His parents had explained how worried they had been but after the initial telling-off, they sat down together and listened to his version of events. They agreed to adopting Giselda as a surrogate Nonna and invited her to Sunday lunch.

He found he enjoyed being at home during his curfew. Even the twins seemed less annoying since his adventure, volunteering to do his job of emptying the dishwasher for five days. Alba knocked on his bedroom door on his first evening back. She sat on his window seat and told him he must always feel free to talk to her if he ever had worries.

'I've had a word with them about the tennis, Davi,' she said. 'It's no big deal. You can stop whenever you want, you know. I sensed you weren't enjoying it much.'

'I don't want to stop completely,' he said. 'It's tournaments and regional stuff I don't want to do anymore. It's no fun.'

'Fair enough. What about school? What's happening there?'

He shrugged his shoulders. ' It'll be okay.'

She'd come over and hugged him. 'You know I went through a bad time after my mum died. I didn't have anyone I thought I could talk to, so I didn't talk for six months. I know what it's like, if you ever need to chat.'

Davide felt she was treating him as an equal and not an annoying little step-brother and he smiled his thanks. He and the twins knew about Alba's real mother dying in a car crash before their father met their own mother, but she'd never opened up to him before about how she felt.

On the following Saturday when the curfew was over, his father took him out walking. It felt special to have Babbo to himself. Usually days out involved all six of them and taking ages getting organised. Somebody would forget something and they'd have to come back to fetch the bottle opener, a jacket, book or mobile phone.

'Where are we going, Babbo?' he asked as they prepared their picnic while the rest of the family was still asleep.'

He had been allowed to choose whatever he wanted to eat. Into his rucksack went white bread and salami, two packets of crisps, two chocolate bars and a can of Fanta orange juice. Francesco added cheese to his own bag, as well as water and a first aid kit.

'It's going to be a magical mystery walk,' he replied, winking at his son.

They left the dented Fiat Panda (now only used for short excursions) outside the bar in Pratieghi. The isolated village was returning to normal after a few weeks of the mainly elderly population being swelled by other elderly guests holidaying in the little hotel. An old lady with large brown age spots on her face, like autumn russets, made a fuss of Francesco, kissing him on both cheeks and calling him her other son. Davide too was paid a lot of attention and given a handful of sweets from the jar on the bar.

'Not too many, Aurelia,' Babbo said, 'or else he'll be asking if he can borrow your false teeth.'

She cackled with laughter and told him off for being cheeky.

Following signs to the source of the river Marecchia, they passed by old stone houses on the edge of the village, their vegetable plots bright with ripening tomatoes, peppers and aubergines. Soon it would be time to harvest and either freeze or bottle the produce for winter. An old man wearing patched, faded blue overalls tied at the waist with a piece of twine handed them two fat ox-heart tomatoes.

'For your picnic,' he said, 'you won't find better than these in fancy supermarkets.'

Francesco thanked him and stood chatting for a while. Afterwards he explained to Davide that old people in this village were lonely because so many families had departed to find work elsewhere.

The first part of the walk took them over stubbly wheat fields, their feet scrunching the stalks. A hare, startled at their approach, bounded off in front of them, its large back feet stirring up dust. At the top of a steep incline they stopped to catch their breath.

'Wow!' said Davide. 'I bet the moon looks just like this.'

The area was arid. Beneath them were folds of friable limestone rocks looking like a miniature Grand Canyon; cones of grey shale contorted by wind and rain into grotesque shapes. Davide slid to the base of the incline and disappeared round a cleft in one of the rocks.

'I'm coming back here for a massive hide and seek game. It's *so* brill, Babbo,' he shouted up, popping his head round the edge of a triangular mound.

Francesco took a photo, telling his son to hurry up back as they still had a fair way to go.

They climbed steadily for another hundred metres or so until they reached the tree line. It was cooler under the canopy of beech and they stopped for a snack. The ground was very dry, ruts at the edge of the path showing signs where wild boar had searched earlier in the season for roots of orchids and wild garlic.

'All right to continue for another hour or so?' Francesco asked. 'You're doing great, by the way.'

The climb was very steep in parts and Francesco adopted a slower pace than usual. But Davide seemed game, keeping up without moaning, enjoying being on his own with his father.

'We're making for Monte della Zucca,' Francesco explained. 'A very important defensive stronghold for the German army in the last war, known as the Gothic Line. Can you imagine soldiers having to walk up here with heavy rucksacks? It's bad enough with these light bags of ours.'

'It's hard to imagine lots of people up here at all. And fighting and stuff – but I bet soldiers hid in that canyon-y bit down there.'

'Maybe. They did use mules as well to carry up heavy equipment. Stolen from local people, of course.'

The track narrowed until they were walking as if in a rut left by a plough, along a ridge where the ground fell sharply away on either side. Francesco waited to let his son pass, holding onto him as they exchanged places. 'I'd prefer you to walk in front where I can see you,' he said. 'Cyclists use this path too but I wouldn't like to wobble off and fall down there.'

'It's ace,' Davide said, extending his arms like the wings of an aeroplane and making engine noises.

After scrambling over boulders and fallen trees, their roots sticking skywards like giant claws, they reached a sign detailing where former trenches and German gun positions had been located. It was nearly one o'clock and they decided to eat their picnic sitting in one of the larger bunkers on top of the mountain.

'We're at 1,100 metres up here,' said Francesco. 'There are plenty of trees now but back then there was far less vegetation on these mountains. And there is hardly any cattle compared with before. So try and picture it without all the green. It would have made an amazing viewpoint – very important strategically for controlling the roads for enemy and shooting at aircraft.'

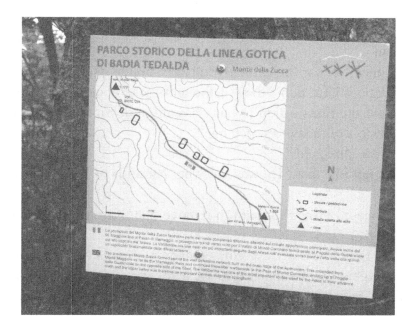

Davide picked up a stick and mimicked gunfire, rolling over and over in the leafy undergrowth to take imaginary cover.

'If you land on my lunch, you'll be in deep trouble. I'll have to lob a hand grenade at you.' Francesco said, joining in with the fantasy game.

They mucked about for a bit, Francesco grabbing hold of Davide, clinching his head beneath his armpit, then tickling him, asking him if he wanted to surrender. Their laughter startled a pheasant in the woods and a wood pigeon flapped its wings. Eventually they decided their hunger needed to be satisfied and munched on the rest of the bread and cheese in their dug-out, happy to be quiet for a while.

Francesco peeled an apple and asked Davide what had been happening to make him so unhappy to want to run away.

'I get fed up with everybody from school calling me names and taking the mick because they think I'm *inglese*…but I'm not, am I? Mamma is really Italian, although she lived in England most of her life…they're so stupid. But don't tell her - it's not her fault if she's different…'

'Names? You mean calling you Harry Potter? But they like the stories about him, don't they? I thought those books were all the rage. And the films - didn't your class all go down to Sansepolcro for Celeste's birthday to watch one?'

Davide shrugged.

'It's not just that.' He was throwing handfuls of leaves into the air.

Francesco leaned forward to remove one from his hair. 'What else, Davi?'

'Oh, I don't know. Just stuff. Annoying things like when they hid the tights I was supposed to wear for the *Palio* last week and the only spare ones were those yucky girls' ones. I felt ridiculous and people were calling me a girl.'

'I didn't notice.'

'It was pants. And when we have an English lesson they think I'm showing off because I find it easy. But what am I supposed to do? Just act dumb? When I tell them we speak English at home as well as Italian, they don't understand. They call me a *clandestino*, but I'm not and I hate that school. I want to leave.'

'Do you really think it would be any easier in another school? Say if you went down the hill to Novafeltria? You wouldn't know anybody. It might be worse.'

'Nobody would know about Mamma living in England, would they? I wouldn't be bullied for that.'

Francesco started to pack the remains of their picnic back into his rucksack.

'I didn't realise you felt like this. It's a shame. You should be proud of who you are, not apologetic.'

'That's what Giselda says too but none of you know what it's like.'

'You're right, I don't but…' Francesco paused, trying to think of the best way of approaching the subject with a ten-year-old. He sat down again with his son on the edge of the gun position and continued, 'I brought you up here for a reason. You're part of all this.'

Davide frowned and his father pointed to the woods. 'Over sixty years ago the Englishman your Mamma thought was her dad was up here in these mountains fighting to help free Italy and he fell in love with your Nonna Ines who lived in the mill. Neither of us ever met her, did we? But she must have been very special. She helped the partisans by taking messages for them and carrying up food to their mountain hideaway, dressed as a boy. If the Germans had discovered what she was doing, they would have shot her. And she knew that. She was very brave. And I think she was also brave to have left these mountains to marry an Englishman and travel a thousand kilometres to take up a new life in a completely different country.'

'What has that got to do with me?'

'A lot, Davide. You're descended from her. You have her blood and her courage.'

Davide frowned. 'I'm not brave...'

'...I think you are - or you can be. Nothing in life is straightforward. And life can be difficult. But it's amazing too. How we face up to difficulties is what makes us into the people we are. I guarantee that people who bully or tease you are cowards. They're ignorant and you've got to find a way to stand up to them.'

'So what do I do next time they call me names?'

'Somehow you've got to show them you don't care – even if you do inside. Mamma and I will have a talk about it and we'll see if we can come up with something.'

'I don't want to talk about it anymore, Babbo.'

With the younger children tucked up in bed and Alba out for the evening, Francesco and Anna lay outside the stable in the dark on sun loungers, watching for shooting stars in the pinpricked sky.

'Davide has to learn that everybody mucks about at school and plays tricks on each other,' Francesco said. 'If he's teased then he should tease back, play some of his own tricks on them.'

'Being teased is really hard when you're only ten,' Anna said. 'It makes me want to go into school and smack Loredano hard.'

'That wouldn't help at all and you know it...'

'Oh, of course I do but seeing him upset brings out the lioness in me. I don't want anybody to hurt my babies.'

'That's exactly why Loredano is the way he is. He doesn't have a lioness to protect him. His mother walked out when he was a baby and his father is always in the bar in the evening, pickled with grappa.'

'I know, I know. But two wrongs don't make a right. I don't want Davide to start bullying too.'

They star gazed, enjoying the sounds of the river flowing gently below them and an owl hooting in the woods.

'By the way,' Francesco said. 'A young American girl joined our research team a couple of weeks ago. She's so excited about being in Europe, never stops taking photos on her phone of anything and everything – from the espresso cups in the bar, my battered leather briefcase, the light fittings in the office... we've nicknamed her Wow because she's so enthusiastic about everything! Apparently her father is an art historian and has made her promise to do the Piero della Francesca trail. So I've told her she can come and stay with us some time to visit Sansepolcro and Monterchi. I should have asked you first. Sorry!'

'That's fine. What's her real name?' Anna asked, thinking it strange Francesco hadn't mentioned her before.

'Donna. She says she was meant to come to Italy because of her Italian name.'

They sat quietly until Anna pointed up at the sky, shouting

she'd seen a shooting star and was going to make a wish.

'Don't tell me what it is,' Francesco said, 'otherwise it won't be fulfilled.'

Anna wouldn't have told him anyway. Her wish was to wake up feeling well again. Her trip to England and the appointment with her sister's doctor couldn't come soon enough, as far as she was concerned. This waiting was torture, allowing her imagination to think the worst. She'd read an article only last night in her copy of "Prima" about the warning signs of ovarian cancer. It had been described as the silent killer and her symptoms of bloating and tiredness matched, although she had no back ache.

'I'd like all my children to have good friends from their schooldays,' Francesco said, interrupting Anna's gloomy fears. 'They spend more time with them than they do with us, if you think about it. I really value my friends from back then. They understand me, know about my past, my mistakes – everything. They've been a great support.'

'I've noticed that about Italians. In the bar down in Sansepolcro where I have my Tuesday morning cappuccino after market, there's a gang of old men. Always round the same table, reading out bits from the "Nazione", teasing each other, flirting with the pretty waitress. They have nicknames for each other like *Capo* or *Rotondo*. Lately, one of them looks as if he's on his last legs and they tend to mother him. After he's left, they sit in a huddle and share ideas on how they can help. It's really sweet.'

'It's normal.'

'Maybe for you. But I went to a stuffy all girls' convent. I've lost touch with my school friends.' She sat up, bubbling with an idea. 'We should do something really fun for Davide - hold a party! Invite his whole class. Hire a bouncy castle…'

'English genius, you are! Look – another falling star! I can make a wish now too.' He leant over from his lounger to kiss her and the plastic arm of his chair snapped, causing him to fall onto the terrace slabs.

Anna jumped up, kneeling down to tend to him. He grabbed her, tickling her but she pulled away.

Just at that moment Alba returned from her evening out. 'Behave, you two,' she said with a huge grin on her face. 'Get a room! You're *so* juvenile.'

Francesco couldn't help thinking that a chance would be a fine thing.

Chapter 16

My Diary - A week of reliving the *transumanza,* by Davide Starnucci

SUNDAY EVENING

I am the head of the family because Babbo has gone away.

In the past, he would have left for five months and Mamma says we'd probably all be sitting around with "long faces". But I'm quite excited about this week. (Babbo is only away for one week, on a university conference in Camerino.)

Alba has gone with him, to compare Camerino with Newcastle University, to see where she'd prefer to go and study next year.

So, it's only me, the annoying twins and Mamma.

Babbo suggested keeping a diary for my school project and Mamma came up with this whole week idea. She says reality TV shows are very popular in England and she remembers seeing one about a family that pretended they were living through World War II. That lasted a month but one week will be quite enough for me.

Paper was expensive and scarce in the 1920s and so the fact I'm writing in this exercise book is not really accurate. It's going to be hard to stick to doing everything they would have done then.

Before he left, Babbo had told me two stories to do with paper. One was how a father tore up the pages from his son's school book to make roll-ups. The other was about a peasant who worked for a really hard master (a *latifondista*) who made his worker get up really early every morning before starting work. He had to walk ten kilometres to and from the local town to buy a daily newspaper for his boss. It was a big chore and he moaned about it to a friend who suggested buying ten papers at a time to save nine more daily walks. When the landowner complained he was reading the same one each day, the peasant told him the news never changed much anyway. The peasant couldn't read because he left school young to work on the land. Most peasants went to school just to learn how to write their name for when they had to sign legal documents.

The first thing I did as head of the house was to put a tablecloth over our TV and unplug it as well as the music centre and radio.

When I told the twins and Mamma the girls moaned a lot, saying it was a pants idea and it wasn't their project, so why did they have to be punished? I wound them up by saying pants wasn't a saying in those days and they'd have to think of something better. So they started on their stupid, secret language stuff: "ants in pants", "don't get antsy with us" and other rubbish talk. Mamma told them off. 'We're doing this as a family', she said.

Emilia argued back by saying Alba had got out of it nicely and Rosanna said, 'And Babbo too.'

Anyway, they calmed down in the end and Mamma got us all kneading dough to make bread for breakfast. It was good fun slapping it round on the kitchen table. We made rolls and pizza bases and that's what we had for supper.

Mamma said, 'We'll use the oven for tonight but in the 1920s there wasn't any electricity here. We'd have used the old bread oven once a week, like one that used to be next to the mill. We knocked it down because it wasn't safe anymore.'

PLAN FOR ANOTHER DAY: There's still an old bread oven up in the village of San Patrignano and I'm going to ask Aunty Teresa if she'll show me how to light it.

MONDAY

It rained all through the night and all day long. Noisy thunderstorms and lightning which made the twins squeal and hide their heads under the settee cushions but I kind of like thunder - it sounds like rockets blasting off.

This morning we put buckets and containers outside on the patio to catch the rain because Babbo and Mamma had already explained there'd have been no taps or showers or washing machines in those days. Water was precious and was usually fetched in buckets each day from wells or natural springs but we would have been luckier than most because of living down by the river.

I don't mind not having a shower for a week but Mamma says she'll miss her long hot soaks with bubble-bath and a glass of wine.

It was AMAZING how much water we collected in the buckets by the time the storms were over. There were a few leaves, dead ants and even a big scorpion floating around (which, as the man of the house, *I* had to remove). I had fun chasing Emilia round for a bit with one. She's scared of scorpions too.

The river was REALLY full after all the rain and the kind of *cappuccino* colour it always is after a downpour. It rushed by noisily and there were lots of branches and even a whole tree or two whizzing past in the fast current.

I remembered Babbo telling me how in the past, when most ordinary people didn't have land or trees of their own to cut down for firewood, they would hurry to the river as soon as water levels in the river had gone down after a storm. They were allowed to collect all the driftwood from the river bed and everybody had their own markers to put on top of their pile so there wouldn't be any arguments. If they cut down trees in the landowners' forests, they were severely punished and could even be evicted from their houses. Not many people owned their own homes in those days.

Tonight I've decided to tear up a strip off an old red tablecloth Mamma said I could use. I know there won't be anybody else rushing down to collect wood because most people round here use pellets in their stoves which they buy in the shops, but at least we can try and do something authentic (Mamma told me to write that word). And she also told me the Forestry Guards don't allow anybody to remove wood or anything from the river nowadays.

The twins have only promised to help 'cos Mamma said they could make gingerbread men after. (It's not very Italian but I suppose we're not a completely Italian family anyway - and we all love gingerbread). I don't think I could cope with controlling the twins without Mamma helping me.

TUESDAY

Today it was really hot and sunny like it often is after a storm. Mamma said it had cleared the air.

It was fun down on the river bed. Mamma came to help collect firewood too and she made us a picnic which we carried down in a basket and not in the cool bag we usually use, because there wouldn't have been any of those in the 1920s. We had left-over pizza from the other night (yummy), and dried fruit and cake. (Actually, ginger).

We gathered quite a load of firewood. Either Babbo or I will chop it up later. Dragging it back to the wood store was such hot sticky work that, even though the water was quite cold, we all decided to go back to the big waterfall for a swim. Mamma said it would do as our wash. She wouldn't let us use soap in case of polluting the river, but she told us in the olden days women used wood ash from their fires to wash clothes down by the river, like a kind of soap. How weird is that?

She was *so* much fun in the river pool – I've never seen her do head stands under the water before and she showed us how to do somersaults without getting water up our noses. She even let me dive off the rocks, which she doesn't usually do. But she said there was more water than usual from the storm and so it was deep enough and quite safe.

As well as the wood we found a few other bits and pieces washed down the river: an old boot (Ma has bagged that and says it'll look good with a geranium planted in it...what????) I joked and said in the olden days a one-legged peasant would have loved to have found the boot because shoes were expensive and most people wore wooden clogs.

The twins picked up bits of strange-shaped driftwood because they said they looked like ghost fingers and they spent ages being boring and pretending to scare each other. When you scream down by the waterfall it echoes all round the place and I hope nobody thought we were being murdered.

In fact nobody came to find out, so it was just as well we weren't being murdered.

WEDNESDAY

Cycled round to my friend's house because Mamma couldn't take me in the car (not authentic and we don't have a donkey) and I couldn't text him either, seeing as we are living in the 1920's) but Tommaso is away - *bummer!* - and won't be back until next week as he has gone down to stay with his Nonna by the sea. I wanted to ask him to come swimming with us. He's the only boy I get on with at school. But he lives quite close to Giselda, so I carried on to hers.

Giselda was in the little room she keeps just for her cats and I told her about my project.

Anyway, she told me that to make it more true to life (authentic), I should have walked all the way up here along old footpaths because the main tarmac road wasn't built then and also hardly anybody owned a bike then, only quite well-off people. She told me some funny stuff about bikes - how people hung them up so the tyres wouldn't wear out and how they even let the air out of them between each ride because they thought it would make their bikes last longer that way.

She made me a *lush* cup of hot chocolate, so thick my spoon stuck in the middle and then asked if she could come and visit tomorrow as she felt she could be of great use to me in the project. I told her it was cool. Well, I couldn't phone Mamma to check if it was alright, because I wanted to do it properly and be authentic. (That's my absolute favourite word at the moment).

'I'll drop in at about 6 a.m. tomorrow,' she said. 'In those days people made the most of daylight and went to bed at sun down and got up at sun rise.'

I hope Mamma won't be cross. Maybe I'll get up at 5.30 and bring her a cup of tea in bed, like Babbo sometimes does. (But he doesn't usually get up at 5.30).

THURSDAY

We overslept and woke up to a weird noise. I looked out of my bedroom window and there was Giselda on a two-wheeled cart and her donkey bridled up. The donkey was making a right old din, *Eeeh Aaaaw*, over and over and Mamma came rushing out ready to tell us off, I think. But she just laughed when she saw Giselda.

The twins ran out with two carrots and Giselda said donkeys used to be known as the little horses of St. Francis.

True to her word, it was 6 o'clock. Giselda held up a paper bag and said, 'I've brought us breakfast. Sweet pizza with a thick sugar coating. And I shall make us all some coffee from roasted barley.'

The coffee wasn't that good and Mamma cheated and went off and made herself a cup of English tea.

'I've brought along some things to make this project of yours more lifelike,' Giselda said, fetching a long bag from the back of the cart. 'This is called a *saccone*,' she explained, 'and each household would have had one to store their flour and beans.'

She held up a longish creamy-coloured bag and Ma was really interested in it, especially when Giselda explained how every housewife in those days would know how to weave the material to make them and darn and patch them and keep them extra clean. Mamma looked closely at the material and said she wouldn't know how to start and how much easier it was nowadays just to be able to use a fridge and freezer and plastic bags.

Giselda pulled out old, fusty clothes from the bag and handed them round: patched trousers and a check shirt - also patched - (there were almost more patches than material) and a piece of string to tie round my middle instead of a belt.

The girls and Mamma were each given a long thick skirt, blouse, shawl and a scarf to tie round their heads. She had some smelly pieces of fox fur which would have been tied round children's ears to keep them warm in winter, but thank goodness it's summer now and we didn't have to wear the pongy things.

'How are we going to run around in these horrible skirts?'
Rosanna whined and Giselda replied that in those days there
wouldn't be a lot of time for playing and that she was going to
keep us all busy for the last two days of the project. Emilia tried to
do a somersault and got tangled up in her skirt and went off in a
strop. Giselda ignored her but Rosanna managed to persuade her to
come back and join in. 'If I've got to wear this hideous thing, then
so have you,' she bossed. 'It's only for today.'

The girls were given the task of finishing off making cheese.
Giselda explained that this normally would start at four o'clock in
the morning when we are usually fast asleep. 'The first task was to
milk all the flock. Well, I picked milk up from the farm at Torriolo
up the hill from you – Alessandro had already done that job on
your behalf – and this has been filtered, ready to heat up in these
pots.'

Because it would have taken far too long to make a fire from
scratch, Giselda said the girls would be allowed to use the gas
cooker in our kitchen.

'I have a thermometer here to check when we should add the
rennet. Between 30 and 40 degrees, but never more than 40.'
Giselda said.

'What's rennet?' asked Emilia.

'It's taken from a sheep's stomach, to help make cheese,' said
Rosanna.

'Well done, Rosi. Now we'll add just the correct amount and
then watch for the point of coagulation, when curds are formed in
the cheese and it starts to go lumpy.'
The fun part came after the girls had broken up the curds with a
kind of whisk.

'I got this down from the wall this morning,' Giselda said,
holding the wooden tool up. Ma was interested in that too and got
out her metal one to compare.

'Ooh, yuck this is all gooey,' Rosanna said, her hands
immersed in the pasty mess of curds.

'It's fun! All squidgy!' Emilia said, wiping a hair from her cheek. She ended up with a splodge of the goo on her face. Ha ha!

'I can't believe this will turn into cheese,' Rosanna said. 'I think I've gone off the idea of eating cheese anymore. And it's stinky-poo!'

When they'd picked out most of the paste (although lots of it landed on the floor and the kitchen units), Giselda produced another old fashioned bit of equipment from her old kitchen.

'These are called *cascine*. They haven't been used for years and years, these forms, but once upon a time, they were used every day to make our own cheeses.'

We all joined in, Mamma too, pressing the paste down into the wooden forms, patting and smoothing it.

'If you had a cellar, it would be the ideal place to store these but modern houses don't have those anymore,' Giselda said. 'Let's try under the stairs, it's quite a cool place. The longer it stays there, the better – to make it strong and seasoned.'

After we'd cleaned up and had an authentic mid-morning snack of *Pan cristiano* (like eggy bread: bread dipped in egg and fried. Quite yummy!) and a drink each of watered-down wine (can't see what all the fuss is about myself), Giselda set me the task of being a day labourer. My job was to '*dicioccare*' – to beat lumps of earth so that it turned into fine soil, removing stones and roots to prepare for planting. In a very short time I had blisters on my palms from the hoe and Ma had to bind up my hands. Giselda apologised but she said she wanted to show us how hard life was for ordinary people in the past.

'At your age you might have been a chimney sweep or a frog catcher or a *spaccapietre*, sitting on a pile of stones and banging them from morning to night until they were small enough to use to rake onto road surfaces. Or a woodcutter, or a boy digging ditches down on the coast where you'd probably have caught malaria while you were at it.'

It was helpful of Giselda to show us all these things but I was beginning to wish the end of the week would hurry up and come and we could go back to normal. It was really, really hard work.

For the rest of the morning, Giselda took us foraging. We walked up to the mountain pass where, underneath beech trees, we found *porcini* mushrooms. I'd already been out mushroom hunting with Babbo several times, so this wasn't new to me, but she showed us some other types I had never collected – tiny mushrooms that looked like rows of teeth and grew beneath fallen leaves so they were difficult to find. Mamma said she would never have the courage to eat mushrooms she found on her own in case she made a mistake and poisoned us all. (Later, when Giselda had gone, we looked them up in our Pocket Book on mushrooms and they are called Wood Hedgehogs!)

Mamma was more interested in the leaves we looked for in the meadows: young leaves of wild chicory, hairy leaves of *pimpinella,* (she said they were called Burnet-saxifrage in English), poppy and dandelion leaves, wild carrot – which didn't look like carrots at all but white frothy flowers - and loads of other stuff I don't remember. Giselda said the leaves would be too bitter to eat raw now as springtime was the best time to collect them. We were getting a bit bored by this stage until Giselda showed us a patch of wild strawberries and we ate loads of those. The girls squashed them in their fingers and smeared the red juice all over their faces and then kept pretending to drop dead and stuff. They are so sad sometimes.

When we got back to the house, Giselda made us clean and chop up some of the plants she said wouldn't be too past it and Mamma boiled them up. In the meantime, Giselda rolled out home-made pasta and we had fun cutting out huge ravioli with an upturned glass and used the plants as a filling. She produced a jar of home-made tomato sauce from her basket and said every peasant household would have had a plentiful supply of this, made at the end of the summer months and stored away for eating during winter when snow was on the ground and nothing could grow. There were no shops round here either. Just the occasional man who came round selling reels of cotton and tins of herrings, or candles - but not when snow was on the ground. She showed us a picture of one – he had this weird thing on his back with pockets where he kept all the stuff he sold. Giselda said everybody had to make do with what they could store up from summer. Stuff like dried pears and apples, chestnuts and maize for *polenta* (which Mamma *hates* - she says she would have died in those days because she can't eat it, it turns her stomach but Giselda laughed and said she would definitely have eaten it rather than exist on an empty belly.)

Lunch was yummy but Mamma said it had taken a whole morning to prepare and kept going on about how hard it must have been for women in those days.

'Everybody helped each other more,' Giselda said. 'In fact, with the men away in Maremma for so long, women and older people relied on each other a lot. And in the evenings, when the chores were finished, they would meet in somebody's house for *veglia*.'

Then she jumped up and clapped her hands and came up with another idea.

'I know – how about we have a *veglia* up at my house tomorrow evening? Maybe you could invite Davide's friends to come around. Get them to dress up like you are – their parents can come along too, if they want. The more, the merrier!'

'It's a bit short notice,' I said. I was trying to put her off really. I didn't think anybody would want to come and I'd probably get teased but Mamma had already told Giselda it was an excellent idea.

When I told Giselda I'd have to use my phone to invite them and it wouldn't be authentic, she laughed. 'In the past you would have shouted from the top of the mountain but I don't think that would work now. Or you could do what the villagers did then - lean against the walls of a house or a tall rock and shout through cupped hands. That was usually done to tell somebody their lost sheep had been found. But no wires would be involved.'

After she'd gone Mamma said we were allowed to switch on the telly and we watched *Harry Potter and the Order of the Phoenix*. She said we deserved it as it had been quite a hard day and then she put some ointment from the chemist on my blistered hands.

We decided we're very lucky to live nowadays.

FRIDAY AND THE VEGLIA

In the end, as it was such short notice, I phoned up a few kids in my class and invited them over. Giselda told me to tell them not to bring any food – she would see to all that. Some of them moaned about having to dress up, but in the end everybody made an effort and Mamma took photos and decided to give a prize to the best costume. Celeste won...she'd borrowed her Nonna's old flowery dress and headscarf and wore short, rubber boots and an old wrap-around apron so we didn't recognise her at first. Mamma gave her a lush gingerbread man as a prize. She'd iced it to make it look like a peasant boy. I was pleased 'cos Celeste took one bite and decided she didn't like ginger and so I shared it with the twins (well, I shared it out so I got the biggest bits).

The Italian grown ups ate most of the food because they remembered eating tripe and *Pagliatella* (the fatty part of lamb's intestines cooked over a wood fire) and bean stew like that when they were little. No way was I going to eat sheep insides and the twins refused too.

Giselda had asked a lady she knew was a good cook to make *acqua cotta* and that wasn't too bad. Except she said the version we had eaten was a bit more complicated and richer tasting than how it used to be made. In the past it was made with stale bread, chopped up mint collected from the fields, an onion – if there was one - and water…

This is Giselda's recipe:

Acqua cotta **from the Maremma**

Ingredients:

Two or three large onions; green vegetables (like cabbage or spinach); tomatoes; one egg per person, toasted bread, some grated *pecorino* cheese.

Put a generous amount of good olive oil from the Maremma into a big pan. Add 2 or 3 large onions sliced up and gently fry them.
Then turn down the heat and cook until the onions almost go mushy.
Add tomatoes cut into pieces and continue to cook, adding herbs such as basil, and some chopped up celery.
When this has all cooked add water (but if there is good broth available, this is better). Boil for 15 minutes.
Fry some toasted slices of bread in a frying pan and sprinkle grated Pecorino cheese on top. Add one egg per person (making sure they don't all join together, so break them into the pan gently). After about one or two minutes, when the eggs begin to set, remove the pan from the fire.
Pour the soup into dishes and put the bread and egg on top.

**

We all LOVED the scrummy sweet *Fritelle di S. Giuseppe* that we finished off supper with.

Ingredients:

2 glasses of water; 2 dessert spoons of very good olive oil; 3 dessert spoons of sugar; 250 grams of wheat flour; 2 whole eggs; 1 sachet of vanilla sugar (1 gram); a pinch of salt; ½ teaspoon of bicarbonate of soda, the grated zest of one lemon.

In a pan, heat up water, sugar, salt, grated lemon and the oil.
When it is boiling, remove from the heat and add all the flour immediately and all in one go.
Stir very well and until well mixed (this will take about 10 minutes).
Leave the mix to cool down and then add both eggs one at a time. Mix well.
ONLY AT THIS STAGE, add the bicarbonate of soda and vanilla and mix again for another 2 or 3 minutes.
Pour plenty of oil into a frying pan and heat to boiling point and throw in the mix little by little (about the size of a large walnut).
Fry – if the mixture has been properly prepared, it will swell in size immediately and turn it with a fork so it cooks evenly.
Remove from the heat and toss it in sugar immediately and then put on a cloth (to absorb extra fat) and eat when still warm and never cold!

Yum yum!

We ate the food in Giselda's garden but when it began to turn dark, she invited us inside the oldest part of her house. I hadn't been in there before. (Her house is actually enormous and it's amazing she's the only person who lives there – except for her umpteen cats).

The windows are tiny and there were candles in bottles on the sill and a huge fireplace, big enough to stand up in. It was really cosy. She told the children to sit on the floor and the adults sat on wooden benches. Then she lit an old pipe and puffed on it. She looked weird with her two long grey plaits and her wrinkled face and I had never seen a lady smoke a pipe and a few of us giggled. Mamma glared at us and we tried not to look at each other in case we started giggling again.

Then Giselda told us a story. One of her cats came to sit on her lap and curled up in a tiny ball and she stroked it gently. You could hear it purring from the other side of the room.

Giselda's story

Once upon a time there was a handsome cowboy, young and strong, who used to ride down from the mountain of Viamaggio to the Maremma coast each autumn.

One spring as he started on his return journey away from the coast, on a day that was hot and sultry, he led his horse to drink water near the site of an Etruscan tomb which had filled up with cool, refreshing water. As his horse started to drink, the cowboy thought he could make out a beautiful young girl, her arm reaching out to the tomb. He thought it was probably a trick of the light but her smile was so alluring and she was so beautiful he just had to try and grasp hold of her and he ended up falling into the tomb. He couldn't manage to climb out and so he drowned.

That night his poor horse kept whinnying with grief and galloped about the Maremma plain, desperate to be reunited with his handsome young rider.

It is said that even today, if you are out and about on a moonlit night down on the Tuscan coast, you can hear the neighing of a horse breaking the silence of the night.

After her story, Gianni's Babbo told another story.

Gianni's Babbo's story

A greedy miller cheated people by taking some of the grain for his own use at the beginning and keeping flour back after it was milled.

One harsh winter, when people were dying like flies from cold and hunger, the miller was the only person comfortable. He sat beside his warm fire with his larder full of bread and he sent packing any beggar that came his way.

One night a woman came to his door. She was cold and dressed in rags and she held a baby in her arms but he pushed her away and shut the door in her face.

He drank a glass of red wine and fell asleep and when he awoke, the fire had gone out in his hearth and his mill was in ruins around him.

He saw the ghost of the woman who had come to his door, now dressed in fine clothes. Her beautiful face looked like the one on the statue of Our Lady in the little church in his village and she told the miller off for earlier sending the poor hungry woman away from his warm fireside.

'You sent me packing,' she told him, 'and now your mill and your bread will be forever cursed.'

'Now, the next time you walk past the site of his old mill,' Gianni's *babbo* told us, 'you will notice that the mill stones are still to this day cracked and useless and you should make the sign of the cross as a sign of respect.'

We spent ages trying to decide which mill it could possibly be but I am sure it isn't our lovely Mulino. It doesn't feel at all spooky and nobody walks past it and makes the sign of the cross. I think it might be the old watermill at the bottom of Rofelle, at the end of a steep stony track. Nobody has lived there for years and Babbo told me he has seen wolves there recently.

SUNDAY

YIPEE!
Today we returned to our normal life. It was great to pour cornflakes into a bowl and not wear scratchy clothes and Mamma said she was going to spend more than an hour in the bath and nobody should disturb her, no matter what. I played a new computer game and the twins watched cartoons on the telly.

But I'm glad we did our experiment of living in the 1920s.

And in a kind of way I miss some things too, like the stories round the fire and not having to have a shower each day and Mamma laughing more.

At least I've done my homework and I've decided that now I've spent a bit more time with them, some of the kids in my class are not too bad. So I might go back to school in Badia in September after all.

Chapter 17

Alba by the river – 2010

The kitchen table was upended, transformed into a pirate ship, and now the twins were performing cartwheels across the living room area.   Their excited squeals and annoying secret language was getting on Alba's nerves. She'd read the same paragraph seven times over before snapping her book shut and shouting to Anna, 'I'm going for a walk.'

Heat bounced off rocks in the river. There was no breeze and cicadas kicked off their noisy protest in the stifling afternoon. Willow trees stood still, their long silvery finger branches drooping in the shallows. She made for her special space in the lee of a high outcrop further along from the pool, near the waterfall where the family often swam. Her head was full of the trip to Camerino. The university had an amazing reputation and she'd liked the old town. There was a lot going on and the students were very friendly. Babbo seemed keen she should enrol in architecture and design and at school they had recommended this too because it would suit her artistic talents. But she was unsure. All of a sudden there seemed too many decisions to make in her life.

Sitting in the shade on her favourite flat rock with its whirls and curls, she began to relax. Babbo had explained when she was little how her rock had once been at the bottom of the sea. She imagined its curious undulations as waves frozen in time. It was hard to take in that the ocean once covered even the peaks of the mountains surrounding her all those zillions of years ago. Thinking about it made her feel insignificant, like a speck of nothingness. She felt she should hurry up and live her life before it passed her by.

The boy was at the pool again on his own. She had seen him arrive with his family at Il Mulino. He was wearing tight trunks, unlike the baggy swimwear fashionable amongst her school friends. He was fit.

But he probably plays English cricket and tennis and rugby and goes to a public school and lives in a big, swanky house in Surrey, like Aunt Jane, she thought. Probs a right snobby nob…

He was climbing to the top of the waterfall now, the muscles in his arms straining as his fingers sought purchase.

More to the right, she wanted to yell. Move your left foot up to the right and you'll find the stone big enough to take your weight. Then grip the reinforcement bar sticking out on the left and you can haul yourself up easily.

She could do it with her eyes closed but you had to take care not to dive straight down once you'd climbed to the top. There was a sharp boulder on the river bed, concealed by foaming spray from the waterfall.

She stepped out from her shady hiding-place, yelling, 'Careful!'

He looked over, cupping his hand to his ear, the din of water tumbling onto rocks masking her words.

And then he dived. A clean slice through the air, piercing the surface of the water with the slightest of ripples marking his entry point.

She waited, holding her breath for the moment when he would reappear. When he didn't resurface, she set off, leaping across the rocks, running through the shallows to plunge into deep water. He could easily have broken his neck; she had left her mobile phone back home; how could she get an ambulance here in time...? And suddenly her ankles were grabbed and she felt herself being pulled into the river. When she came up for air and screamed at him, he laughed in her face.

Standing up, she was incandescent with fury - because she'd been dragged in and her shorts and T-shirt were soaking; because he'd tricked her into thinking he had drowned or cracked his head open on a boulder and because she fancied him and she'd gone and made such a stupid wally of herself.

He took in the sight of her: skimpy wet T-shirt clinging to big breasts, shorts transparent from her dunking, revealing skimpy panties underneath, maybe a thong? She had a great body. Shame about the peculiar streaks of blue in her long, brown hair. And that stud. He'd never liked nose piercings; had always wondered how bogies didn't get stuck to the metal bits. He could tell she was well angry with him. Seriously angry, shouting something about concealed rocks. Did she think he was thick or something? He'd sussed the depths out before he'd dived in.

'*Mi chiamo Danny*. My name's Danny,' he said, extending his hand.

He knew Italians were touchy-feely and planted kisses on each other's cheeks when they introduced themselves. He'd watched men doing that in the bar in Badia Tedalda. Men even kissed men. You wouldn't catch him kissing his mates like that. Not even for two crates of beer. Well, maybe he might for two – but defo not for one. But it didn't look as if she was going to let him anywhere near her face – or anywhere else, for that matter.

'It's short for Daniel,' he continued, his hand still extended. 'I'm staying in your mill.'

'I know you are, you idiot,' she retorted and started to walk away from him along the bank.

'Er - excuse me,' he said, a grin on his face as he observed the string of algae hanging from the back of her wet shorts, 'you seem to have grown a tail.'

She felt behind her, pulled the weed away, scrunched it into a ball and lobbed it hard at him, smacking him square on the nose. 'And you seem to have grown a beak,' she said, continuing her walk back along the river track.

It was the Saturday evening barbecue – a tradition started eight years previously by Anna and Francesco when they had started up their holiday business. New arrivals were always invited and it was an opportunity to tell them about local market days or concerts and festas. Francesco acted as meat chef for these informal suppers, while Anna rustled up her famous Anglo-Italian puddings. Tonight it was tipsy trifle with Amaretto biscuits and peaches but with absolutely no jelly in sight. The children waited on the guests and everybody mixed in at the long trestle table set up under the shelter of a willow tree at the edge of the river and laid with a gingham cloth. Candles in painted jam jars hung from the branches and as well as the flames from the barbecue pit, Francesco lit a bonfire nearby and placed chairs around for people to sit and chat after the meal.

'Take this plate of meat to the table, Alba,' her father said, 'and there's a tray of roasted peppers and aubergines in the kitchen for the vegetarians.'

He picked up an old cow bell from the ground and swung it back and forth, '*A tavola, tutti!* It's ready, come and sit down to eat.'

By the time Alba returned with the dishes, the only seat left at the long table was next to the insufferable Daniel. She tried to wriggle as far away as possible from him but his mother was a big woman, taking up a place and a half, and Daniel's legs nudged hers.

'Can we be friends again?' he asked.

'I never thought we were friends in the first place.'

Emilia sitting opposite frowned at her. 'That's not very nice, Alba. Babbo's always saying we've got to be nice to our guests.'

Danny laughed, reached over and tweaked the little girl's long plaits whereupon she added, 'but I can see why she might not want to be nice to you. Leave my plait alone, please.'

'Whoops!' he said, tucking into a pork chop, 'are all the females in this family prickly?'

As soon as she could, Alba left the table with a pile of crockery and escaped to the kitchen to start stacking the dishwasher. Every now and again she stole glances at Danny through the window above the sink. He'd moved nearer to the fire and was prodding embers with a long stick. Sparks flew up like fireflies, lighting up his tanned face and blond hair. She watched him cup his cigarette with one hand while he fetched a can of beer from the table. He caught her looking at him and she moved away from the window.

'I'm tired, Mamma,' she said, 'I'm off to bed.'

She lay on top of the covers, too hot and unsettled for sleep, wishing the next fortnight would pass quickly so new guests would arrive and she could say goodbye to Danny and his family forever.

The next day was hotter than ever.

'There'll be a storm before too long,' Francesco told his family at breakfast. 'Make the most of the sunshine today because the weather's going to break. I hope it doesn't rain for the concert this evening.'

They were going as a group to Anghiari to listen to the Southbank Junior Symphonia. It was a free annual event and a calendar fixture always enjoyed by guests.

The girl playing the clarinet in the quartet swung from side to side, immersed in her private world. As she conjured her screeching music, she bent her knees and arched her eyebrows at some meaningful note that meant absolutely nothing to Alba. Instead she watched with fascination as three white moths were caught in the glare of spotlights, dancing and flapping as if riding on crotchets and quavers.

She stole a sideways glance at her parents. Babbo had his eyes closed as he listened, Anna's hand clasped tightly in his lap. Alba consulted her programme. "Divertimenti by F. Bridge." She'd never heard of him.

Daniel was sitting on the white plastic chair next to hers. He leant nearer to her, wrinkling up his nose and whispered, 'Let's go to the next venue in Piazza del Popolo before everybody else gets there to grab the best seats. This is crap…'

They were at the edge of the row so could sneak away without having to clamber over anybody's legs. She was still annoyed with him for tricking her in the river, but anything was better than sitting through this boring caterwaul.

They climbed steep alleyway steps past tall mediaeval houses, their window ledges decorated with pots of frothy coral geraniums, and arrived in the piazza. A stage had been set up at the lower end and there was another scattering of plastic chairs on the incline. Daniel pointed to the bar in the corner and steered her towards it.

'Wait outside and I'll fetch us a drink.'

But she went in and made her way to the balcony at the back of the bar to take in the view. There was a full moon and the air was still warm. The Apennines were a moody blue backcloth to lights twinkling from houses on the plain. Car headlights and city lights from distant Sansepolcro added to the night sparkle.

Notes from the quartet's instruments continued to float towards them from the piazza they'd left.

Four alley cats dressed like humans yowling to the moon, she thought and not music to relax to. It was discordant, 'hiccough music' leading the listener to somewhere and then letting them down, pointing them in unexpected directions.

Daniel returned, carrying a bottle of Sangiovese and two plastic beakers. They found a place at the back of the piazza and leant against the wall of a house, its stones still warm from the sun.

'Cheaty music,' she said gulping the wine.

'You what?'

'I guess it's supposed to mimic tension or something. I prefer music I can sink into.'

'You don't have to like it. You sound guilty for not liking it.'

'Everybody else seemed to,' she said, turning to him, 'I felt ignorant looking round at their rapt expressions. As if I was missing something important.'

He laughed. 'How do you know they weren't just bored and wondering when it was going to end, or thinking how hard the chairs were or how tight their best shoes were?'

'Do you think the musicians noticed us sneaking off?'

'What does it matter? You worry too much.' He topped up her wine. 'Cheers!' he said, touching his beaker to hers. 'Who cares about anything?'

The music stopped. There was the sound of clapping and then a crescendo of voices as the audience began to crowd into the square from the last venue. Alba and Danny stayed put against the wall, happy to remain at the back watching people panic-scrabbling for chairs in front of them.

The next piece of music sounded better to her ears. She looked up the name of the composer: A. Piazzola, from South America. It was a tango. About twenty-five musicians wandered onto the stage, strolling together, chatting and laughing. They were dressed casually, but all in black. A beautiful blonde wore brown espadrilles and an elegant black halter neck evening-dress. Then, from amidst all the chatter, a young Japanese violinist walked to the front of the stage and plucked a few chords. The pretty blonde moved further forward, replying to his introduction and then, one by one, the others joined in.

The music was magnetic. Daniel put their beakers on the ground and pulled her to him. They moved in time, kick stepping up the alleyway leading out of the square, improvising, guessing at tango moves together. She let herself be guided by him, her body responding to his, giggles bubbling up from deep within her.

'Look serious!' he hissed in mock melodrama, 'the tango is *deadly* serious…' And then he swept her downwards into a backbend. She squeaked but he held her tight so she wouldn't fall. He pulled her up again in time with the brusque melody that soared from high to low, low to high and then, on the final chord, he kissed her on the mouth. Long and slow.

She liked it.

He tasted of wine and excitement.

A clap of thunder joined the music, followed by heavy drops of rain that splashed onto their faces as they remained fused together.

'Oh, there you both are,' her father said, emerging from the alleyway with an umbrella.

And they sprang apart.

In the car park Danny slipped into the back seat next to Alba and held her hand for the entire drive back up the mountain.

Forty-five minutes later the car pulled into the gateway of Il Mulino.

'Can we see each other tomorrow night?' Danny whispered.

'I can't,' Alba said. 'I've arranged to go out with my father. But the day after tomorrow's good.'

'Shit – my parents want to drag me to Urbino for the day.'

She shrugged an apology but there was no way she was going to cancel tomorrow's outing with Babbo. It was a belated birthday present: a night time trip to listen for wolves.

Chapter 18
Alba and the wolves

'I'm sorry to disappoint you, Alba,' Francesco said next morning, 'but I have to take Donna and the team to Arezzo for a meeting really early tomorrow and you know how late it gets when Mirko gets whiff of his wolves and wants to stay out half the night observing them. Is there anybody else you could take?'

She tried not to make herself sound too eager when she suggested Danny. 'He's leaving next week,' she said, 'and it would be an amazing experience for him.'

Francesco winked at her and she smiled back, glad he didn't tease her.

'When are you going to introduce us to this Donna?' Anna asked. 'I thought you said she wanted to do the Piero della Francesca trail.'

'There's still plenty of time,' Francesco said. 'She's managed to extend her visa for another three months. She's fallen in love with Italy, big time.

Anna remembered how the charm and beauty of Italy had captivated her ten years earlier and how easy it had been to leave her old life in England behind. She was curious to meet this Donna to compare notes. Maybe she too had fallen for an Italian. She stacked the dishwasher thinking how time had flown and along the way stolen some magic from those early years.

Mirko had a daytime job in a jewellery shop down in the town of

Sansepolcro but his heart lay in the countryside. He kept a census
of wildlife and his preferred attire was camouflage trousers, jacket
and walking boots. They met in the square at 11 p.m. and drank a
small beer each in the Dori Bar, although Danny grumbled about
them being lightweights. One beer wasn't enough, he said. Earlier
he'd complained to Alba about having to go with Mirko. 'I'd rather
be on my own with you,' he'd said, 'I'll be gone the day after
tomorrow.'

'Of course we can't go without him,' she'd replied. '*I* don't
know where the wolves are.'

When he'd wanted to stay longer in the bar and drink, she'd
told him they needed to stay awake and alert. 'An espresso would
be better, really,' she said, beginning to wonder whether it had
been such a good idea to ask him along.

Two Pointers lay asleep in the back of Mirko's jeep and she
couldn't resist leaning behind to stroke the youngest, Storm, curled
on top of a box of equipment. His tail thumped against the metal
wheel shields and he gave her a little whine and then yawned. She
had read somewhere that dogs yawned when they were
embarrassed.

Mirko was telling them how he'd had to rescue Storm in the
woods the previous week. He'd been carrying out a census on the
caprioli. These roe deer were down in numbers because of the
shortage of wild boar, decimated by the previous harsh winter and
the wolves had switched their preferred prey from boar to deer.

'I came upon a kill - a dead roe,' he explained, 'and the dogs
were off the leash. We came round a huge rock and there was a
pair of wolves with six cubs right in front of us on the path. Storm
wanted to play with them, silly young pup – and of course the
female wolf wasn't best pleased.'

He turned round, taking one hand off the steering wheel,
waving around his free hand as he emphasised the peril his dog had

been in, 'I had to go right in, scoop him up and get out of there fast.'

Alba translated to Danny who looked at her, mouth wide open, incredulity in his voice. 'You're joking me,' he said.

Mirko turned the jeep off the tarmac road and got out to unlock a gate guarding the entrance to a dirt track. They travelled higher and higher, through dense forest where distant lights from houses in Badia blinked on and off as they passed gaps in the trees. The jeep navigated holes gouged by large tractor tyres made by woodcutters' vehicles. Sections of the track had been washed away by mud landslides after rain storms. Tracts of the road seemed impassable but Mirko always found a way through, even if it meant diverting via a space in the trees. Alba enjoyed this part of the adventure almost as much as the hunt itself. To be awake when the rest of the world was safely tucked up in bed or slumped in front of boring television sets; to have an out-of-the-ordinary experience that made her feel she was alive and connected with something important. She loved it. She stole a glance across to Danny who was very quiet, hanging onto the strap above the passenger door.

You okay?' she asked.

'Just glad I didn't have a big supper before climbing into this crazy jeep! The dogs would have an extra snack if I puke up.'

Mirko swung the jeep off the track into a siding, telling them wolves had been in this area three days earlier. He gave them a torch each to switch on as a signal if they heard anything during the recordings of wolves he was about to play. Once out of the car he put a finger to his lips, motioning them to stay as quiet as possible and to move ten metres further away from where he was positioned at the edge of the ridge.

When Danny slammed shut his passenger door he couldn't see Alba's furious glare in the dark but when they were standing close together, she leant near and whispered, 'Dickhead! Next time, shut it quietly.'

'Whatever!' he shrugged and moved further away, making no attempt to tread quietly.

She considered going over to stand next to him but remained where she was, preferring to keep as still as possible, as Mirko had instructed.

The howling of wolves from Mirko's recording broke the night's silence, sending shivers down Alba's spine. Sad, primeval, haunting, scary, magical - adjectives that didn't conjure the half of what she felt. After a two-minute wait and no response, Mirko switched on the recordings again and soon afterwards flicked on his torch and moved cautiously over to them, his feet barely making a sound, despite the twigs underfoot.

'Did you hear that?' he asked, 'down there in the gulley, behind the lowing of the cows? A couple of cubs replied to the recording.'

Neither of them had heard even the cows and Alba felt angry she had let her annoyance with Danny interfere with her concentration.

'Bit of a con, if you ask me,' Danny said to her as they climbed back into the jeep. She was disappointed in his lack of appreciation. He obviously wasn't that bothered about the whole experience but she decided not to let him spoil it for her.

Mirko told them he was going to drive to a better spot, where they would be nearer the wolves.

'We have to move fast now,' he said, 'they'll hear our vehicle and start moving out of this area in no time.'

At a new site, above a huge drop where Alba warned Danny to stay still because in the dark it would be easy to fall down the precipice, they heard the shrill, yelping reply of wolf cubs. Mirko was satisfied he had located his first group of wolves and immediately used his mobile to inform a member of his team doing a census further down the valley.

'Any luck your end?' By this stage Alba stopped translating everything for Danny. It didn't seem important to do so anymore.

'Now we're off to Sasso Simone,' Mirko said, climbing back up into the driver's seat.

'He's not wearing his seat belt,' Danny remarked.

'Neither are we,' she replied.

It was now twenty past two in the morning. The few houses in the lonely hamlets they passed through were locked into the night. Mirko paused his jeep at the edge of a cornfield, shining his powerful torch over the grass.

'Look over there, at the edge of the meadow,' he said, handing his binoculars to Alba. She located a pack of boar foraging in the crops close to a copse.

'The boars will soon pick up in numbers,' he told them, 'they always have several young in their litter which usually all survive, whereas deer have one, maximum two young at a time. There are very few boar this year but nature will sort that out.' He laughed. 'It usually does.'

Slipping the jeep back into gear he drove on higher and higher until they were above 1,000 metres. At the edge of a path blocked by barbed wire, he stopped. The wind was up causing him to mutter, 'It might be difficult to hear the wolves if the wind gets much stronger.'

They all put on another layer of clothing before trudging upwards in the darkness through gorse and scrubby grass. Wearing head torches made the going easier, the narrow dried mud path dropping away steeply on either side. Mirko led them off track down through a wooded area and then stopped at the edge of a sheer drop. Looming in the dark were the two outlines of Sasso Simone and Sasso Simoncello. He told Danny that on these two high plateaux, far back in the 15th century, Cosimo de' Medici had built a Fortress of the Sun. After a mere ten years it had been abandoned due to inhospitable terrain and the ruins were barely discernible now beneath the scrub of juniper bushes and brambles.

'Fascinating!' Danny said in a bored voice, followed by, 'when are we going back?' Alba could hardly believe his rudeness and when she felt him squeeze her bottom, she dug her elbow hard into his side. 'Jesus, Alba!' Danny yelped and Mirko told him to be quiet.

They waited for a while in silence and suddenly the wind dropped. Alba had never been to this spot before. She thought that she wouldn't care if she didn't hear the wolves. She was in a place of magic: the flat rocky outcrops before them stood like two towers marking the entrance to a secret world. It was like waiting to start an adventure within an exotic tent, its roof embroidered with stars and streaks of the Milky Way. Two shooting stars tumbled down as she gazed upwards. She didn't want to say anything or point out to Danny what she had seen but kept it to herself. It was a special moment to store away like a favourite chocolate to savour later when she needed a sweet moment. She gave up trying to find words to describe her feelings. It was enough to sink into, to live and love the whole experience.

And when Mirko played his recording, this time the wolves responded almost immediately. Their cries floated over to her echoing from the ridge of the plateaux. She pictured them – maybe nine in number, Mirko had said - some standing, heads raised to the sliver of moon and the roof of stars, howling out their warning cries. It was as if they were proclaiming this as their territory and not to venture nearer. And the high-pitched squeaky howls of the cubs were copying their elders. The amazing episode lasted for about a minute until the final whimpers of the wolves faded and ordinary night sounds took over.

Mirko switched on his recording once more and she almost wanted there to be silence so the spell wouldn't be broken. But the wolves repeated their howling, clearer this time, more insistent. A single tear trickled down her face.

In the jeep afterwards, Danny said he was knackered and couldn't wait to hit the sack.

But she knew she wouldn't be able to sleep a wink.

The next day they met at the river. He stood on the weir facing away from where she was sitting, knees hunched up to her chin. He was skimming stones in the shallows, holding a roll-up in the other hand. She realised he only ever seemed to smoke when his parents weren't around.

'It was all a big con,' he said. 'I bet there was another nature weirdo up there on the opposite hill with his old recordings too, switching his machine on at convenient intervals to time it with Mikel's.'

'Mirko,' she corrected. She didn't know whether to slap him round his stupid, sunburned face or push him into the river.

Instead, she got up and hurried away from him without saying goodbye. As far as she was concerned he had failed the wolf test miserably.

THEN

Chapter 19
Spring 1922 – Marisa and the *festa*

Five years had passed. In those days, time was measured by seasons and not by the clock.

On May 3rd we celebrated the feast of the Holy Cross. Willow branches two metres long had been cut from the river's edge, stripped and fashioned into crosses. Then they were dipped in olive oil and taken to church to be blessed by Don Mario. These crosses could now be seen dotted around the meadows and fields surrounding Montebotolino, a witness to our hopes and prayers for hard work on our land. They would remain until harvest time, at the end of summer.

Yellow *ginestra* bloomed again with its sweet perfume and as I knelt by the river scrubbing Nonno's bed sheets clean, shadows on bleached stones cast by a pair of swallows swooping and diving reminded me it was almost time for the men to return from their five month sojourn on the Maremma.

This year I had decided to join in the celebrations for their homecoming, instead of hiding in the kitchen to help other women chop vegetables and stir sauces for the *festa*. At twenty-eight I felt life trickling away from me, like a stream tumbling relentlessly down the mountain to disappear into a vast ocean. I wanted a taste of life before it passed me by. Recently I had taken to wearing my Sunday veil over my face whilst working on our vegetable plot and covering my arms from the sun's glare with one of my old nightdresses. I hoed thistles and tangles of Old Man's Beard away from my precious plants. There was chamomile to cure stomach pains and insomnia, mint to wrap in poultices to disinfect festering wounds, nettles for hair loss, sage for tooth ache, juniper berries for coughs and rosemary for sciatica. Elena laughed as I passed by her house on the way to fetch in our hens and asked me what the devil I thought I was doing dressed up like an old scarecrow.

'Keeping the jays away from my plants,' I replied, not wanting to tell her the real reason.

I didn't feel like revealing how I wanted to try to look my best for the home comers' *festa*. I wanted my skin milk-white instead of my usual scorched leathery look from working outside. It was easier to accept scarecrow taunts than be teased.

At the beginning of March I bought a length of fine soft cotton in the shade of blue chicory flowers and I'd sewn a dress with puffed sleeves and full skirts to hide my ugly legs. The travelling salesman who sold it to me had accepted three rabbit skins and some honeycomb in exchange as I didn't have any *lire* to pay for it. I'd promised him three more skins when he returned later in the summer. The wide skirts wouldn't disguise my limp but I reasoned I would be sitting down most of the time watching the dancers, so it wouldn't matter. I'd found a strip of thicker cotton in a darker shade of blue in poor Mamma's bundle of cloths and I'd embroidered a pattern of white flower petals to make a belt to tie around my waist. When I'd tried it on after my Sunday bath and peered at myself in the cracked mirror leaning against my bedroom wall, I had to admit I didn't look too bad. My waist looked tiny in proportion to my bosom and the colour of the cloth suited me. Even if I never wore the dress again, I'd enjoyed making my outfit during evenings by the fire. It made a change from weaving and darning heavy cotton *sacconi* for storing our beans and flour.

All of the women left behind in our village had kept back some chestnut flour from their winter stores to bake cakes and rolls for the *festa*. I had filled baskets of *prugnoli* mushrooms collected from the fields and lanes and dried them on racks hanging from the kitchen ceiling so we could add them to sauces for *polenta*. If we were lucky the men would bring back fresh ricotta to go with *pimpernella*, wild carrots, poppy and scabious leaves which Elena would add as fillings for her famous *ravioli*. *Borlotti* beans, tripe and tomatoes would provide another main dish, served with slices of *pancristiano*, dipped in egg and fried in oil. We'd all been working hard for hours to prepare this feast and it would disappear in minutes. This was always the way.

I couldn't wait for Loriano to return so we could once again listen to music from his accordion. But most of all I was looking forward to seeing Giuseppe.

Our house was always used for hosting important *feste*. Situated just off the square, it was also the largest house in Montebotolino and the grassy area in front was spacious enough for men to spill out and drink their wine, away from the disapproving glares of wives and sweethearts. The village bread oven stood nearby too, making it easy for us to fetch and carry baked dishes and *foccaccia*.

This evening, the large oak kitchen table we used for our meals, food preparation, birthing and even laying-out of our dead had been pushed back against the far wall and our rushed-seated chairs, as well as those of our neighbours, arranged round the room. This was where I and the older women would sit, chat and watch the dancing after our kitchen work was done. The younger ones would wait to be asked to dance. This would happen only after the men had swallowed glasses of Chianti to loosen limbs and inhibitions.

Earlier in the day I helped tidy away our precious copper pans and hid them under the bed in the front bedroom. In their place I hung garlands of ivy, poppies and spring flowers round the empty plate racks. Yellow rattle, dog roses, charcoal burners' broom and bundles of dog daisies gathered from the meadows on my favourite slopes turned our humble kitchen into a place of beauty. I'd picked perfumed red roses and placed them in a vase in the niche next to the plaster statue of the Madonna and swept the floorboards clean. There was nothing left to do now save wait for the men to return.

The village children perched on grassy mounds below the village were the first to spot the straggly line of men and beasts appearing over the rise known as the Three Bishops. Four white shepherd dogs ran on ahead barking their arrival; the bells of San Tommaso pealed a welcome and everybody rushed from their houses to wave and shout. Some of the younger girls hurried to greet sweethearts, wives removed pinafores and adjusted headscarves over straggly curls or greying hair. Elderly folk shaded their eyes with age-blotched hands to peer better into the distance. The numbers of sheep and cattle were much reduced from those of the outward journey, which was either a sign of business well transacted or an indication of disease and decimation. We all waited anxiously to learn the outcome and the smiles on the faces of the home comers, together with their general good cheer, told us the story was good.

I remained leaning against the warm stones of my house, observing. Each year Giuseppe matured from the gangly youth who had left five winters ago, into a handsome young man. His body had filled out from hard physical work down on the coast and the stubble on his face was that of a man's. Feeling suddenly shy, I hurried inside to stir the *polenta* simmering in the big black cauldron hanging over the fire, searching for something to occupy my butterfly thoughts.

Late in the afternoon when the remaining stock had been safely penned and the men had scrubbed their tired bodies and changed into fresh clothes pulled from old chests scented with lavender and lemon balm, the celebrations began.

Flagons of wine that had been stored away purposely in backs of barns were uncorked and ladles of delicious bean stew heaped onto tin platters. Giuseppe thanked me as I served him a dish piled high.

'I've been dreaming of this for months,' he said, 'I swear I never want to see another artichoke again for the rest of my days.'

The men around him laughed and agreed, explaining they had eaten their fill of them, the fields around the town of Alberese being ideal for growing that crop and providing seasonal work for some of the men who were not shepherds.

'That and bread-and-water soup,' Giuseppe added, toasting his friends before knocking back a beaker of wine.

I understood what he meant about the joys of a change in diet.

Through the winter months, women and children who remained up in the mountains survived on a diet of chestnut flour and *polenta*.

We all filled our stomachs that evening until not a crust was left. And then it was time for the dancing.

I watched as at first the only dancers on the floor were three middle-aged couples, sure-footed, their bodies used to each other's movements. They were joined a little later by Gianni and Stefania and Piero and Manuela, two betrothed couples to be married later in June. Gianni was not a natural dancer and peered down at his feet as if not quite believing what they were doing. But Stefania guided him round to the music, encouraging him with her patient smile.

Soon the floor was crowded, colour from dresses, scarves, shirts and ribbons whirling around in rainbows, the whiff of sweat mingling with scents of flowers and wine. The floorboards in our old kitchen bounced up and down with the rhythm of stamping feet and even dishes on the table danced in time to music spun from Loriano's deft fingers. Save for a line of old ladies dressed in black, I was the only woman not on the dance floor. Feeling awkward I moved outside for fresh air. Beneath the branches of a crab apple tree planted by the bread oven, I sat on a stone seat and gazed up at the stars scratching the sky. It was cooler out here away from the throng of warm bodies and I pulled my shawl tighter round my bosom.

'Let's leave this dump and go down to Badia Tedalda.'

I recognised the voice from amongst the group of youths clustered round the wine barrel nearby. It was Ivo's, son of the man who helped us slaughter and joint our pig each January. 'The only free bit of meat round here is Marisa,' he continued, 'and who'd want to taste her?'

I heard them laugh and shrank back against the stones of the bread oven wall, wishing I could disappear.

And then Giuseppe was in front of me holding out his hand, asking me to dance.

'You don't have to, Giuseppe,' I said, 'but thank you.'

'I know I don't have to,' he replied. 'But I haven't danced yet and I like this tune.'

It was a slow, haunting song about leaving for work down in the Maremma. All of us knew it well.

> *"Tutti mi dicon Maremma Maremma*
> *Ma a me mi pare una Maremma amara,*
> *L'uccello che ci va perde la penna*
> *Io c'ho perduto una persona cara*
> *Sempre mi trema il cuor quando ci vai*
> *Dalla paura che non torni mai."*

Loriano sang the words in a deep baritone, describing the bitter life on the Maremma plains. Even birds lost their feathers there, he sang, and he had lost someone dear to him too. Every time he went down, he feared he would never again return home.

I stopped at the edge of the dance floor.

'I can't dance, Giuseppe,' I whispered, tugging at his shirt. 'I've never danced in my life.'

He bent down and murmured for me to place my feet on his and to hold on tight.

'I'll do the dancing for both of us,' he said.

In one way it was like the flying I'd always yearned to do: I felt weightless and a freedom my crippled legs would not normally allow. Even when I'd been a toddler, no older than two or three years old, I would come hobbling out of the church after Sunday Mass in a furious rush and shuffle on my bottom down the thirteen stone steps. It was all my parents could do to stop me from rolling down the grassy slope to the fencing - the only barrier against a precipitous drop to the valley far below.

'You'll kill yourself, child,' they'd shout. And I would cry, telling them I only wanted to drop off the edge to fly like a bird and dip my wings into the silver thread of river sparkling in the distance.

We danced like that for a further five tunes and I remember Giuseppe complimenting me on my fine voice as I sang along with Loriano. I could see my Montebotolino neighbours nudging each other and heard them commenting about me and my new dress.

'Why, she almost looks pretty,' I heard Elena say.

Finally I stepped off Giuseppe's feet, worrying I was hurting him.

'Don't be foolish,' he said. 'If I could count the number of times I've danced like this with my little sisters, you wouldn't worry. It's a game we've played since they were tiny!'

That night, trying to find sleep in my single bed, I replayed each tune in my head. Each move, each step, each time Giuseppe held on to me tight as he twirled me round, my hand tiny in his strong grasp; how he laughed when I shrieked as he spun us faster and faster. My brain wouldn't let go of these thoughts.

I was in love with this boy, even though he was ten years younger and thought of me as an older sister. I loved him.

Chapter 20
October 1922 – Giuseppe

When the first sprinklings of snow whitened the peak of l'Alpe della Luna across the valley from Montebotolino, I knew it was time to leave again. Despite the fact I had now made this trek down to the Maremma five times, it was still hard to leave my family, but once we were underway and had put distance between our mountain village and home comforts, the going became easier. However, little did I know how the *transumanza* of 1922 would change my life. I am not proud of what happened but *"sbagliando s'impara"* - one learns by one's mistakes. If I had to choose an epitaph for myself, this would be the very one.

She told me later that it had been quiet in Bar Paradiso that night and she was bored - bored with her job and bored with her life. She said Bar Inferno would have been a better name for what she termed "this dump of a place". As far as she was concerned it made no difference if customers spat on the straw-covered floor as it was never swept clean and she was not about to volunteer ... not on the pay she received from mean old Augusto, the owner of the bar. She'd been working in Alberese for seven months and the malaria-infested town, plus clod-hopping peasants with their rough words and even rougher hands, were getting to her. Augusto encouraged her to flirt to make the men drink more wine, but she said it was hard to flutter eyelids at toothless old men in smelly breeches. If I had not entered when I did, she would have hitched a ride out on the next cart bound for Grossetto, for she was sure there would be more excitement and a better way of life in the city. And then I never would have met her…

It was the first time I'd stepped over the threshold of Bar Paradiso but I'd wanted a change from sitting by the camp fire in the evenings. I'd changed into a clean cotton shirt that Mamma had patched for me over the summer and made an effort to scrub my hands clean. I decided at the last minute to take my copy of *Orlando Furioso*. There was bound to be a quiet corner in that place where I could enjoy my book, I thought.

It was about half past nine when I entered and I chose to sit myself down at a table in the corner, next to a cobweb-curtained window. A young woman was half heartedly wiping down the wooden barrels, that served as table tops, with a filthy rag and I caught her eye. She dawdled over. When I asked for a bowl of pasta and a pitcher of cold water, she pulled a face and told me the kitchen was shut.

'Cook's ill,' she said.

Her accent was guttural, harsh. I guessed she was probably a *romana*. One of the monks at the seminary had been from Rome and this girl swallowed her final syllables in the same way.

She leant towards me, revealing an ample bosom and deep cleavage. I felt my face redden.

'I'll see what I can do for you, darling,' she whispered. 'There's yesterday's *pagnotta* and some dried sausage if you're desperate for a bite.'

Then she winked at me, saying, 'And you could do with a bit of grease on that sunburned face too.'

I heard myself stammer a polite reply, 'That would be kind, signorina.'

'My name's Luisella, *tesoro*,' she said, pushing a curl behind her ear and flouncing off to the kitchen.

While she was away I opened the volume Fra Michele had given me and carefully traced the letters, mouthing the ancient words. Luisella told me, much later, that she'd watched me from the kitchen doorway. She said I reminded her of one of the paintings on the walls of the chapel back in her home village of Ponte Mammolo, north of Rome. Like one of the angels in the frescoes, she said, with the same dreamy eyes. Nobody had ever said such things to me and I was flattered, even though I thought she was talking rubbish.

She brought me over a plate piled high with sausage and despite the bread being rather dry, I tucked in with relish.

'Not been feeding you, then?' she asked, laughter in her voice.

I stopped chewing, a hunk of bread half way to my lips. 'I'm sorry,' I said, 'but I don't much like camp food. I'm as hungry as a wolf.'

'Cooked water and stale bread on their menu, right?'

I grinned and she smiled. There was a gap where one of her canine teeth should have been and she sucked at it with her tongue.

'As I said, my name's Luisella and...' She broke off when Augusto shouted at her from behind the bar to get on with her work. With her back to him she stuck out her tongue and rolled her eyes so that only I would notice, and smiled her gap-toothed smile.

As she walked back to the bar, I watched the sway of her hips as she skirted the tables. Her ankles were slim. My mother and sisters wore longer skirts covering their legs and I found myself wondering if Luisella's calves and thighs were slim. But then I felt myself redden again and I concentrated on the pages of my book instead. I brushed away the breadcrumbs and was pleased I hadn't smeared sausage fat on the ancient letters. This book was the one treasure I had salvaged from my two years at the seminary.

On the following Sunday I returned. It was certainly not for food or wine (which tasted more like vinegar) or conversation from other drinkers. I told myself it was because Bar Paradiso was a place where I could read my book in peace.

Luisella beamed a welcome and I made my way to the same corner seat. Her lips seemed redder and her breasts strained higher against her tight, grubby blouse. The plate she set before me was even bigger than last week. As she bent down to whisper to me, I felt her bosom brush my shoulder.

'I sliced you three more pieces of salami while Augusto wasn't looking and topped the jug up with extra wine.'

I stayed in my corner late that night, alternately glancing at my book and ogling Luisella, until Augusto started to blow out candles and pull shutters closed, ordering everybody home to their beds.

She was waiting outside in the shadows and we walked together across the deserted square, the shutters on the tall houses firmly locked. I kept my distance and we prattled about nothing in particular. She was very different from mountain women and I found I had no wish to share information about home with her. She grumbled on about Augusto, swearing in her guttural accent about how he had tried to put his filthy hands up her skirt as he climbed the cellar steps behind her.

'The next time that dirty old *porco* comes near me, he'll regret it,' she said. 'I've nicked a sharp knife from the kitchen and it's staying in my drawers. I'll stick it in him where it hurts and then he won't ever be able to use his wrinkly little sausage again.'

She lifted her skirt to show me the blade tucked into her bloomers and I looked away from the sight of her thighs. They weren't slim as I had imagined, but round - with flesh bulging above her stockings.

On the third Sunday I walked her home again. As we turned a corner she stumbled. I caught her and she pulled me to her. I felt the weight of her breasts against me once again and it made me hard.

On the fourth Sunday we walked away from the square in the direction of the beach and when I asked her if I could kiss her, she replied, 'I thought you'd never ask.'

One kiss led to another. She lifted her skirts as she leant against the wall of a house on the edge of town. I heard sounds of a family preparing for the night: somebody scraping plates clean, a man gargling and a baby crying, but when I pushed myself into her, the slippery wetness of her, I was aware of nothing else except release.

I couldn't stop thinking about her in the days that followed and especially about the oblivion of the moment when I came inside her. People called it making love but I knew I didn't love Luisella. It was nothing more than lust, which I would have to confess before I could receive the Holy Eucharist into my mouth at Mass again.

So the next time I saw her and watched her flirting in Bar Paradiso with another customer, I knew I shouldn't have felt anger. I shouldn't have clenched my fists or let my stomach knot up in a jealous twist of fury. I shouldn't have stood up so my stool crashed to the floor behind me and I shouldn't have hit the stupid drunken lout so hard that his nose was smashed into a pulpy mess and blood streamed down his clothes.

Afterwards Luisella had smiled and cooed at me as she bathed my bloodied knuckles, kissing each one gently, telling me nobody had ever stood up for her like I had. She took me home to her attic room and sat astride me on her cheap metal bed, her plump thighs warm and soft against mine and I sucked her nipples until she moaned. I had to stop her cries by covering her mouth with my bruised hand lest Augusto heard.

For three long weeks after that I managed to keep away from Bar Paradiso. I found a derelict stable in the fields behind the camp where I could read in peace. But I found myself reading the same passage over and over, whilst images of Luisella tormented me until I had to reach inside my breeches to relieve myself. The sticky stain was there for everybody to see so I sneaked away through the trees to the shore and jumped into the salty shallows, rolling over and over fully clothed to clean myself. Across the water near the spot where we had found poor Fausto, the moon glinted on the island of Giglio and I thought of how many places there were to explore in the world and how small and lost I felt.

I needed to talk over my problem with Paolo. Our paths didn't cross so often now I was working for Matteo – only when his mules needed new shoes.

'What's up?' he asked me when I found him. 'You look peaky, lad.'

I lowered my voice and told him how I'd met a girl and how I couldn't stop thinking about her but I wanted to stop thinking about her - more than anything in the world.

He looked at me, scratched his chin and puffed on the pipe he never seemed to light. After a while he asked me a strange question. 'Does your heart feel strong?' he said.

When I shrugged my shoulders and stayed staring into the flames of the camp fire, Paolo took his pipe from his mouth and prodded me in the chest with its stem, firing off several more questions.

'Would you want to take this girl back to Montebotolino, Giuseppe? Could you picture her at a *veglia* seated at your family's hearth mending your shirts, sharing stories and jokes with everybody? Could you imagine her in the company of your mother and sisters, or hard at work, hoeing and planting seeds in your meadow?'

My silence in the face of all these questions must have spoken the truth and when Paolo asked me who the girl was and I told him, he laughed outright, 'You must be the only one round here she hadn't tried out, Giuseppe. She's nothing but a *puttana*. You'd best make sure you've not picked up the pox from that one.' And he spat into the fire and laughed even more.

With my mind made up, I waited next evening in the shadow of a lime tree outside the bar for the end of Luisella's shift. I rehearsed over and over what I would say to her and why I could no longer go on seeing her.

At midnight while she was pulling closed the shutters of the bar windows on the street side, she caught sight of me as I leant against the tree, tossing my cap from one hand to another, scuffing dirt with my clogs.

'Oh, that's nice,' she shouted, 'the boy from the mountains has decided to put in an appearance at long last.'

I walked over to her but before I could open my mouth to speak, she told me she was pregnant, demanding to know what I was going to do about it.

Chapter 21
May 1923 – Giuseppe

How to describe my troubled mind during those subsequent months? I retreated into myself, turning down invitations from my friends to spend time together. Even my best friend Luciano gave up on me eventually, at a loss to know why I'd changed so much. I'd told nobody about Luisella's condition, not even Paolo. I visited her on the odd Sunday and we slept together, but I didn't enjoy her company. She moaned and moaned at me to sort something out and bring her money.

Late one afternoon at the end of April I sat hunched on Alberese beach and it came to me to swim out towards the Island of Giglio. Tidying my clogs and clothes into a pile near the shore's edge, I walked into the sea until I was out of my depth. I wanted to drown in the salty water and for the sea to take away my torment. I started to paddle water. Spray stung my eyes, the sea was cold and I wondered how long it would take to grow numb and sink below the surface. I turned onto my back, extending my arms and legs like a cross. The sky was a spangle of stars, the moon almost full, and a picture of my family flickered into my brain. Mamma was by our hearth, the fire unlit. She was dressed in black, wringing her hands and wailing, my siblings were clustered around her trying to offer comfort. And they were crying too.

In that moment I asked myself how I could let my family suffer another tragedy and I struck back to shore. The current was strong and it carried me to the beach where I knelt and sobbed before pulling on my clothes.

Two weeks later in early May, disconsolate, I waved farewell to my mountain friends as they set off on the long trek back to Badia Tedalda. I invented an excuse for not accompanying the caravan. 'I need to stay down here to make extra money for mother,' I said 'There's plenty of work for me on land reclamation. Maybe I'll manage a trip up to see you before the end of summer.'

But I wondered if I would ever see Montebotolino again and once again cursed the evening I'd wandered into Bar Paradiso.

It was six a.m. on a Sunday morning and already sweltering in the hut I was now sharing with labourers from the north, near Venice. Last night there had been celebrations for somebody's birthday and I was the only one awake. My new acquaintances were sleeping off last night's wine. I hadn't joined in. These days, I kept to myself.

I'd sat far back from the camp fire, deep in worry, slumped against the trunk of a Mediterranean pine. I was still angry with myself about Luisella. Of course I hadn't been ignorant of what our coupling might produce. I'd helped often enough to bring the huge Chianina bull to cover our neighbour's cows and, later on I'd pulled blood-caked calves from their haunches. Luisella had always told me not to worry, that she would douche herself with vinegar afterwards. But I shouldn't have trusted her and cursed myself for my foolishness. I felt sure she'd tricked me into getting her pregnant.

Sunday Mass was no longer part of my weekly routine since sleeping with her. I'd been once since she'd told me of her pregnancy and the downcast eyes of the plaster statue of Virgin Maria in the little chapel of Villa Gran Ducale seemed to show disappointment in me. The words from the *pater noster* – "and lead us not into temptation", screamed hypocrisy as I recited them. Instead, I'd taken to spending Sunday mornings in bed with

Luisella – worshipping her body instead of the Holy Eucharist. It felt more honest to take her nipples into my mouth than to receive the consecrated host on my tongue.

Two nights earlier we'd had a huge row and so this Sunday I'd decided to leave her alone. I didn't like her waiting on tables in Bar Paradiso and told her it wasn't a suitable job for a pregnant woman.

'What am I supposed to live off, then?' she'd shouted, hands on hips, mouth turned down in a sulk. 'Just because I'm pregnant it doesn't mean I have to stay cooped up all day and night in that hole of a room you've found me, waiting for you to come and see me whenever you want to get your leg over.'

She was right. And I didn't like the person I was turning into.

Emerging from the hut, leaving the Venetians to their snores, I splashed cold water on my face from a trough and pulled on a half-clean shirt. Pulling my cap down over my curls, I set off in the direction of Alberese.

The ornate gates to the Villa Gran Ducale were wide open in readiness for the arrival of Sunday worshippers for Mass. I found myself dragging my feet towards the chapel, my boots stirring up puffs of dust.

It was a small squat building that could only house half a dozen uncomfortable pews and benches. These were always occupied by the family of the Estate and their domestic servants. Everybody else spilled out from the back and hovered near the entrance. I remembered a dark haired beauty I'd gazed on in the front pew and how I'd concentrated on her shapely back, my eyes tracing a perfect line of pearl buttons fastening her raspberry pink dress. Paolo, standing next to me, had nudged me, whispering that I should stop my drooling and dribbling, that she was the *padrone's* daughter and well beyond my reach. 'And shut your mouth,' Paolo had hissed, 'you look like a baby teething.'

All that seemed an innocent lifetime ago.

Padre Giacomo, the elderly parish priest, was hoeing round a neat display of lettuce plants, humming to himself as he worked. He wore a battered straw hat pulled well down over his head, the rim split at the front, affording two peep holes.

'You're too early for Mass, my son,' he said, straightening up and leaning on his hoe. 'So you can come and help me get rid of these dock roots. They seem to grow while my back is turned.'

I removed my jacket and hung it over a stack of firewood at the side of the vegetable patch. Rolling up my sleeves I set to, attacking weeds with a hoe handed me by the priest. I jabbed at the soil, the blade clanking as it scattered stones in all directions.

'You need to dig sheep manure into this, Father,' I said, lifting a handful of the poor, friable soil and letting it sift through my fingers.

'Well, you can bring me plenty of that, can't you? After you have told me what is troubling you.'

The priest moved to work on the next row of salad plants and then pronounced, 'You are in trouble with a woman.'

He spoke in a matter of fact fashion; the statement could just as easily have been, my *borlotti* bean seedlings are a disaster this year.

'How did you know?' I asked, stopping my mutilation of the soil and shading my eyes from the already fierce sun to better view the old priest's face.

'I didn't sprout wispy hairs and deep wrinkles overnight, my son.'

We worked together for another ten minutes or so. I was grateful for the priest's silence; I couldn't have put up with a lecture.

'That will do for today,' he said eventually. 'Come inside and we'll drink some water and then you can help me prepare for Holy Mass.'

The water was cool and slightly sweet. He told me it came from a spring behind the house and was stored in pottery bottles in a back scullery. As he poured two more tumblers of water, he asked me if the woman causing so much worry was married.

'No, Father.'

'Well, that's something, at least. And are you married?'

No, Father.'

'I thought not. How old are you?'

'Nearly nineteen,' I replied.

The old man sighed and then said, 'I will marry you both.'

'Yes, Father.'

'And now help me serve at Mass. And say an Act of Contrition and three Hail Marys for your penance.'

Five days later, in the tiny chapel of the Villa Gran Ducale I, Giuseppe Starnucci, married Luisella Sciotti.

The sole witness was the priest's house keeper, a plump middle-aged woman called Iole. She had a streak of flour on her face, having been called away in the middle of preparing potato *gnocchi* for the priest's lunch. All through the ceremony her fingers worked away at her rosary beads, her lips pursed in disapproval and every so often a deep sigh escaped from her.

I felt as if I might suffocate. My marriage should have been one of the happiest days in my life but my heart brimmed with misery. My dreams of one day becoming a primary school teacher were now shattered for good. My family wouldn't take to Luisella, of this I was absolutely sure. They might be civil to her and my mother would help with her grandchild. In turn she would expect Luisella to join in with household chores. But they wouldn't love her as a daughter and I knew I would always feel ashamed of her.

At the same time, my upbringing told me it was the correct and moral thing to do, to marry this girl who was expecting our child. I could hear my mother tell me, 'You have bought your bicycle and now you must pedal it.' I thought wryly of how many others must have used Luisella as a bike, remembering Paolo's smile when I'd told him I'd fallen for the village tart.

I'm sure Luisella must have felt she was set up for life. Up until now she'd been like a stray cat, used to living in ditches and scavenging for scraps at the butcher's door. Now she had found herself a roof over her head and me to protect her. I imagined her just like a cat, licking clean her whiskers, curling herself up as near to the fire as comfortable and purring herself to sleep.

Our wedding supper took place in Bar Paradiso. Grudgingly, Augusto set down a litre of rancid red wine on our corner table. 'On the house,' he announced, before placing a heel of bread and a plate of slightly off Maremma black boar next to the bottle.

Luisella had kept on her cream lace veil, set saucily on the back of her head and fastened with a gaudy clip. She told me she'd found it on the sawdust floor of the Bar one night. A few days later she admitted to having pinched it from a market stall.

I moved out of the hut into a tiny room above Augusto's bar. In the middle stood a single bed with sagging springs that sang out squeakily whenever we coupled, which was a rare event as Luisella grew bigger. Although we were now married she found a variety of excuses to keep me off her, 'My back hurts; you'll hurt the baby; he'll get a hole in his head; poo, you smell of sheep.' And in truth I no longer felt like bedding her.

One small window, its pane cracked and held together with a piece of tape, a wobbly wash-stand with a chipped bowl and jug, my cardboard suitcase which served both as table and container for clothes: these were all the furnishings that made up our first home.

Luisella had taken to pestering me about living in Grosseto. 'Buy me a smart new apartment in the centre,' she whined. No matter how often I explained that there was no way on God's earth

I could afford this, she refused to believe me.

'We'll return to Montebotolino up in the Apennines,' I told her, 'that's where we're going to live and you had better get used to the idea.'

Then she shouted and threw things at me. My copy of *Orlando Furioso* landed on the floor. A handful of pages came loose and I picked them up, slamming the door to our room as I stormed out. Another pane of glass dropped to the floorboards and smashed as I clattered down the stairs.

I walked to the beach again and sat by the sea's edge, hankering after my days of freedom with my *garzoni* friends. I had nobody to unburden myself to, but the rhythm of the waves lapping back and forth on the sand began to calm me down. Gradually my heart stopped its crazy thumping and hope stole back. Maybe Luisella and I would grow to like each other eventually and settle down to something resembling happiness. She was very pregnant and her hormones were all over the place. I'd heard women at *veglie* confide to each other about such matters and complain often enough about their men and how marriages took time and patience. My mother would help smooth the waters. Once we returned to Montebotolino life would be easier, I convinced myself.

With these positive thoughts lifting my spirits, I made my way back to Bar Paradiso. As I approached, I heard Luisella singing, accompanied by wolf whistles and raucous cheering. Peering through the smeared window, I saw my pregnant wife standing on an upturned wine barrel, hands on hips, the top buttons on her blouse undone to reveal more of her bosom than modesty allowed. She was clearly drunk and she began to sing the words of a bawdy *Maremmana* song:

Io me ne voglio andare in Maremma,
Mi voglio sposare una maremmana,
Non mi importa se non ha soldi,
basta che abbia una fresca fontana...

(I want to go down to the Maremma,
I want to marry a girl from there,
It doesn't matter if she has no money,
Just as long as her fountain's moist...)

I pushed my way through the throng of men ogling her, knocking three youths at the front sideways and yanking Luisella off her makeshift stage.

'Take your dirty shepherd's hands off me,' Luisella said, slurring her words, 'you're a boring, spotty youth of a husband. I'd rather sleep with a sheep than with you.'

Her audience roared with laughter. I punched the man nearest to me in the mouth. As he fell, spitting teeth and blood as he collapsed to the floor, a couple more drunkards fell down with him like falling dominoes.

'More, more, hit them some more,' screamed Luisella, enjoying the mayhem she was causing.

I dragged her away from the laughing men towards the door. Her words were filthy and coarse. She tried to bite my hand clenched round her wrist and then she suddenly collapsed like a rag doll, clutching her hands to her belly.

At first I thought it was a trick to make me let go of her and I shouted at her to stand up, to get up from the floor.

Then she uttered a high-pitched, terrifying cry and I saw blood spreading across the soiled floor where she lay.

Chapter 22
Giuseppe

The midwife came out to me where I sat hunched on the steps. Shaking her head, she thrust a bundle of rags at me. My son.

'It was too early,' she muttered, 'and she lost too much blood. And what's more the stupid girl was wearing a chain round her neck. Did nobody warn her that the cord would wrap itself around the baby's neck if she wore a chain? Don't expect the infant to last the night either. And you owe me six lire.' She held out a blood stained hand to me.

I didn't know how I would scrape together that amount. It was more than I'd earned in the whole of March and April. I hadn't been able to save anything, with Luisella always grabbing any money I made. In a matter of hours I had become a father and a widower. I could hardly take it in.

'I'll bring it in the morning, signora,' I muttered and she brushed past me clattering down the steps in her clogs, grumbling about the folly of the young and how she would believe the money when she saw it in her hands.

I stood watching her for a few moments as she waddled down the alleyway in the early morning light. The fresh air offered little comfort as I stood cradling the baby in my arms. It weighed hardly more than a new born kitten. The last thing I had imagined was the death of Luisella; she'd always been so loud and lusty, so full of life.

And there was no way I could cope with bringing up a child. I decided to leave it at the convent. I wouldn't be the first or the last.

But there was something I needed to do first. I pushed open the door at the top of the stairs to our room; the place where Luisella had taken me to bed and taught me so many tricks. Now she lay still, her hair tangled on the pillow. The room smelled of metal. I knew this odour, the iron smell of blood. It conjured memories of New Year when we killed our pig and Mamma would hurry to the kitchen with her basin brimming with freshly-spilled blood to make sausages. And I remembered spring in the Maremma, when the shepherds had slaughtered the first lambs and we'd eaten *budelluzzi.* But here in this bedroom, the smell of blood was sour.

With the baby in my arms, I knelt to pull the sheet from his mother's face. It was waxy white, her lips were slightly parted, eyes wide open, staring at me from who knew where. I couldn't bring myself to kiss her. Instead, I brushed back a strand of her matted hair, closed her eyes and whispered I was sorry, that she was better off without me. Her gold chain carrying the medal of the Madonna's face caught the light from the dwindling moon through the cracked window. I put the child down beside her and supporting the weight of Luisella's head, I removed the chain from around her neck, already marble-cold. And I took the gold earrings from her lobes. The child should have something of its mother, besides the knowledge she had died giving birth.

I hunted about for something warm, for he had started to cry, a mewling, whimpering sound. It stopped when I swaddled him in a shawl and held him close to my body. I found myself whispering words of comfort that I'd heard women at home use and which came to me from somewhere better and kinder.

'There now, little one,' I crooned, '*shhh* now, soon be better, there, there, there…'

The convent of Santa Maria Magdalena was not far away, in a small *piazza* behind the elementary school. The town was beginning to stir. It was market day and a handful of stall holders were arranging their merchandise. Under the *loggia,* sacks of maize leant drunkenly against each other. A bag had keeled over, spilling shiny fat chestnuts onto the cobbles. I thought back to more innocent times as a boy, nicking fistfuls of chestnuts from old Rucca in Badia, when he was looking the other way.

A pot mender sat half asleep slumped against a brick column, patched copper pots arranged around him. With one hand I pulled my cap further down on my head in an effort to hide my face and I clutched the bundle of rags tighter, willing the baby not to cry, hoping nobody would guess the nature of my cargo.

The ancient wheel beside the convent door stood waiting to be pushed open like the mouth of a hungry beast, ready for me to place the baby in its wooden drum and push it to the inside of the orphanage where the nuns would take over. I didn't even need to scribble a note. The child, if it survived, would continue in life never knowing anything of its origins. I'd met a couple of orphans in Maremma. Their names – Innocenzo and Addolorato – were a giveaway. Our baby would doubtless be afflicted with a similar label. I whispered again what I had muttered to Luisella, 'It's for the best' and made sure the gold chain was linked through the weave of the shawl. I stretched my arms towards the wheel and then the baby opened its large, brown eyes and yawned. I gazed down at my son, noticing for the first time his curl of dark hair and tiny mother-of-pearl fingernails. Deep in my belly I felt a pang and I was smitten.

Clutching him tightly to me, I made my decision. I had to get him home to Montebotolino before it was too late.

I knew the quickest way to return was by train to Arezzo, from where I could catch the new *Appennino* steam train. From there to Palazzo del Pero and onwards, to Sansepolcro. From the city I could ride on the *corriera* up to Badia Tedalda. It would be easy to find some means from there, even if it meant 'borrowing' a mule to carry us up the steep track to my home village. The journey would take the whole day, if we were lucky, and my son would need milk and napkins. I couldn't manage this without help and I hurried back to the midwife's house.

The door knocker was shaped like a cherub's head. I hadn't noticed it when I'd fetched the old crone for Luisella's labour.

'I'm coming, I'm coming,' I heard her grumble from behind the thick oak door, '*Madonna buona*, why can't babies wait to come at a decent hour?'

With her straggly hair unpinned and her headscarf removed, she looked even uglier than I'd remembered – more like a witch than a midwife.

'Oh, it's you,' she said, 'if there are any problems, I told you already, you take him to the doctor. I've done my bit.'

Before she could close the door on me, I wedged my foot to block it open. 'I need *your* help, not a doctor's.' I said, dangling Luisella's gold chain before her. 'And you can have this.'

Her greedy eyes widened and she grabbed the metal, biting it to check its worth. Then she opened her door wide, 'Come in, come in,' she said.

With a long strip of cotton, she showed me how to bind the baby from his chest to his feet, like an Egyptian mummy. 'Otherwise he'll not grow straight. That's if he grows at all. This one's had a bad entry into the world.'

She handled the baby with sure hands and when she had finished, placed the 'papoose' in my arms and showed me how to get my son to suckle from a teat fixed to a glass bottle containing goat's milk.

'He'll gag at first, mind,' she explained, 'this is bigger than a woman's nipple and this milk will have to do, poor creature.'

She gave me enough milk for one day. 'It'll not go off,' she said, 'you're lucky it's not high summer.'

When she asked what would happen when we arrived in the mountains, I told her not to worry and that I had somebody up there to help me. Before I turned to leave, to my surprise she handed me back the gold medal and chain.

'I can't take this from you,' she said and muttered something under her breath. Then she made the sign of the cross on his little forehead.

'Thank you,' I said. 'Take these instead, signora.' I pulled Luisella's earrings from my pocket. 'They're no good to a boy but I can give him the chain when he makes his First Holy Communion.'

Before she ushered us out into the early morning, I added as an afterthought, 'Remember my poor wife's soul in your prayers.'

The journey to Arezzo passed in a blur. The midwife told me of a neighbour of hers who was taking a cart load of animal skins to the station and when I explained my predicament he gestured to me to climb up beside him, pulling the shawl from the infant's face and smiling. I was grateful he was a man of few words; there was nothing I felt like talking about that morning.

I caught the little *Appennino* train just in time, running down the platform, the station master shouting at me as I pulled open the first door I reached.

The compartment was occupied by a woman and a tangle of children, cardboard cases and bundles tied up in scraps of cloth. There was also a basket of seed potatoes and three chickens, their heads poking from a box under the wooden seat. I hoped to blend into the confusion but half an hour into the journey, my son started up a noisy protest.

'That's a hungry cry,' the woman in the corner seat commented to everybody and nobody in particular. I lifted the wriggling bundle of bindings out from within my coat and balanced the baby on my lap, whilst trying to sort out the task of feeding him the first bottle. The woman watched us struggle for a few moments and then thrust her own baby into the arms of a young girl. She came over to me, steadying herself as the train clattered round a bend, '*Mi permetta, signore,*' she asked. 'Will you give the baby to me?'

She returned to her corner seat and loosened the cloths from around the baby. Then she pulled open the drawstring on her blouse, whereupon my son latched on to her nipple for his first proper feed, one fist punching the air whilst the other little hand rested on the woman's breast.

'I've always too much milk, signore - it's a help to me too, if you don't mind,' she said and then she asked me where his mother was.

I shook my head, whereupon the baby received his second sign of the cross of the day and she rocked him gently as if to protect him from a distress he was too tiny to know about. Then she changed the soiled bindings, talking to him all the while, telling him he was beautiful, that he must grow up big and strong to help his father, who was a good man. Her four children watched her, the older girl jiggling her baby sibling up and down on her little hip.

'I'll top him up for you before we get off,' she said, handing him back to me. 'I expect you've a wet nurse lined up for him once you arrive home?'

I smiled vaguely in response. In my head I said a prayer of thanks for the kindness of strangers, thinking God might not have abandoned me after all - despite my not having paid much attention to Him of late.

The child slept for the rest of the journey. Maybe this was due to the woman's rich milk or maybe it was because of the rocking and bouncing of our rides by bus to Sansepolcro and afterwards by mule up the stony track to Montebotolino. I'd borrowed the animal from Valentino, the miller's son. By now it was quite dark, the path lit only by a waning moon, but I could have found the way blindfold. We passed the cemetery, votive candles flickered, keeping the dead company. Over the weir where spring water splashed into a clear pool where women of Rofelle beat their washing clean. Along Bettino's strip of meadow planted with *erba medica* for his two cows. Then by a stretch of prickly bushes which would be laden in late summer with blackberries for jam. And finally, the steepest part of the climb, where the mule had to work harder to keep her foothold on slippery slabs of rock studded with quartz that glistened in the moonlight. I clutched my son to me within my jacket and held fast to the reins with one hand. Then the familiar outline of Arturo the barrel maker's house loomed over us and I slithered down to lead the animal into our stable, tying her to a metal ring forged by myself with Nonno's guidance. Finally, I pulled down a bundle of hay for the tired beast as a reward for delivering us safely home.

It took half a dozen pebbles tossed up at her window before Marisa appeared, 'Who is it?' she hissed, 'what do you want at this time of night?'

'*Shhhhh!* You'll wake everybody. It's me – Giuseppe. Let me in.'

Chapter 23
Marisa

Do you think I could refuse to help Giuseppe? Of course not! I did what came naturally, what my heart cried out to do. I climbed down the ladder from my bedroom without a moment's hesitation and let him into my house. And when he explained the situation, instinct took over.

I lifted the lid of the trunk that smelled of lavender, where poor Mamma over time had added item upon item to my wedding dowry. I hunted beneath linen sheets which had been waiting to be embroidered with nuptial initials and pillowcases, and towels and pot holders all edged with fine crochet, until I found rolls of thick cotton bindings. Taking the baby from Giuseppe's arms, I unwrapped the soiled cotton strips from around his tiny body. He was perfect, beautiful, the baby I longed to bear. I gazed on his fists, stroked his starfish fingers and the baby clasped my finger more tightly than I had imagined possible for anything so delicate and small.

'Here's what we shall do,' I said, moving to the fire with Giuseppe's son in my arms. It felt as if I had been a mother all my life as I placed a small pan of ass's milk on the ashes to warm. 'We'll tell everybody he's ours. If they say anything, I'll tell them you came back to help me. You called for the midwife but the baby came too soon. I'll tell them I was ashamed I'd gone with you out of wedlock, so I didn't tell anybody.'

I poured warm milk into his bottle that I'd scalded with boiled water and I attached a teat we used for orphaned lambs.

'This will have to do for the time being. In the morning we'll fetch Paolina, the wet nurse. We'll tell her my milk just won't come.'

Testing a few drops on the soft skin of my wrist, I coaxed the baby to drink. It came too fast at first and the child spluttered, his fists fighting the air, cries of protest bringing Giuseppe to hover over us.

'He's strong for a baby that came too soon,' I said, adjusting the teat so the milk flowed more evenly. 'He obviously couldn't wait to make his mark in this world.'

I moved to the side of the fireplace to sit in my grandmother's chair and the baby settled in my arms, finishing the bottle, bubbles of milk at the corner of his tiny blistered lips.

Giuseppe was staring at me and I looked at him square in the eyes. 'We'll have to get married,' I told him. 'And we'll call the child Dario, after my brother who died in the war.'

And Giuseppe went along with my decisions. What else could he do? He told me months later that when he had looked down at me holding Dario, we reminded him of a painting. We looked like a Madonna and child, he said, on a holy picture he'd seen in the seminary and he said he knew I would be a wonderful mother to his son. I wondered if he felt I could be a good wife.

At six o'clock in the morning ten days later, a group of figures straggled over the dew-drenched grass and up the worn steps to our little church of San Tommaso. A thorn from the rose bush at the entrance snagged on my veil, which was the only item of wedding apparel I agreed to wear. 'It will hide my face,' I told Giuseppe, 'because my eyes would tell the real story.'

Don Mario, my father and poor old Nonno and Nonna huddled close to keep warm, for there had been a storm during the night and the mountains were shrouded in cold mist. Giuseppe's mother Vincenza, his little brother Angelo and his two giggling sisters, Maria Rosa and Nadia, made up the wedding party.

Vincenza cradled Dario during Mass. He was dressed in the same christening gown and shawl I'd worn as a baby. They were yellowed at the edges because I'd found no time to launder and starch them. Don Mario performed two sacred sacraments of marriage and baptism that morning.

After we had exchanged vows there was a moment of confusion, for we'd forgotten entirely about rings. Vincenza stepped forward and slipped her own wedding ring off her middle finger. She no longer wore it on her ring finger as she had lost so much weight since her husband and her oldest son had passed away. 'It's no use to me now,' she said as she handed it to Giuseppe, 'take it as my gift to you both.'

It was the first of her many acts of kindness and over time I grew very fond of her.

When Don Mario announced we were man and wife the children started to clap, but when no adults joined in, they stopped abruptly. No bells rang out but I smiled as a single shaft of sunlight burst through the tiny window high up in the church, lighting up the spot where Giuseppe and I stood together. I took it as a sign and I watched dust motes circling round in the sunbeam and imagined I saw a smile on the downcast face of San Tommaso on the glazed tiles behind the altar. Giuseppe squeezed my hand instead of lifting my veil to kiss me and because my veil covered my face, nobody could see the tears in my eyes.

There was no dancing at my wedding. There were no bawdy comments from the few guests present; no preparations of the wedding bed which normally would be strewn with rose petals or orange blossom or whatever flower was in bloom at the time.

Vincenza had killed a chicken for lunch and roasted it with garlic, rosemary and sage and served it on a bed of sun-yellow polenta. Babbo found a bottle of *vinsanto* and we dunked hard *cantuccini* biscuits that Vincenza retrieved from her corner cupboard.

Babbo moved into my single room and Vincenza helped to make the matrimonial bed up with more of my trousseau that I'd painstakingly sewn but never believed I would ever use.

'Why didn't you tell me you were expecting, *cara*?' she whispered as we smoothed linen sheets over the mattress and folded the corners neatly underneath. 'I would have helped you with the birth.'

I lowered my eyes and my mother-in-law took my hands in hers. 'There's no shame, you know,' she continued. 'It's happened many times before and it will happen again.'

She moved over to the wooden cradle at the side of the bed, love written all over her face as she gazed upon her first grandchild.

That night I sat in bed feeding Dario with another bottle of ass milk and Giuseppe came to sit next to us. He had drunk almost two jugs of strong red wine but he seemed quite sober.

'Does he look like her?' I asked.

'I hope not,' was his reply.

He was quiet for a few moments and I asked him no more questions about the woman who had given birth to his son. Then he rose from the bed, saying, 'I'll sleep on the floor tonight.'

I smoothed the baby's downy hair. 'If that's what you want, then sleep on the cold floor by yourself. But there's room enough next to me.'

But he pulled a blanket from the chest and on our wedding night he slept on the hard floorboards.

Chapter 24
September 1923 – Marisa

At the end of summer, everybody in the village set to, stripping leaves from their harvested maize, throwing cobs into large baskets arranged around the square, making sure to leave two leaves on the end. This was so we could tie bunches together to dry from hooks and nails on the walls of our houses.

I laughed at a group of children who were playing with the black strands, making pretend moustaches and fringes, impersonating people from our village. Softer outer leaves were put to one side to make into fresh stuffing for bedding and I helped my friend Rossella lay these out to dry upon the ground. The sun was still warm. Before long the walls of the houses in our village of Montebotolino were daubed with yellow cobs hanging from all the houses. They represented security for winter and this year the harvest had been good.

Giuseppe filled a bag with our share of the corn that had fallen from the husks. On the following day he would take them to the mill for grinding into maize flour for *polenta*. I stored some into clean *sacconi* to take down later in October when the first rains arrived. And the empty husks would be used as firelighters. Nothing was wasted.

After the work of *scartocciatura* was over, we celebrated with a small party. In a couple of weeks the men would start preparations for their annual journey down to the Maremma and cold nights would set in, changing Montebotolino to a mournful place. So this gave us an excuse for an open air *veglia.*

The last portions of beans and tripe had been scraped clean from plates and the fire we'd lit in the middle of the square began to die down. I stirred the embers. Sparks spluttered into the star-canopied sky along with my thoughts and dreams. I watched Gianni and Stefania seated together on a low stone bench next to the bread oven, half hidden by branches of the laden apple tree. They'd been married a month and Stefania's swollen tummy told the age-old story of premarital love. For the whole evening their hands had been intertwined, except for moments when they shared supper from the same plate, feeding morsels to each other, whispering secrets, needing no other company save their own.

Giuseppe was over by the wine cart. Every now and again his distinctive laugh carried over to me. I knew he had drunk the best part of a litre of strong Sangiovese wine. Now he was holding court, recounting stories that met with guffaws and backslapping by his old friends circling him. He drank a lot these days and I wondered if it was a habit he'd picked up in the Maremma or whether I might be the cause.

Baby Dario was fast asleep in the basket I used for carrying washing to the fountain, his long dark eyelashes closed on plump cheeks, one fisted hand stretched out above his head and his mouth twitching in his dreams. I wanted to scoop him up, hold him against my aching heart. I loved him as much as if I'd given birth to him myself.

'Asleep at last,' Giuseppe said, creeping up behind me. He touched my shoulder and leant over the basket, his breath sour with wine. 'Shall I carry him to the house?'

'I'll do it,' I said. 'You keep your friends entertained.' I stood up, ignoring his helping hand.

'But I've had enough of them. My wife and son will do me just fine for the rest of the night.'

He swayed a little, blinking, his eyes red-ringed and bleary.

I knew he would fall fast asleep as soon as his head touched his pillow and I hoped he wouldn't keep me awake again with his snoring. If so, I would move into Dario's little room, warm above the inglenook situated directly below. I'd taken to keeping a thick counterpane beneath his cot and folding it double to use as a mattress on the floor.

The first time I'd slipped from our matrimonial bed had been exactly one month after our hastily-arranged wedding ceremony. Giuseppe hadn't tried to make love to me once. Each night we lay together like two stone figures, carefully keeping to our own sides of the mattress.

One morning I woke before him. In his sleep he'd thrown his left arm over me. I could hear the steady beating of his heart. I watched the rise and fall of his chest and gazed on the hair where his nightshirt buttons had come undone. His mouth was slightly apart, his breath morning-stale, and there was stubble on his chin and upper lip. I tried to imagine what it would be like to feel his roughness against my face, neck and breasts. Then the cockerel crowed in the barn next to our house and my husband opened his eyes. Seeing me staring at him, he rolled over and turned away.

That evening I boiled water in the cauldron in the hearth and after Dario was settled in his cot, I sponged my body clean and washed my hair, adding fresh rosemary sprigs to the water to release oil and sharp perfume. Then I sat by the fire in my nightgown, brushing my long hair until it shone. Giuseppe found me waiting when he came in for his supper. I was hunched on a milking stool staring into the flames and he pulled me gently to my feet and led me upstairs.

But it had been no good. I could tell he was only being kind. He kept his eyes closed all the while he held me in his arms, saying nothing. I wanted to melt into him but my mind wouldn't let my body abandon myself to him. All the while I thought of the girl who had died, Dario's real mother, and images of her and Giuseppe making love filled my head. I lay there rigid, like the wooden doll Babbo had carved for me one Christmas when I was quite little. With its stiff smile and arms clenched tightly at its sides, Babbo had even thought to make its little legs misshapen like my own.

Eventually Giuseppe gave up with his love making and returned to his side of the bed. 'Don't you like it?' he asked.

'No,' I whispered back, tears trickling down my cheeks, unseen in the dark. 'No, I don't.'

If he couldn't understand that I wanted him to make love to me with passion and not because of a sense of duty or pity, then how could I explain? It was better not to be loved at all. But I said nothing.

Since that time he'd tried once more when he was very drunk. On that occasion he was clumsy with me and I pulled the counterpane from the bed and moved to Dario's room, positioning the nursery chair against the latch so he couldn't enter.

I wondered how it was possible we could talk about so many subjects – plants, books, livestock and of course little Dario – but we couldn't talk about us. In my heart there was a storm that needed to break and my heart hurt like thorns on the wild *rosa canina* growing in the hedgerows.

NOW AND THEN

Chapter 25

Late August 2010 – Anna and Alba travel to England

Francesco left Anna and Alba at Arezzo station where they were to start their journey back to England. On the train to Pisa airport Alba sat in her own world, eyes closed, ear-phones plugged in to her music. Anna thought she was so beautiful; her long, thick lashes looked almost false, fanned above sun-bronzed cheeks. She loved her as fiercely and protectively as the children she'd had with Francesco, but she knew it was no good to wrap them in cotton wool. Alba was nearly nineteen now, ready to spread her wings and start her own journey but, like any loving parent Anna feared for her vulnerability and safety.

Despite the latest Donna Leon mystery on her lap, Anna had no energy even to pick it up to read. Tense and fatigued, her skin felt stretched across her face, tight like a rubber mask. She'd promised Francesco to let him know straight away about the doctor's diagnosis and told him not to worry - although she herself was more than anxious. As they pulled away from the station she stared out of the compartment window. An assortment of graffiti defaced once beautiful buildings lining the tracks and everywhere was grimy, as if nobody cared about the world they inhabited. In the outer suburbs, flats were like boxes piled on top of each other: rubber gloves, brooms and cleaning paraphernalia decorating most of the balconies. Through an open window she glimpsed a woman folding laundry from a basket, a bicycle parked in the middle of her tiny living room.

They changed trains at Florence and the districts along the railway lines were even uglier. Washing hung down the sides of filthy *palazzo* walls, more graffiti tattooed every building, pigeons huddled on crumbling ledges. It was all very different from shiny tourist brochures depicting the sights of Ponte Vecchio and Piazzale Michelangelo. Although desperate to get to England, Anna was already missing her beautiful fresh corner of rural Tuscany.

The scenery improved slightly as they approached Pisa. Sunflower fields dotted the flat landscape and ancient abandoned farmhouses bore witness to an exodus from countryside to city.

On the plane they grimaced as they drank stewed tea from polystyrene cups.

'Who'd want to be an air-hostess?' Anna remarked, watching a pretty girl and slim young steward manoeuvre a cumbersome food trolley along the narrow gangway.

'Why do you say that?' Alba asked, looking up from the in-flight magazine she was flicking through.

'It's not exactly a glamorous job, is it? They're just like waiters – except they work in difficult, restricted spaces.'

'At least they get to travel,' Alba retorted, 'and see new places.'

'You've really been looking forward to these few days away, haven't you?'

'Yep!' she said, stuffing the magazine back into the seat pocket in front of her. 'I can't wait to get to Newcastle to see what the university is really like. I've looked at all the info on line, but glossy photos and the real thing might be different.'

'Very wise! Keep an open mind.'

They held hands as the plane descended – each convinced it was the other who needed reassurance about bumpy landings. The Italian passengers broke into applause as the wheels touched the runway at Stansted and Anna smiled at the idiosyncrasy. She'd only ever come across Italian passengers who applauded the pilot for a safe landing. Once they had gone through passport control and customs, they kissed each other before catching separate trains.

'See you in a week in Newcastle, then,' said Anna, waving her stepdaughter goodbye. 'Make the most of it.'

'Good luck with Aunty Jane.'

Anna smiled, although inside she was a wreck. The prospect of her sister's bossy company was as nothing compared to her fears about the upcoming appointment with Jane's doctor.

Jane offered to accompany her to the surgery but Anna turned her down. 'It's only a routine check-up,' she lied. 'You're better off staying here and packing a couple more boxes while I'm gone.'

It was good to be away from her sister's incessant chatter and gossip about her bridge-playing cronies. She had forgotten how domineering a personality Jane was. She constantly admonished her for not using the bubble wrap and tissue paper efficiently and if Anna had had to listen once more about the next-door neighbours' inconsiderate lighting of bonfires or untidy guttering, she would have happily dropped Jane's precious Wedgewood ornament collection onto her quarry-tiled kitchen floor and walked out to let her get on with the move by herself.

The walk through the smart neighbourhood to the Edwardian building housing Doctor William's practice took under ten minutes. Along the way she noticed front gardens with neatly clipped hedges and weeded beds brimming with colourful plants. She couldn't help thinking that if these gardens had been in Italy, tidy rows of vegetables would be growing where this palette of roses and frothy flowers bloomed.

At the doctor's she leafed through a dog-eared sailing magazine in the waiting room while rehearsing what she would say to the doctor. The walls were hung with amateur paintings of seascapes and an assortment of still lives. She admired a naïve water colour of a jug of sunflowers, wondering where she could hang it in Il Mulino and then decided against its purchase, the price tag of £250 putting her off.

'I'm Doctor Pennington, the locum. How can I help you, Mrs Starnucki?' The lanky young doctor had made the typical English mistake of mispronouncing her surname. He looked hardly older than Alba, she thought, wondering for how long he'd been qualified.

'My name's Italian - pronounced with a 'ch' sound, doctor,' she corrected.

'Ah, so sorry! Languages never were my strong point and we have an increasing amount of difficult surnames in this practice.'

He asked her a little about Italy and where she lived. Then he told her he'd only been to Italy once - to Rimini for a stag-do - and he'd managed to miss his flight home. All the while Anna was half relieved she was getting no nearer to the issue of her fear of dying from terminal cancer and not being around to see her children grow up. And then, totally unexpectedly, she started to cry. The young doctor handed her a box of tissues and she began to voice her worries while he listened, his legs stretched out beneath the desk and his too long arms folded in his lap. When she had finished and apologized several times for her tears and blown her nose, he smiled kindly.

'Please don't say sorry. That's what we're here for - to listen and see how to help.' He looked at the notes in front of him. 'I see from the forms you filled in at reception that you're in your mid-forties, Mrs Starnucci,' he said, pronouncing her name correctly this time. 'You might be going into early menopause... But your symptoms are indicative to me of a number of things, so I'd like to examine you first and I'll tell you where we go from there.'

After he'd finished, he spoke to her from behind the curtain he'd pulled round the couch so she could dress again in privacy. She thought it quaint after he'd been feeling all round her pelvic area and asking intimate questions about her sex life. But his respect was professional and comforting.

'In view of the fact that you're returning to Italy next week, I'd like our nurse to take blood samples and send them off immediately to the lab. I'll mark them as urgent,' he said, looking up from his notes. 'One is for the ovarian cancer you're so worried about. The lab can measure the level of a protein called CA-125 produced by ovarian cancer cells... '

Anna leant forward in her chair to say something but he interrupted her. 'I don't believe that's what is wrong, however. But we need to allay any concerns.'

She watched as three phials of blood were extracted from her left arm, thinking how amazing it was that this dark red liquid, her life-force, might soon provide answers.

'We should have the results back in two days' time,' the young nurse said, 'so make another appointment to see doctor then.'

Standing up to open the door, Doctor Pennington shook her hand and told her to keep busy and try not to brood. 'We're having lovely weather at the moment. Go for walks in the park, go shopping, visit a garden centre - anything but sit at home and worry.' His handshake was firm, confident and Anna walked away with her fingers metaphorically crossed, desperately wanting the next two days of helping Jane to fly past.

***

'Down it! down it! down it!' the students shouted, thumping on the bar tables, bottles and glasses vibrating with every hand beat. A tumbler toppled over spilling brown liquid into a boy's lap. He stood up and stared at his wet crotch. 'Fuck that!' he shouted and tipped another half pint over the head of the girl leaning into him.

Screams, laughter, whistles as the girl stuck out her boobs, her wet T-shirt revealing she wore no bra. She clambered up onto the bar, gyrating to David Guetta pumping from loudspeakers.

'Off! Off! Off!' he shouted and the rest of the mob took up the chant as she moved her hips provocatively to the music.

Alba slipped out of the university Union building. Icy air blasted her after the student fug. Not being used to northern weather, she'd left her denim jacket back in her room in Ricky Road, the Halls where she'd been allocated a room for this late Open Weekend.

She had tossed and turned most of the night and finally giving up on sleep, she crawled out of bed at 6 a.m. to plan her itinerary from leaflets left on the desk. It had turned out to be a long busy day and she was tired now, as well as shivery cold. She'd sat in on a sample lecture on the Romantics given by an attractive post-graduate from the English department, been shown round the vast library, computer clusters, sports centre, various cafes and the beautiful quadrangle. Afterwards she went into town. A volunteer student had given her a whistle-stop tour of some of the city, which she had really enjoyed, including the Sage building and the new Millennium Bridge over the Tyne, pointing out the best bars. The city was sparkly steel and a pleasing combination of modern and industrial Victorian and she'd enjoyed its cosmopolitan atmosphere more than viewing the university departments.

It was now approaching midnight. and she'd had enough of today. To keep warm she decided to jog back to her room, pretty confident she knew the way. There were plenty of street lights to help her – unlike back in Rofelle where nights of full moon or a torch were the only way to see the way after sunset.

She took a left, past an all-night Londis store. A huddle of young lads wearing thin shirts, despite the raw weather, were arguing on the pavement over what midnight snack to buy. She avoided a puddle of vomit and stepped out to cross the main road. A car screeched as the driver slammed on the brakes, swerving to avoid hitting her. Automatically she had looked left at oncoming traffic, forgetting that in England cars drove on the opposite side of the road. The driver kept his hand pressed down on the horn, lowered his window and shouted, 'Bloody students, look where ya gaan', before accelerating into the night.

She stopped half way across the road on a traffic island, her legs wobbling from the near miss. When she felt ready, she checked for approaching traffic, making sure to do the opposite of what she would do in Italy. Safe on the other side, she turned left again and found herself on a path flanked with parkland. There were no street lights here and it felt wrong – the path seemed to be leading away from the built-up area of the city and into countryside. So she turned round to retrace her route and promptly collided with a cyclist.

Alba came to, unsure whether the stars were in her head or in the black sky.

'Ya alreet, pet?'

A Hoodie, a scarf tied bandit-style over the bottom half of the face was bent right over her, frowning with concern. 'I didna see ya at all, like.'

Alba liked the Geordie accent; it would go well set to music, she thought randomly and then immediately winced, hoping she hadn't broken anything.

'I've been and called for an ambulance, pet,' the Hoodie continued, 'it's on its way now. Don't move until it gets here, like…if it ever does, mind.'

Hoodie pulled down the scarf to reveal a pretty young girl wearing bright red lipstick, a stud in her right nostril just like her own. Or was it her left nostril, Alba wondered. It was too complicated to work out, lying on her back. She felt woozy as well and hoped she wasn't going to be sick, because these were her only clean clothes.

'I'll stay with ya now, until they come. Are yas a student? What's ya name? I'm Manda. Stay awake for me now, pet...ya might have concussion. I'm not a nurse or nowt but that's what I've seen on the telly, in Casualty, like.'

While they waited for the ambulance to arrive, the two girls exchanged details. Manda was sweet and friendlier than any of the students Alba had met at Open Day. She worked in a boutique selling vintage clothes and chatted away about her favourite Forties outfits, determined to keep Alba awake. Most of the students Alba had met that day had been stand-offish. She had given them the benefit of the doubt, thinking they might be shy. But a lot seemed immature and self-absorbed.

At A and E, a kind nurse phoned Anna. There was nothing broken but they made Alba stay in overnight in hospital to check the bump on her head was nothing serious. Manda left as soon as she knew Alba was going to be fine and they swapped e-mail addresses, promising to keep in touch.

When Anna arrived before lunch the following day, Alba was already up and dressed and sitting in the visitors' room leafing through old magazines, a box of painkillers in her pocket and a bandage supporting a sprain to her right wrist. She was surprised when she burst into tears the moment Anna hugged her, but her stepmother assured her it was delayed shock.

Later on, sitting in the Slug and Lettuce, eating a large burger and chips, Alba apologised once again. 'I'm so sorry, Anna. I've dragged you all the way up here away from your sister.'

'You dragged me away just in time. Before I committed a gruesome murder,' Anna replied, setting down her cappuccino, thinking how unnecessarily huge it was compared to cups of coffee in Italy.

'How come?' Alba asked, adding another squirt of spicy relish to her burger, enjoying the chance to eat "fast food rubbish", as her father disparagingly described it.

'I couldn't do a thing right. I was given lessons at the start on how to wrap china tea cups and saucers in tissue paper, how to clean out a cupboard with bleach, how to use a duster more efficiently – she told me off for flicking mine. When I wanted a break she wouldn't let me drink my tea from a mug, saying it was common. And when I tried to throw out her manky dried flower arrangements - well past their sell-by-date - I thought she was going to have a heart attack.'

Alba laughed, 'Sounds a whole bundle of fun - *not.*'

'Oh I could go on, believe me. But I won't. Just take it from me I was more than pleased to have a genuine excuse for leaving early.' Anna left the remainder of her tureen of cappuccino and called for the bill. 'What would you like to do now? Are there any more lectures or talks you need to attend?'

Alba shook her head. 'I'm done,' she said.

'What about a spot of retail therapy? We've got a good four hours left, I reckon, before they close. Let's hit the shops... if you feel up to it?'

Alba wished later she'd filmed the fun they'd had. She could have sped it up, set it to honky-tonk piano music, faded the colours to sepia and edited it with those scratchy features old films had down the sides of the screen. Charlie Chaplin, eat your heart out, she thought.

They tried on hats: trilbies, cloches, deer-stalkers, wedding extravaganzas covered in lace and flowers, fascinators and bobble hats. Alba's wrist was too sore to pull on trousers, but in Primark Anna tried cheap skimpy jeans that took no prisoners and expensive designer dresses in Fenwick's, wondering when she would ever wear them back home in Rofelle. They sprayed themselves with perfume testers in the Beauty department until Anna said they were starting to smell like a brothel.

'What's a brothel smell like?' Alba asked, genuinely curious.

'*I* don't know…it's just something my mother always used to say. Now, lead me to the next shop.'

In the end the only purchase was made by Anna. She treated Alba to a pair of purple Converse trainers and then they headed for the water front and found a bar where they ordered a bottle of crisp white Chenin blanc, instead of a pot of tea.

Anna kicked off her shoes and wiggled her sore feet.

'I'm out of practice with shopping,' she said, raising her glass to her stepdaughter, 'but I've enjoyed every single minute of this afternoon. Thank you so much!'

'Thank *you*!' Alba smiled, 'It's been great.'

'I wasn't going to say anything before telling Babbo,' Anna said, 'but I can't keep it to myself any longer. You can be the first to help me celebrate.'

'What are we celebrating?' Alba pulled a horrified expression. 'Oh my God - you're not expecting, are you?'

Anna spluttered on her drink. 'No, no, nothing like that! I'm celebrating being well.'

She explained how she'd convinced herself she was seriously ill and how Aunt Jane's young locum doctor had checked her over, sent her off for tests and then told her she was suffering from an under-active thyroid. 'I should have worked it out for myself really, because my own mother and maternal grandmother suffered from the same problem.'

'Is it serious? Will you get better?'

'Of course, darling. The doctor took blood tests and he's very confident of his diagnosis. It explains my tiredness and the reason I've put on weight,' she said, patting her stomach. 'I'll have to take tablets – forgotten the name of them, Levo-something or other. But he's sending all the results for me to give to *dottor* Renzi. So, *alla salute!* Literally - good health!' They touched glasses and Anna topped them both up.

They were quiet for a while. Anna leant back into the squishy mock leather sofa and looked round the wine bar. It was only 4.30 in the afternoon but, save for a couple of silver haired ladies tucking into strawberry cream teas, most customers were on the wine. She wondered if anybody else was celebrating good news like hers.

'Cocktail hour obviously starts earlier here than in Italy,' she commented.

'The English like their drink. Last night it turned wild in the Union bar. I felt a real outsider. I mean, I like a glass of wine too and we always have it with our meals at home, don't we? But last night they were drinking like they were never going to see alcohol again. I didn't like it.'

'Apart from last night, what do you think of the university?'

Alba wrinkled up her nose and helped herself to a handful of salt and vinegar crisps. 'I'm in a muddle.'

'What about?'

'I *love* Newcastle. It's great - so different from home. I mean - sorry, don't get me wrong, Rofelle's fine and everything. But it's too far from anywhere and every time there's a party or film or whatever, it means driving down a million and one bends wherever you want to go to – Rimini or Sansepolcro…'

'Everything's on tap in a city like this,' Anna agreed, resisting reaching for the snack bowls. She knew once she started on peanuts she wouldn't be able to stop, and the mirrors in the changing rooms had shown her she needed to start tummy exercises right now.

'Exactly!' said Alba. 'I like the idea of studying somewhere like this, but I'm going off doing English or architecture.'

'What would you prefer to study? Italian, maybe? You'd get a place, no problem.'

'No, no, no – not Italian. What would be the sense in that?' Alba threw up her hands and shrugged, looking so much like her father that Anna wondered why she had never noticed the resemblance before.

'I feel I need to leave Rofelle for a while,' Alba continued, 'but where to and doing what, I just don't know.'

Anna settled the bill, staggered that half a bottle of ordinary enough wine could have bought a couple of good bottles of Montalcino back home.

As they pulled on jackets and gathered bags, Anna suggested Alba ditch her university digs and come and share her comfortable B&B room in Jesmond Dene. They took a taxi to pick up her belongings from Ricky Road and Anna sat on the bed in the grubby single room, watching her stepdaughter stuff her toilet bag and change of underwear into her rucksack.

She pulled open the safety door and helped carry Alba's bags because her wrist was hurting now the painkillers had worn off. Together they walked through the twilight streets, joining the throng of people hurrying home.

'Your best subject at school was Art and I've always thought you were a talented painter,' Anna said. 'Why don't you follow that route, Alba?'

'I do still love my art but I thought Babbo wanted me to do something academic. Art seems so … self-indulgent.'

'That's a silly thing to say and he would agree with me,' Anna said, tugging Alba to a standstill, causing a mini pile-up as two shoppers bumped into them.

As they walked on, she advised Alba to follow her heart and pursue her talent.

'But what if I'm no good at it? It's one thing your own family thinking you're good at painting. But what if the rest of the world thinks I'm crap? It would be a waste of time and money.'

'What-ifs go nowhere, Alba. And that sort of talk isn't like you! You're normally adventurous, a free spirit. What's up?'

'It's all so daunting and confusing.' Anna said, digging her hands deep into her jacket pockets.

Back in the B&B Anna flicked on the little kettle to brew a hot drink for them both. As they sipped Earl Grey and dunked ginger nuts, Anna said she'd come up with an idea. 'I'll make a quick phone call and then I'll tell you about it.'

'But…'

'Just wait and see. Trust me!'

'Okaaaay,' sighed Alba, flicking through the channels with the remote control.

Once they'd returned to Rofelle and Anna had thrashed over the idea with Francesco, plans for Alba were finalised. A couple of weeks later, she waved goodbye to all her family at the airport, on her way to Stansted for the first part of her homespun Gap Year. André – Anna's hairdresser from her England days – was meeting her at the other end with his husband Marcus, the manager of a highly successful Surrey Art Gallery. The couple had been toying with the notion of buying a retirement home in Tuscany since renting Il Mulino and falling in love with the Italian way of life. However they would need to subsidise their pensions with a business and learning Italian was definitely going to be necessary for their idea of running a gallery in their new dream home. So, three months board and lodging in exchange for Italian lessons and part-time help in their Surrey gallery had been agreed with Alba.

'Yes, darling girl,' Marcus had gushed over the phone to Anna. 'Absolutely brilliant! Send her to us. We'll soon find out if she's got talent in the art department. We shall simply *adore* having her. Lovely, sweet girl!'

And André was heard to ask, 'Has she still got that vile blue hair? We might have to adjust that slightly - always with her agreement, of course.'

One fledgling was fleeing the nest and embarking on her own life journey, like many others before her, Anna thought as she enveloped her stepdaughter in a hug.

'Don't forget, if it doesn't work out, we're always here for you in Tuscany,' she said, stepping back to let Alba go.

They watched her as she snaked away from them through the security queue, waving and blowing kisses each time they caught sight of each other. And then she was gone.

Returning to the car park, Francesco caught hold of Anna's hand. 'I hope she'll be all right.' he said.

She touched his cheek with her free hand. 'Of course she will, *tesoro*. Don't worry!'

'She's never been abroad on her own. It's a big step.'

'I know. But it's what we talked about last night, remember? The time has come to let the first of our chicks try her wings. She needs to go; she's more than ready. Come on, let's get these other babies home.'

Chapter 26
Anna and Francesco - 2010

Anna was up first next morning. After she'd laid the breakfast table, she propped an envelope for Francesco against a jar of fig jam. While she waited for the rest of her family to surface, she went outside to dead-head geraniums in terracotta pots dotted round the patio, wondering as she worked how Alba was enjoying her new independence.

'What's this?' Francesco called from the kitchen, waving the envelope.

'Open it and see!' she said, coming in to wash her hands to chop strawberries and bananas for the twins' cereal. Davide was up too, his curly hair tousled from sleep.

'That's enough, Davi,' Anna said as he dipped his knife deep into the jar of Nutella. 'You've more spread than bread on your plate.'

'*Uffa*!' he grumbled. 'Without Alba here you're now going to notice everything we do even more.' He scraped off some of the thick hazelnut spread and wrinkled his nose at his mother. 'You're making me waste food, Mamma. And that's worse than eating too much Nutella.'

Anna winked at him and shrugged a very Italian shrug.

Francesco read out his card: 'Keep next weekend clear for a child-free *Great Escape*! Love from a secret admirer xx.'

Emilia jumped up to read over his shoulder. 'Can we come too?' she pleaded.

'It says 'child-free'. *Doh!*' Rosanna said, tugging her twin's plait. 'Mamma, you can't be a secret admirer if we all know your handwriting. Silly you!' she said.

'Babbo and I are going to have a little break on our own,' Anna said. 'There are no guests in Il Mulino this week, so it's perfect timing. And while we're away, Aunt Teresa is taking you to Aqua Splash in Rimini. It's all been arranged.'

'Yay!' came the chorus from all three children. The twins high-fived and, amidst all the fuss, Davide scooped Nutella back onto his bread.

With breakfast cleared and the kitchen to themselves, Francesco took Anna in his arms. 'It's so good to see you happy again, my darling,' he said, nuzzling behind her ear. 'I've got my old Anna back.'

'Less of the old, please!' She kissed him long and deep and he murmured appreciation. 'Mmm! Pity I've got to go to work today. I can think of plenty of other things I'd prefer to be doing.'

She slapped him playfully and laughed. 'Right! Especially with children running in and out all day long.'

'I wish you'd talked to me before about your health worries, Anna.'

She put a finger to his lips, 'Don't start again, Francesco!'

'Don't forget Emilia's medicine, Teresa.' Anna said, zipping up the picnic cool bag for Aqua Splash. 'She needs to take another 5 ml. dose this evening and...'

'You've already been through this twice with me,' Teresa laughed, hugging her sister-in-law. '*Don't* worry! We'll be fine.' Picking up the bag, she turned to the siblings. 'Come on then, gang! Kisses and hugs all round and then into my pickup, or we'll be late and miss all the fun.'

Anna took her time filling her leather weekend bag. Usually packing was a hectic affair. Alba used to do her own but, although the twins and Davide tried, Anna invariably had to sit with them and start again from scratch. She selected a couple of dresses she'd hardly worn. There were few occasions to dress smartly in the mountains. A new silk nightdress, pretty lace underwear, sandals and, at the last minute a bikini, were folded into the bag.

Despite Francesco's protests Anna drove. 'This is *my* surprise trip,' she said. 'You can drive us back.'

'I wanted to plan a trip for you,' he said. 'Anyway - where are we off to?'

Pulling on her sunglasses and adjusting the mirror she told him all would be revealed in due course. 'Unless I get lost – in which case you'll have to map read.'

They drove south via Sansepolcro, stopping for a coffee break on the outskirts of Arezzo. To Anna, the landscape was picture-postcard Tuscany. Fields of sunflowers, olive groves, neat lines of vines and cypress trees punctuated with squat farmhouses with terracotta roof tiles. The kind of clichéd image on labels of Italian food products. It was picturesque in its own way but she found it tame and structured - less natural than the countryside they called home.

Over coffee and brioches she finally told him their destination, hoping he would be pleased. 'I've booked a two-night stay in an *agriturismo* just outside San Quirico d'Orcia.'

'Wonderful! I've never been.'

'I remember you saying that and I wanted to choose somewhere to explore together for the first time.'

'I'll drive next,' he said, 'then you can enjoy the scenery.'

'I *am* a little tired. It's so much hotter down here.'

She'd planned a straightforward route along the *Autostrada* but Francesco opened the map and showed her alternative roads further inland. 'It might take us an hour or so longer,' he said, tracing his finger south to a town called Lucignano. 'But we could stop for lunch in this pretty hilltop town. And afterwards loosely keep to the old *transumanza* route.' He pointed to a minor road on the map.

'I'd love that. But I told the lady at the guest house we'd arrive at about six o'clock. Is it do-able?'

'*Perfettamente!*'

Their lunch was a simple affair - slices of mushroom and artichoke pizza with bottles of water bought from a bar. After wandering round the mediaeval town laid out in a maze of interesting piazzas, they sat under the scented shade of lime trees to eat their snack, preferring to save their appetites for an evening meal.

'This is a little jewel,' Anna said. 'There must be hundreds of places like this dotted round Italy waiting for us to explore.'

'This is just the start then, *tesoro*. We'll have to take more time-out.' He pulled her to her feet and she reached up to kiss him. 'I'm bursting with kisses,' she said, finding his lips.

'And I'm not complaining.'

The scenery after Lucignano changed as they entered the undulating landscape of the Crete Senesi, the rolling hills in the province of Siena. At one point, near San Giovanni D'Asso, Francesco stopped the car at the side of the road so Anna could take photos. 'I need a better camera to capture this view,' she said, gazing at the unfurling hills. A welcome breeze blew along fields of wheat so they looked like rolls of unfolding yellow fabric. Clouds above were frayed and ragged and, where crops weren't planted, the hills were ash-coloured and lunar.

Francesco pointed to a huddle of white dots on a far hill. 'A small flock,' he said. 'What a timeless scene! Just imagine thousands more sheep trailing down this road. It would have been a rough *strada bianca* in the time of *bisnonno* Giuseppe, their hooves stirring up dust like thick smoke.'

It was approaching six thirty when they pulled into the parking area at *Agriturismo Girasole*. The location at the edge of town with its pretty stone buildings was even better than Anna had imagined. The owner showed them to their room in a former hay-loft. 'This is for your exclusive use,' Signora Leonetta said, indicating a tiny kitchen area and stylish sitting room with a sofa covered in fresh white linen. She pointed to a log-burner in the corner. 'But you won't need that,' she laughed. 'Tonight it's very *afoso* – this sultry weather means we're in for a storm.' She showed them the switch for the ceiling fan and indicated the wrought-iron spiral staircase disappearing into the roof space. 'Your bedroom is up there - and your bathroom.'

'It's beautiful!' said Anna.

'Very comfortable! And what time is dinner?' Francesco asked.

Signora Leonetta frowned. 'I am so sorry, *signori*, but the kitchen is closed tonight. My cook is ill but there's an excellent *ristorante* in town. And I can book you a taxi – on the house – as we have let you down.'

'How far is it?' Francesco asked.

'A fifteen minute walk.'

'Then we'll walk,' Anna said 'and work off all the calories from our meal.' She patted her tummy and the signora laughed.

While Francesco collected their luggage from the car, Anna climbed the winding staircase to explore where they were going to sleep. The bed was king-size and positioned opposite a wall-to-ceiling window overlooking vineyards that climbed towards the town walls of San Quirico d'Orcia. The golden light of sunset bathed the scene.

Francesco returned with the case and placed it on the luggage rack before coming over to stand next to Anna. 'This is a good find, *tesoro*! It's stunning.'

'I'm so pleased you like it.' She twined her arms round him. 'Shall we have a quick change and then wander up to the old town for dinner? I'm quite peckish.'

They walked through the bustling tourist town hand in hand until they found the restaurant. "Da Maria" was down a narrow cobbled street behind the imposing seventeenth century Palazzo Chigi. They opted to sit at a table outside and decided on the menu of the day, quite happy not to have to make choices themselves and they weren't disappointed. It was delicious homely food with starters of colourful *crostini* topped with peppery tomatoes, basil, mushrooms, local cheeses and cold meats, followed by a plate of homemade *tagliatelle* sprinkled with shavings of truffles. Afterwards there was a main course of a selection of roast meats with oven-baked aubergines and peppers.

'I think we'll splash out on good local wines to go with our meal,' Francesco decided, choosing white Pitigliano and a red Morellino of Scansano.

'This is nice,' Anna said after the waiter had left them alone. 'I don't know why we haven't done this before.'

Francesco took her hand and kissed the palm. 'We'll make time to do it again.' He gazed up at her. 'Anna?' She knew what was coming and withdrew her hand, busying herself with opening a packet of breadsticks. 'Don't spoil it, Francesco!'

'I'm not going to let you retreat into that shell of yours. Please try to explain why you didn't tell me what you were going through with your health.'

'I've said I'm sorry. Leave it!'

'You push me away when you're like this. We should be able to talk.'

She ran her fingers through her hair. 'You know what I'm like.'

'Yes, I do. And I should have probed more, but…'

'…life takes over with four children and jobs to think about and there's never any time and we end up talking in shorthand.' She sat back while the waiter went through the procedure of opening a bottle of Morellino, pouring a dash into Francesco's glass and waiting for his verdict. Francesco nodded his approval and the young waiter deftly poured wine into both their glasses without spilling a drop, before disappearing into the restaurant.

Anna tasted the potent wine and leant back in her chair. 'I promise to confide in future,' she said. 'But it's still hard for me to open up. You know what my childhood was like – the big age gap between me and Harry and Jane and my parents rowing all the time. I was left on my own so much and that's how I learned to cope with stuff - by being quiet and getting on with it by myself.'

'I know, *tesoro*, but your life is us now: me and the children and you. The past is over…'

'…it wasn't easy…it has its repercussions.' She put down her fork, no longer hungry.

'I don't want us to quarrel and I'm not judging you. But it's important to bring things into the open.'

'Like about you and Donna?' she blurted out, annoyed with him for spoiling the holiday mood. He wasn't Signor *Perfetto* either and shouldn't be lecturing her.

He stopped chewing and raised his eyebrows. 'What did you say?'

'You and Donna! I'm sure you were having an affair. Classic scenario: man in his fifties working with a nubile, long-legged young blonde with frumpy, stressed wife back at home...'

He roared with laughter. 'Are you being serious? *Donna?* She's only two years older than Alba!'

'Exactly!' She took a huge swig of the strong wine.

'If you think such rubbish, Anna, then that's all the more reason to open up to me about what's going on in that head of yours.'

'Don't be so patronising!'

The young waiter reappeared and hovered near their table. He cleared his throat. '*Signori*. Can I clear away your plates?'

Anna had left all her meat but Francesco told him to come back in five minutes. She watched him eat. Her kind, patient husband's hair was even more salt and pepper now, the lines round his eyes and mouth more pronounced but he still made her stomach flip. She wasn't really angry with him. She was angry with herself - for being catty and shutting him out.

'Deep down I knew there was nothing going on between you,' she told him eventually as she folded and re-folded her serviette. 'But I wasn't in a good place. I am sorry, really I am. I'll try to open up more.'

He took both her hands in his, stroking her palms with his thumbs. 'It makes me smile when I think of your imagining me and Donna having an affair. Mind you, I'm flattered you think I've still got pulling power!' He gave her a wicked wolfish wink and she pulled her hands away and picked up a knife, pretending to stab him. 'Oh, yuck, Romeo!' she said.

'I'll come clean,' he said and for a moment she was worried.

'She wasn't tall and blonde, Anna. She was short with shaved hair and she didn't believe in wearing deodorant, even on the hottest of days. Not my type at all!'

And then they both laughed.

A huge clap of thunder followed by fat drops of rain sent them scurrying inside the restaurant for shelter. As they stood waiting in the doorway the storm intensified, until channels of water flowed past on the cobbles like a mountain stream. The proprietor, a handsome young man in tight, fashionably-ripped jeans and crisp, tailored shirt, assured them it would soon pass and, after they'd settled their bill he offered them coffee and *liquori* on the house. They chatted for a while, comparing notes on the state of the tourist industry.

When the rain stopped, they decided to chance the walk back to *Agriturismo Girasole*. They were half-way down the drive when there was another intense downpour and they broke into a run, arriving at their room soaked through and out of breath.

'You have the shower first, *tesoro*,' Francesco said.

'We could have one together?'

She suddenly felt shy at her suggestion and as they undressed, she knew her embarrassment was ridiculous. They'd been married for more than ten years. But it had been a while since they'd had quality time on their own. At night their door was always kept slightly ajar in case one of the children should cry out and need them. When they made love it was with controlled passion, with the light off and the concern of early starts in the morning impeding any adventure in their intimacy.

Francesco turned on the shower and when the temperature was right he held out his hand and pulled her into the cubicle. He poured bath gel into his hands and gently rubbed soap into her shoulders, moving down slowly to her breasts. She gasped at the sensations his hands were playing up deep inside and pressed herself against him, kissing him passionately. He grew hard against her and then it was her turn to massage him, pleasuring him with soapy fingers until they could wait no longer.

Afterwards they laughed as they used towels to mop up the pools of water they'd managed to splash outside the shower tray.

Lying entwined on the bed, he stroked her tummy lazily. 'I love your curves - your undulating *crete senes*i...'

'...I have definitely more undulations and hills than when we first got together,' she giggled before feeling his stomach, 'but is this the beginnings of a paunch, *tesoro mio*?'

'But I especially love your tummy that has carried three beautiful *bambini* for us to cherish,' he moved down to plant a dozen kisses on that part of her.

She pulled his hand to her mouth and kissed each finger in turn. 'I love you so much,' she whispered.

Propping himself up on one elbow, he looked down on her. 'I love you too.'

She envied his ability to fall asleep so quickly. Before switching off the bedside light, she lay for a while on her side watching the rise and fall of his chest as he drifted into sleep, thinking how precious this break was proving to be; how important it was to work at keeping their magic from fading. A prayer her own mother, Ines, used to recite to her at night before she tucked Anna under her bedcovers suddenly came to her:

"I lay my body down to sleep, I pray to God my soul to keep. And if I die before I wake, I pray to God my soul to take."

She shivered, thinking how terrifying it had sounded to her as a little girl and how terrifying it still was. She didn't want to die for a long while yet. There was too much life to live with Francesco and her adored children. And for starters, there was the whole of tomorrow to enjoy before returning to La Stalla. She smiled as she switched off the light, thinking that maybe they could spend the morning in this king-size bed.

Chapter 27
Christmas Eve 1932
Marisa

Life followed the pattern that mountain folk from the Apennines had kept to since Etruscan times. Each year our men, boys and sometimes whole families continued to leave for the Tuscan coast, as autumn deepened its hold on the peaks.

Old sayings are founded on truth and experience and the elderly would mutter as they cast their gaze to the mountains: '*Quando l'Alpe mette il cappello, vendi la capra e compra il mantello*'. And indeed, when the Alp of the Moon donned its hat of snow, peasants who knew they were bound for the coast would sell a goat to buy a cloak and prepare for their journey.

They would return with the swallows in early May to let sheep and cattle loose on a mix of wild flowers and fresh grass sprouting on our mountain slopes. And families had to learn to get to know each other again after months of separation. While the men had been away, women had grown used to independence, chopping kindling and logs for the hearth and shovelling paths through metres of snow. On cold grey days, which we called 'wolf season', we locked up hens and roosters early on crisp nights and took to carrying stout sticks in case predators should venture near.

At first it was strange for us when these tasks were resumed by our men in the summer months. In turn, they felt hemmed in by white-washed ceilings instead of open skies. As a result of homecomings, babies were conceived. After the desire of first urgent couplings were satisfied, a few shepherds would decide to sleep once again in the freedom of open meadows above their villages, together with their sheep and dogs. And there were some women who breathed sighs of relief when the men departed from their beds. They fingered rosary beads in church and prayed for forgiveness from Our Lady whilst beseeching Her to send their monthly periods, for there were already too many mouths to feed.

At thirty eight years of age I still hoped for a child of my own. So far it hadn't happened. But Dario was my pride and joy and I thanked God each day for our little son.

Giuseppe was away in the Maremma again and I was putting the finishing touches to Christmas gifts for Dario, humming as I worked. I'd unpicked an old jumper of Giuseppe's that he no longer wore because the elbows and cuffs were worn. I'd dyed the wool a deep emerald green from the leaves of sweet reseda gathered from the slopes of Montebotolino. Before sewing the pieces together, I planned to embroider a line of steam engines across the chest from new wool I'd combed out with teasel heads.

Despite never ever having set foot near a railway station, our son was train mad. At the end of autumn Giuseppe had carved a tiny steam engine from a log of soft wood found floating in the river and we'd concealed it at the bottom of the trunk at the end of our bed. I'd also knitted a pair of cosy bright red socks and, later on I would stuff walnuts and biscuits into the toes. It was a shame Giuseppe was always away over Christmas and couldn't see the joy on his little son's face as he found his gifts.

December had been unseasonably mild. Usually Montebotolino was cut off from the rest of the world by snow and the roads became impassable even for the little horses of *San Francesco*, as we liked to call our donkeys. Mountain people enjoyed a special affinity with snow. It was harsh but precious at the same time, beautifying our landscape, turning it soft and dreamlike. Icicles hung from gutters like crystals and snowfalls were plentiful, bringing a silence and enchantment that gratified the soul. Children used planks of wood to slide down the shaggy slopes, tying them to their feet with laces 'borrowed' from adults' boots to fashion makeshift skis. And woe betide if laces weren't replaced. It was an interlude of innocent fun snatched by little people usually occupied with household chores. When snow impeded the routine of fetching water in heavy copper jugs, setting snares for pole cats for their highly prized fur or looking after animals up in the meadows, our children could enjoy a brief taste of freedom. For a while they could own the mountains instead of the other way round.

But this year snow had still not fallen. The sun shone. Primroses had started to open yellow faces prematurely to the sky and there was spinach beet still being harvested from summer vegetable plots.

I planned to finish Dario's jumper later, after I had rolled out pasta for the first course of our Christmas lunch. In the larder I'd left chunks of boar to marinade in rosemary, garlic, olive oil and white wine. Last week I'd baked a *panettone* which was sitting on the shelf below. *Borlotti* beans were ready in a round bottomed bottle to cook overnight in the embers of the hearth. All that remained was a trip into the woods to hunt for our Christmas log.

Dario was playing football with a pig's bladder on the grass in front of our house.

'Come with me to look for the *ceppo*,' I called. But he was having too much fun with his little cousins, Stefano and Simone, so I told him I would take Chicco the dog, instead. 'I won't be long. Be good and don't make a nuisance of yourself,' I called.

Giuseppe's youngest sister, Maria Rosa, waved me off, telling me not to worry. 'He's a treasure, aren't you, Dario?' she said. 'Don't worry, Marisa. He'll be as good as gold with us.'

I smiled as Dario's cousins started to tease him, pretending to kiss him, 'as he was such a good *tesoro*,' asking me when they should change his nappy and wipe his nose. It was good natured fun and I liked to see him playing with other children. He was too often in the company of old people. That was the way it was with our style of life in those days. There was insufficient work during winter months and more and more families were leaving villages to find work elsewhere. Giuseppe's other sister, Nadia, and his younger brother Angelo had departed a couple of years ago, taking my mother-in-law with them. Life on the coast was easier now that malaria was almost eradicated, they said, and they'd found permanent work and a house to share on a big farm near Alberese. We only saw them when they returned in August for the summer holiday.

But this Christmas was a special treat for they had come up to stay, hearing about the mild weather. The village had come alive again. I hadn't appreciated how much I'd missed ordinary sounds of other families' routines until they weren't there: mothers calling to their children to come to table, the scraping of chairs on stone floors, the clatter of a saucepan being dropped, followed by ripe swear words. I feared the mountains themselves would also become an echo of the past. The landscape was changing, reverting to woodland, with pockets of untended meadows slowly swallowed by untamed undergrowth and saplings.

Wrapping my shawl around my waist, I fetched a length of rope to drag the Christmas *ceppo* home. This Christmas log would be ceremoniously burnt as we gathered round our fire. Then, calling Chicco to heel, I set off for the beech woods.

In November whilst foraging for nuts and acorns for our pig, I'd earmarked an unusual log, half covered in moss. When it first caught my eye I'd stopped, heart hammering in my bosom, legs turning to jelly, thinking it was a corpse. One end resembled an outstretched arm, twiggy skeletal fingers pointing to the sky. When I realised it was my imagination playing tricks, I'd laughed out loud in relief. With its protuberances and strange shapes, it would be perfect once flames started to lick at it. The more fantastical and mysterious its form, the better the flames would dance. I imagined sitting by the hearth on Christmas Eve taking it in turns to blindfold Dario and his cousins and guiding them towards the fire. Then they would beat the log with sticks, chanting: *'Caca ceppo, caca ceppo...'* urging it to cough up in the hope that when they opened their eyes, the log would magically have produced little gifts for them all.

Afterwards we would climb the steps to our church for midnight mass sung in Latin. Last Christmas Dario had been fascinated by everybody's breath in the cold stone chapel and asked me why they were smoking invisible cigarettes. But this year it was too warm.

I'd left a pile of stones as a marker to remind me of the turning. It was darker here under the trees, the undergrowth musty. Mouldy fallen leaves were slippery underfoot. I had to bend to avoid snagging myself in a bramble bush and I stumbled. My left hip made contact with a boulder and I screamed in pain. Winded, I stayed where I was for a minute or so, biting my lip in agony, tears stinging my eyes. When I tried to get up, I couldn't put weight on my legs. Chicco came over, licking my face and whining. To try and right myself, I grabbed hold of his neck. 'Good boy, Chicco. Stay and help me.' My old companion waited as I tried to heave myself up, but the pain was excruciating and I passed out.

I don't know for how long I fainted but when I came to, darkness was falling. I tugged my shawl from around my waist to wrap around my shoulders. Even that was an effort. And Chicco was nowhere to be seen.

Chapter 28

Christmas 1932

Giuseppe

My old friend and mentor Paolo passed away half way through December. The malaria fevers he'd dreaded so much had returned to his body. We had a saying, we mountain people, that it took one whole year to grow rich in the Maremma, but only six months to die - "*In Maremma si arricchisce in un anno e si muore in sei mesi*". Paolo's holiday in the Maremma, his *vacanza maremmana*, as we sarcastically described it, had come to an end.

I made up my mind. Word had filtered down about the lack of snow in Montebotolino. For this reason and because of Paolo's death, I decided to surprise Marisa and travel up for Christmas Eve. I would also be able to offer personal condolences to Paolo's widow, Rossella. The journey to the mountains was normally out of the question at this time of year because of ice and snowdrifts, but with the tracks being clear, I would be able to visit Rossella and tell her how peacefully Paolo had met his end. I'd omit the truth about his suffering: the fevers, delirium and painful stomach cramping he'd endured. By the time the priest had arrived to administer Extreme Unction, Paolo was unconscious, the malaria had taken its evil hold. I'd stayed with him to the end trying to offer comfort, holding his hand and talking to him about old times in case he could hear.

I packed up the couple of tins of salted herrings he had purchased at Grosseto market before falling ill, as well as two lengths of cotton material for his twin daughters. For myself I kept his *bastone del febbricone*, the special stick he'd proudly and successfully used several times on sick sheep. It was a shame he'd been able to use its powers to cure animals but not on himself.

Christmas in the camp was normally celebrated without fuss. Don Mario would come down a few days before the feast to say Mass for us if he could, and we would spend the day itself resting. If we were lucky, *polenta* would be supplemented with a hunk of sausage or *Cotechino*. In the evening as we relaxed round the brazier, a couple of shepherds might play tunes on their mournful *zampogne* bagpipes made from sheep's hide, and if there were any spare chestnuts, we would roast them in the embers. How good it would be instead to be home sitting at my hearth with the people I loved best.

I managed to hitch part of the ride home on the back of a cart laden with cheeses and hams bound for the festive season in Arezzo. The driver had known Paolo and, as we parted at the edge of the city, handed me a whole *Pecorino* cheese, telling me to give it to his widow and daughters. The city was bustling with shoppers and travellers, people were in good spirits and the smell of roasting meat and spice filled the air.

As luck would have it, I spotted the son of the owner of the *osteria* at Viamaggio Pass, his cart laden with casks of sweet Vinsanto, and he made a space for me on the back. I nodded off for much of the journey as the horses pulled us up the winding roads. The fresh mountain air woke me as we arrived at the top of the pass and I spent an hour inside the hostelry warming up and chatting to old acquaintances. Everybody was commenting on the strangely mild weather, wondering what we were in for afterwards. After lingering over a couple of glasses of red wine, I decided to walk the rest of the way home. I loved my mountains, their peaks sketched against a clear sky and I breathed in the crisp air with greedy gulps, smiling as I imagined how surprised Marisa and Dario would be to see me. I couldn't wait to see the look on their faces.

After just over one hour of brisk walking, and with light fading fast, I turned the corner into the square adjoining our house. Nobody answered when I knocked on our door, so I popped over to Maria Rosa's house, where a candle glimmered at the kitchen window. Peeping through the panes I saw my son and his young cousins playing by the fire and I tapped on the glass.

'Marisa? Is that you?' my sister asked as she pulled open the door, baby Flavia on her hip. When she saw me she gasped and covered her mouth with her hand. She pulled me into the kitchen, embracing me as she whispered, 'I didn't want to worry young Dario but something's wrong.'

She glanced over to my son who hadn't yet seen me, engrossed in a card game on the floor. 'Marisa went off to look for a Christmas log on the ridge two hours ago but she's not back. I'm sorry, Beppe, I couldn't leave the children alone to go and search for her. Thank God you're here.'

It took me less than five minutes to fetch a paraffin lamp and length of rope from the house. At the last minute I grabbed a bottle of *grappa* from the corner cupboard in the kitchen. The sun would soon be gone behind the peak of Montebotolino and I had to hurry. Even though a full moon was due, conditions and visibility would be far from ideal for a night search. I had a good idea where she might have gone and as I started up the steep path, a shape bounded towards me out of the gloom. Instinctively fearing it was a wolf I drew out my knife but urgent barking made me drop to my knees. 'Chicco! Good boy! *Good* boy! Where is she?' I patted his head and he scampered away up the slope.

If it had not been for the dog, I wouldn't have found her that night. She was wedged behind a rock about ten metres off the path and when I got to her, her eyes were closed. I thought for a moment she was dead and knelt on the forest floor, taking her frozen hands in mine.

'Beppe, is it really you…? Or am I dead and gone to Heaven?' she murmured, opening her eyes to peer up at me.

I was to repeat her phrase many times in the future when telling people the story of how Chicco and I rescued my plucky wife. She would slap me in embarrassment, blaming her confusion on her pain and fear. But all the same, everybody teased her each time the tale was told.

'You were the last person I expected to see in the middle of the woods on Christmas Eve,' she would say in her defence, 'you can't blame me if I was delirious…'

The children of the village knew our story off by heart. It was retold countless times at the fireside.

Later on at home, sitting by the hearth with the fire blazing and a blanket tucked round her knees, she sat and watched me as I moved about the kitchen. I tapped old tobacco from my pipe, packed fresh leaves into the bowl with my thumb and asked her if she was feeling any better.

'A little,' she said. 'But this bruise is painful. It's not helping my sciatica either. If you boil up a handful of rosemary leaves for ten minutes for me, Beppe, and then rub the liquid on my hip morning and night, that will help.'

I fetched sprigs of the herb from the patch outside the back door. Marisa said shyly when I returned, 'You know the best medicine is to have you home with us.'

It was unusual for her to talk this way and I smiled at her

sentimentality. While the leaves boiled in a little pan, the fire beneath it crackling and snapping, we sipped the remainder of the grappa I'd taken up the mountain. Dario was already tucked up warm in his bed. We decided to miss Midnight Mass as I'd promised to take him with me early next morning to fetch down the log that Marisa had taken so much trouble to find. In view of her accident we'd agreed it didn't matter if traditions were altered this year. We'd burn the *ceppo* on Christmas night instead of tonight.

'I like the smell of your pipe,' she said. 'I miss it when you're away. Did you know Rossella had started to smoke one? She looks so funny puffing away. She coughs and splutters all the time.'

I told her more about Paolo's death. She was very upset although we both knew his health was poor and talked about inviting his family to eat Christmas lunch with us the next day.

'I think we should leave them to grieve a while,' Marisa said in her typical wise way. 'But we'll keep an eye on her. Poor Rossella!'

She stared into the fire, her fingers working at a tuft of wool sticking up from the blanket. And then she laughed aloud. 'How many strange beliefs we have,' she said. 'Christmas Eve is when I'm supposed to receive special graces to strengthen my powers as a healer. Just look at the state of me! I can't even heal myself.'

'There must be some truth if the belief's been handed down over all these years. And it does no harm to anybody.'

I'd seen enough of these old superstitions over the past ten years of travelling with the shepherds to see the merit of practices that dated hundreds of years. If they worked it seemed foolish to discard them.

The rosemary infusion was ready and she pulled up her skirt to reveal a livid bruise. As carefully as I could, I dipped a cloth in the liquid to make a poultice. She winced as I put it into position, telling me not to take any notice of her whingeing, and then rearranged her clothes and settled down again on the bench.

It was very warm by the fire. Outside the wind had picked up, whistling at the cracks in the door.

'It wouldn't surprise me if we have snow soon,' Marisa said. 'But the weather has been strange. Do you remember how my father always used to say that snow in December meant a fruitful year? *Dicembre nevoso, anno fruttuoso.*'

'And mine used to say we were more likely to have bread on the table if there was snow; that rain brought hunger. *Sotto la neve pane, sotto l'acqua fame.*'

'They did know what they were talking about, our old folk. But I hope snow doesn't fall quite yet, Beppe,' she added shyly. 'We're so enjoying having you home unexpectedly.'

I smiled.

After a while I asked her how Dario had been while I was away. 'I tried talking about school when I put him to bed, but I couldn't get much from him. All he wanted to know were details about the *Appennino* train – how big the engine was, how much coal it burned. I kept reminding him the fare was too expensive for the likes of us and how I'd had to hitch rides on carts to get home. But he kept firing train questions at me.'

'He's not enjoying school. Did you know he now has to attend the youth movement on Saturdays? They all do. He's in the *Balila* brigade and they have to wear black shirts and caps.

'They're stuffing their little heads with propaganda,' I said, 'I don't like it.'

'He hates the military exercises. They have to march about with wooden guns and he said as there were only six in his group, when they make mistakes the *professore* sees straightaway and he's always shouting! Horrible little gnome of a man.'

'He's always been a bully.'

'Dario was in trouble last week for not learning his homework by heart.'

'A poem, was it? I could help him.'

'No, not a poem. If only it had been.' She sat forward in her chair, wincing with pain. 'I can quote his homework word for word because I tried to help him memorise it: "I believe in Rome..."' Marisa enunciated sarcastically, ' "...the Eternal, the mother of my country...I believe in the genius of Mussolini...and the resurrection of the Empire...".' She broke off, shaking her head and grimacing.

'Brainwashing! Like catching sardines in a net,' I said. 'And what he learned is not too different from our prayers, if you think about it. Very similar to the Credo. Just replace "Rome" with "God the Father".' I pushed a log further into the centre of the hearth with my boot and replenished my glass.

'I'm not happy about it either. But what can we do, Beppe? If we want him to attend school, then this is now a part of it. And we would be punished if we stopped sending him. I heard that Pierluigi kicked up a fuss in the *osteria* the other week about his boy having to attend military exercises on Saturday. He wanted him to stay at home to help. Somebody must have reported him because a group of older boys in the *Avanguardista* turned up the following night and he's disappeared. They say he's probably been sent down to Rome to work on the Pontine Marshes. It's supposed to be worse down there than the Maremma for malaria. And all simply for wanting his son to help on the farm.'

'*Porca Madonna,*' I swore. 'Mussolini promised us so much. It looks like we'll have to suffer before Italy will be strong again in the future.'

'Yes, but for how long do we go on suffering, Beppe? They talk about children begging in the streets in big cities...that's surely not right...what sort of progress is that?'

This was the old Marisa from the days I remembered when we were young and used to sit for hours discussing how to change the world. Her cheeks burned pink and her eyes flashed with anger as she spoke

'Best to keep this kind of talk within these four walls, from what you say.' I warned.

'And not in front of Dario either,' she added. 'If he mentioned at school that we disapprove, there'd be trouble for all of us.' She leant forward again, whispering, 'Do you know what he actually quoted to me the other day, Beppe? "War is to the male what childbearing is to the female." And then he asked me why I hadn't done more childbearing... I nearly choked on my food.'

'So much propaganda,' I replied. 'Get them while they're young and then you have them for life - just like in the seminary.'

'It's hard to know what to do for the best. Over my dead body will he become a little warrior for our nation. Maybe he will have to become a train driver, after all.' She stared into the fire.

'And what's so wrong with that?' I asked.

'He's too bright. I want more for him. Perhaps we could send him away to your seminary?'

'There is no way my son is attending that place.' I left the fireside to reach again for the grappa bottle but it was empty.

'There's a bottle of wine in the larder,' Marisa said. 'But I was saving it for Christmas lunch.' She looked at me before continuing, 'You promised me you would cut down on your drinking.'

'Then I'll go to the *osteria* and drink with the men. They won't nag me,' I wanted to bite back the words as soon as they left my mouth.

'Please, Beppe,' she said softly, patting the space next to her on the bench. 'It's Christmas Eve. Don't spoil it.'

I stood for a while staring down at her. Firelight danced off her curls; her face, so deathly pale when I found her lying in the forest, was now flushed from the warmth of the fire. She was a pretty woman and I felt ashamed of the way I was with her. My respect for her had grown and grown since the time she'd taken on Dario with never a complaint.

I sat down again. It was stifling in the little room and I was more used to sleeping in a hut or on the ground with a dozen men. I pulled off my thick jumper and rolled up the sleeves of my vest.

'It's boiling in here,' I said.

'If you want fresh water to quench you, I fetched it from the spring yesterday. Get a bottle from the larder – that'll cool you down. I'll have some too.'

As I handed her a tumbler of water, she held on to my hand. 'What *did* happen to you at your seminary, Beppe?'

I pulled my hand away and sat down next to her.

'You've never talked about it, have you?' she persisted. 'But I know something went horribly wrong. Otherwise why are you so dead set against Dario having the education you wanted.'

I shook my head and remained silent.

'Well then,' she said, 'we shall drink something stronger than spring water. I made walnut liqueur and Christmas day can begin early. It's on the top shelf.' She pointed to the corner cupboard.

It was fiery, brewed the usual way from pure alcohol, watered down to half its strength. She told me she'd added sugar and soaked a hundred shelled walnuts in it for the whole of November. It was good and strong and helped loosen my tongue.

I knocked back several glasses and began to tell her what had happened all those years ago, sparing no detail of the abuse. I spoke softly in case anybody should be listening, even though I knew there was only Dario upstairs and he was fast asleep. When I told her how I'd always felt it was my fault, she put her arms around me.

'How could you ever think you encouraged him?' she whispered. 'He was a wicked, vile man and you were too innocent to know about the evil he was intent on.'

'Exactly, Marisa! That is why I've no wish for our son to go through the same torture as I did. How can we protect him if he's so far away from us?'

She turned my face to hers and kissed me on the lips, long and slow. Our kiss grew more passionate and my tongue played with hers. She tasted of walnuts and honey and as I cupped her face in my hands, she moved deeper into my hold.

'I'll bring the bedcover from downstairs,' I whispered.

Over and over I asked if I was hurting her, if her hip was too sore and I made love to her as gently as possible.

It might have been the walnut liqueur; it might have been because I knew I had come close to losing her to the mountains, I don't know. But for the first time in our marriage, Marisa relaxed as she lay with me. The fire crackled and spat in the hearth and our lovemaking made shadows on the walls of the kitchen. When she came, I covered her mouth to still her whimpers in case Dario awakened and came down the ladder from his room.

Afterwards she cried soundlessly in my arms. Tears streamed down her face and I pulled her closer, wiping them with my thumbs, worried I'd yet again done something wrong.

'Did I hurt you?' I asked. 'Was I too rough? It's been too long...'

She shook her head. 'No, you didn't hurt me, Beppe. I'm just happy.'

It worried me that when I went to drink at our *osteria* on Christmas day, one or two of the men gave me the fascist salute instead of shaking my hand as we'd always done. I laughed at first, thinking they were joking, but they scowled at me. I wondered what would become of us all. On the wall behind the counter hung a poster of Benito Mussolini, *il Duce,* in his battle helmet. The Great War had taken lives but it had happened at a distance from most of us. But now, twenty years later, our nation seemed to be preparing for another war. Our children were being groomed to be part of a nation of warriors. Dario had proudly shown me his colourful exercise books. One of them displayed a picture of a young boy in uniform, with the caption: "Book and rifle make the perfect fascist." Mussolino was bent on recreating the glory of the old Roman Empire which seemed to lurk as the background to our children's lessons. My son had shown me his uniform hanging on the back of his bedroom door and stood to attention. 'I'm a legionary', he'd said, clicking his little heels together. And my heart sank to my boots.

On the feast of Saint Stephen, I left once more for the coast. Storm clouds threatened in a sky pregnant with snow. If I stayed, it might be months before I could return to my work.

Before leaving, Marisa and I talked and talked about Dario's future. We agreed not to send him to any seminary but to let him continue with his schooling in Badia. She persuaded me to make this my last journey down to the Maremma and urged me to bring Nonno's forge in Montebotolino back to life. There was still blacksmithing work to be picked up from a few small farmers and shepherds who had decided to overwinter their stock in barns up in our mountains. We would manage, she told me.

'Our little Dario will fall right,' she persuaded me, 'with the two of us to guide him. As long as we are careful, we can instil in him the values we believe in.'

Marisa and Dario clung to me at the door. My wife begged me to come back soon, telling me she couldn't wait to be together with me again. For the first time in all these years I left for the Maremma with a lighter heart and hope for the future.

Chapter 29

A trip to the Tuscan Coast

September 2010

At five o'clock on a Sunday morning, Francesco, Anna, the twins and Davide boarded a coach bound for Alberese, down on the Maremma coast.

Most of the passengers were pensioners and they greeted the youngsters with smiles of delight. Francesco explained they were coming along because of Davide's school project and Anna chipped in, telling them she was coming along out of interest in the *transumanza*.

'But *we're* only coming because we have to, *uffa*!' piped up Emilia.

Rosanna dug her in the ribs, 'Shut up! Babbo promised us big ice creams if we behaved, remember?'

'If you want to know about the *transumanza,* come and talk to us,' said a slight, elderly man with a beard. 'My father and his father before him went down to that godforsaken malaria infested swamp each year. Bless their souls!'

There were murmurs from several of the older passengers, which set off an exchange of information and reminiscences all round the coach.

Stars were still shining overhead as the coach set off down the bends towards Sansepolcro. Anna couldn't help eavesdropping on the elderly couple sitting in front of her. Their silver heads inclined towards each other as they chatted, most sentences were prefaced with, 'I remember... 'as they shared stories from their youth. The passengers all knew each other and seemed a happy band of old friends. She listened to their chatter as they exchanged news of who had been in hospital, whose grandson had just graduated and who was the latest of their pals to be afflicted with dementia and, once again, marvelled at the sociable nature of Italians.

They passed by the rambling house of the Chiozzi family on the way to the Viamaggio Pass where Giselda now lived with her cats and where, once upon a time, shepherds and flocks joined the caravan as it straggled along from villages and hamlets tucked into folds of the Apennines. Near the house and clustered beneath a huge oak stood a group of fallow deer, one huge stag with impressive horns standing guard. They scattered as the headlights of the coach picked them out.

Dawn broke as they reached the plains, the coach speeding along the straighter road to Arezzo. Birds perched on telegraph wires like rows of pegs on washing lines and mist hovered over newly ploughed fields. A scattering of sunflowers bent under the burden of their heavy seeds, floated above the morning mist and resembled rusty shower heads.

It was a long journey. Francesco dozed but Anna enjoyed gazing out of the window, taking note of names of towns crowning the Tuscan hilltops: Monte Amiata, San Galgano, Roccastrada, the names like phrases from a poem. Davide was engrossed in his Harry Potter book while his twin sisters made friends with an elderly couple on the back seat, every now and again reporting to their parents on how wicked their new friends were. Signor Micheli had taught them a couple of rude jokes, whilst Signora Micheli had described how naughty she'd been as a little girl.

'Babbo,' said Emilia, 'do you know what she and her friends used to do in the piazza?'

'Shock me,' Francesco said, opening his eyes.

'Well - they used to wee on benches and then hide and spy on people who came along. The people would wipe the wee away with their hands and say stuff like, "I hadn't realised it had rained..." And then they'd sit on the wee...' Emilia burst out laughing as she finished her story.

'But they didn't ever wee on the bench their own Mamma used to sit on,' interrupted Rosanna.

'Thank heavens for that!' laughed Anna.

'And they used to knock on the orphanage door and run away,'... took up Emilia.

'...until one day the nuns opened the door as soon as they'd rung because they must have got fed up and been waiting for them and this huge boy orphan ran out to chase after them...'Rosanna continued.

'...and Signora Micheli's little cousin lost his shoe while he was running away from the big boy and they all got told off when they got home but they didn't tell their parents how it happened,' finished off Emilia.

'All much more fun than being slumped in front of television,' said Francesco.

'But quite naughty, don't you think?' Anna glared meaningfully at her husband.

Four hours later the views from outside the coach turned to flat landscape. Reclaimed ground that had once been marshland early in the twentieth century was now planted with olives and vines. Small flocks of black and white sheep dotted the gentle slopes. The road ran along a canal and as the coach trundled past, dozens of egrets fluttered up from the water like large white handkerchiefs.

Anna was disappointed with the centre of Alberese. She'd expected more than the bland wide square lined with tall unattractive buildings. A parched palm tree drooped in the middle of a patchy grassed seating area, its benches covered in graffiti and rubbish littered the ground. And Francesco was peeved to find the museum closed. A notice on the door explained that, due to lack of funds, it would remain closed for the foreseeable future.

'That's a great shame,' he said. 'I was hoping to show you lots about the *transumanza* - photos and documents and old tools. How very frustrating!'

'*Pazienza!*' Anna said. She found it a useful word. She found many ups and downs to living in Italy, not least the bureaucracy. It was frustrating the way anything that should be easy had to be complicated. It seemed there was no sensible reason for this other than to keep pen-pushers busy in their hidden-away government offices.

'Never mind,' said Davide, who was secretly pleased he didn't have to poke around a museum. 'I've already got enough information from Babbo and Giselda.'

'And we'll be fine on those swings over there, won't we, Emi?' said Rosanna.

With an hour to spare before the special fish meal that was a part of today's coach tour, Anna and Francesco opted to drink *aperitivi* at a bar next to the playground.

'*Cin cin!*' said Anna, clinking her tall glass of Aperol against Francesco's. He was still fuming about the museum. 'I definitely wouldn't have dragged you all down here on a four-hour coach journey if I'd known the museum was closed. It's a long way to come just to eat fish.'

'I don't mind, *tesoro*. I'm enjoying being out and not having to think of cooking. Cheer up! We'll have fun today, don't worry.'

Lunch was the usual gargantuan Italian feast. After a glass of Prosecco served with trays of crostini, there were numerous starters, each plate whisked away as soon as it was empty: mussels, razor shells, morsels of tuna steak with tomatoes in an oil dressing, clams and giant prawns. On came the *primi*: linguine with baby lobster claws and risotto with fresh mussels. When Anna thought there couldn't possibly be any more to eat, the waitress appeared again with a plate piled high with fried octopus and more giant prawns. All this was served to the fifty or so people from the coach who were chatting and laughing, knocking back wine and sharing nostalgic memories of how life used to be down on the coast for their ancestors. At one point Francesco was invited to referee an animated discussion between a couple of hunters as they bantered about the differences between hunting boar up in the mountains and down at the sea. He held up his hands in surrender after a couple of minutes and said he preferred to remain neutral.

Amazingly, the children had room for ice cream but Anna and Francesco opted for strong *espressos* and Anna vowed she would never, ever eat again.

'But you know you will,' Francesco said, his fingers massaging the back of her neck. 'Do you think we should be offering meals at Il Mulino?'

'That would be a definite N - O,' Anna said. 'Far too much work.' She pulled Francesco up from where he was sitting, 'Let's go for a walk and work off some of this meal. I can't sit here all afternoon. In fact – lead me to the cemetery!'

He groaned. Anna's interest in graveyards was something he still couldn't fathom. When she'd taken him to England on a winter break before the twins were born, he couldn't believe it when she'd dragged him off to look round grave stones dotted around Norman churches. She'd read out names and old-fashioned inscriptions to him and it gave him the heebie-jeebies to think of bodies buried so close to a church and nearby houses and not in cemeteries at the edge of town, as was the Italian way.

'The children won't want to come,' he said, hoping to dissuade her.

'We'll promise to take them to the beach afterwards. They'll be fine. They could do with a walk too.'

**

Alberese was a small town so the cemetery wasn't far. The children refused to enter until Anna set them tasks to discover the strangest names. 'But no running off!' she warned. 'Stay in sight.'

Emilia found a *Famiglia Scoccianti*, translating as "annoying family"; Davide a *Bellabarba* - "beautiful beard"; but they all decided Rosanna's *Famiglia Gattamorta* or "dead cat", had to be the winner.

The name that Anna stumbled upon was the most intriguing.

'Hey, here's one of our long lost relatives,' she called to Francesco, gently pushing aside russet petals of fresh chrysanthemums in a vase in front of a gravestone. They were in the area where Francesco had explained poorer people were buried; below ground as opposed to in family vaults where plots were more expensive and generally preferred. Anna had laughed when he told her his mother always asked to be buried where there was a good view. And he had made sure of that for her in the little cemetery in Rofelle. They went together regularly to tend the family grave and Anna liked the way the dead were never forgotten.

'Look,' she continued. 'Starnucci! And she was married to a Giuseppe. Wasn't that your grandfather's name?

'That's a coincidence,' said Francesco, let me see.'

He knelt on one knee and read out the inscription:

'STARNUCCI LUISELLA, NEE SCIOTTI
WIFE OF GIUSEPPE
DIED MAY 1923, AGED 23

OUR SON, YOUR PARTING GIFT
PAX

'She died in May 1923.' Francesco paused before he turned to Anna with a frown and added, 'The same month and year my father was born!'

'Another coincidence?' Anna said.

'Must be!' He stared at the plain stone grave. There was no enamelled photo displayed on its surface like on other tombs nearby.

'Aren't you curious?' Anna asked, 'wouldn't you like to meet another possible relative of yours? I'd be itching to - it shouldn't be difficult to find out more about her, Francesco.' She altered the arrangement of flowers so the inscription was more visible. 'These are fresh flowers that somebody's arranged.'

'We can't wait around to see who comes to tend her grave,' Francesco said, standing up and brushing soil from his trousers.

'No, we can't,' said Davide... '*please* can we go now? This place is soooooo spooky.'

'And I'm starving again,' Emilia said, rubbing her stomach.

'You're *always* starving,' Rosanna retorted.

'Come on then, everybody,' said Anna, 'for now, we'll take it as a coincidence – the beach calls.'

As they all walked towards the sea, Anna put her arm through Francesco's. 'You're not going to leave it like this, are you *tesoro*? It's like ignoring a whole possible chunk of your history.'

'It's probably a coincidence. Somebody else's history...'

'...but, what if it's not? Don't you want to at least try and find out more? You'll be forever wondering who this young woman was otherwise.'

'Now's not the time. The children don't want to go poking around that cemetery anymore. It's not fair on them.'

Several fellow diners were now wandering down the dusty lane between Mediterranean pines towards the beach. Blue-green water lapped a clean sandy shore and Anna and Francesco sat together watching their children run free at last, splashing at the sea's edge.

Francesco was very quiet. He skimmed pebbles into the waves and seemed deep in thought.

'You're thinking about that girl, aren't you?' Anna asked, snuggling up to him. 'I think we should go back.'

He smiled at her, 'You know me so well. Give me a minute.' He stood up to brush sand off his chinos and went over to talk to the twin's elderly friends.

Without hesitating, signora Micheli came over to Anna with Francesco, 'Don't worry about your beautiful children. We'll keep an eye on them for you.'

'Please, pretty please,' Rosanna said, joining her hands in prayer. 'We want to stay here, Mamma - we'll be as good as gold.'

'But - ' began Anna.

'No buts, signora,' cut in the old lady, 'it will be an absolute joy. You can trust us.'

Her white-haired husband added, 'Our three grandchildren live in Australia now and we miss them, so it would be an absolute pleasure for us to be grandparents for the day to yours.'

'Please Mamma and Babbo...' This, from Emilia.

'Look what lovely new grandparents we've found. Aren't we clever?' Rosanna added.

Francesco and Anna walked back towards the cemetery entrance where an elderly man was tidying fallen leaves and dead flowers into a bin next to a water stand. Large empty detergent bottles stood ready for use as watering cans.

Francesco went over to him. Anna watched as in answer to her husband's questions he shook his head and then spread his hands in the Italian way. Then, as Francesco turned, the old man shouted after him, 'Try Perpetua. She knows everybody and everything! You'll find her in the church.'

'Listen, Anna - if Perpetua's not in church, I'll leave it be.'

'Fingers crossed then we find her'

Then he laughed and said, 'Perpetua – it's a nickname traditionally given to a priest's housekeeper who would faithfully serve him.' He winked at Anna. 'Possibly serve him in more ways than one...'

The church door was open and, after adjusting to the gloom they made out a stout woman in a polka dot pinafore bending over a metal candle rack. She was chipping dried wax from the holders and on the gleaming marble floor beside her was a bucket containing rags and cleaning products.

'Signora Perpetua?' Francesco asked, as he approached her.

'*Signorina*,' she corrected, as she turned round. She had squint eyes that were difficult to focus on, bow legs and a cross face sprouting a creditable moustache.

Anna stifled a giggle, determined not to look at Francesco in case her giggles turned to uncharitable laughter, thinking the old lady would have made a prickly mistress.

'How can I help you?' Perpetua asked. 'The crypt is closed to visitors and I've only two minutes to spare before I leave.'

'I'm looking for any relatives named Starnucci who might live here. I'm Francesco Starnucci. There's a grave in the cemetery...'

'...I'm sorry,' she said, collecting up her cleaning paraphernalia, 'I don't know that name. But there are plenty of newcomers in this town. Including foolish foreigners who buy up ruins for holiday homes. Our town has changed too much over the years.'

'It's just that there are fresh flowers on that grave...'

'Signore, I'm very busy.'

Francesco fished a visiting card from his wallet and handed it to her. 'Here's where you can contact me, signorina, if you come across any information.' He shook her hand and placed two Euros in the offertory box next to the candles.

'Oh well, at least you tried.' Anna said, as they linked hands outside in the bright sun.

They were almost back at the beach when Francesco's mobile phone rang out. 'This could be Alba,' he said, 'I hope so. We haven't heard from her for a few days.

'No news is good news, remember!' Anna said.

It wasn't Alba. She heard him arrange a meeting with somebody called Carla in half an hour's time and after making sure with Signora Micheli that all three children would be safe for another hour and promising to be no longer, they made their way back to a bar in the *piazza*. Buckets, spades, lilos and plastic beach shoes hung from a rail outside. A blackboard displaying exotic cocktail drinks served in coconut shells and umbrellas draped in raffia completed a tired and tatty décor which had nothing to do with Italian seaside.

Carla was a petite brunette in her mid-twenties. Her hair was plaited round her head and she wore frayed denim shorts with a skimpy white peasant blouse that showed off a tattoo of dove's wings on her left shoulder. The only other customers were four old men playing cards on a corner table covered in Formica. Carla's eyes lit up as Anna and Francesco entered and she came from behind the counter to welcome them.

'Signori Starnucci? Can I offer you something? A *digestivo?* Coffee?'

'Nothing at all for me,' said Anna, covering her stomach with her hands.

'We've just finished eating for the whole week!' Francesco added.

Carla laughed, 'You've obviously just had the Sunday Special at Belmare. Let's sit outside. It's quieter.' She indicated a table and chairs shaded by a luxuriant bougainvillea. 'Signorina Perpetua called me and told me you are relatives of Luisella? I've often wondered about her. But my great-grandmother used to say it was a secret whenever I asked about her and nobody dared persist. *Bisnonna* was scary.' She chuckled. 'All our family had to do was keep Luisella's grave tidy. But it's always made me sad to think she had no family who cared about her. On the *Festa dei Morti*, when my parents visit our relatives' tomb, I make sure I go to Luisella .'

'I'm not sure if we are related,' said Francesco, 'but it's uncanny her husband was called Giuseppe – as was my grandfather who used to come down to Alberese. And on her grave it shows her baby was born in the same month and year as my own father.'

'It wouldn't be impossible,' Carla said. 'With families separated, all kinds of things happened all the time - bigamy, children born out of marriage... And I know many babies were left in the orphanage here during the time of the *transumanza*.' She shrugged her shoulders.

'But why does *your* family put flowers at her grave?' Francesco asked.

'Well, *bisnonna* was a midwife. Mamma told me the story of how she'd delivered a baby boy to a Luisella Sciotti all those years ago and that she was paid to take care of her grave after she died in childbirth.'

'What a sad story,' Anna said.

Carla showed them an intricate gold ring on her right hand. 'I had this made from a pair of earrings that Luisella's husband gave *bisnonna* by way of payment. I inherited them when she died. They weren't my style and so I had them adapted into this.' She started to pull the ring off her finger, 'I should give it back to you if you think you're related...'

Francesco covered her hand with his, 'Absolutely not! You're very sweet but I'm not at all certain I'm related to this poor girl.'

'Anyway, a pair of gold earrings can't have been sufficient payment for all the years your family have tended her grave,' Anna said.

Carla pushed the ring back onto her finger before getting up to return to her bar work. 'She's become part of our family now. I think of Luisella as an adopted relative. And it would feel strange not to tend her grave. It's never been done in the hope of payment, you know.'

Anna hugged her. 'You're a good girl. It's been so special to meet you, Carla.'

'We'll see you again, I'm sure,' Francesco said, clasping her hand in his.

The children waved at them as they approached the shore but continued happily with what they were doing. There were several driftwood structures dotted about on the sand and Anna and Francesco sat watching as the twins ran up from the waves and started to weave in and out of the sea-bleached sticks. They draped seaweed flags over the top and then returned to the water's edge, hand-standing near the waves. Their adopted grandparents, the Michelis, stood watching them nearby, clapping when Emilia performed three perfect cartwheels. Davide had joined up with a boy of his age he'd met in the restaurant and they were engrossed in building a huge Tower of Pisa out of sand.

'How lucky we are,' Anna said, snuggling in to Francesco's arms. She reached for a shell, fingering its smoothness, admiring the way it curled into a secret interior, before slipping it into her pocket as a souvenir of the day.

Chapter 30
Francesco - 2010

On a mild and sunny Sunday in early October, Francesco left La Stalla after lunch to clean the footpath that led from Montebotolino to the remains of fortifications along the Gothic Line.

He needed the workout after an indulgent lunch and relished the chance of a couple of hours' solitude. The view of Alpe della Luna across the river valley was like a watercolour in the autumn haze. He hacked at brambles blocking the path, wondering who might have been the last walker to come this way. Maybe it was himself, the last time he had pruned and clipped, for there were never many walkers in these parts. This area was a tourist route waiting to be exploited and as he worked he thought through some guided walks he could present to the tourist office.

Fluffy white seed heads and tendrils of Old Man's Beard were beginning to strangle saplings and juniper bushes and he cleared away as much as he could. It was satisfying to see the difference his labour was making. At the top of the peak of Montebotolino he stopped to pick an apple from a tree that sprouted a couple of metres from the bank of an old gun emplacement. As he bit into it he mused on how it might have come to grow in such a remote spot. Had it perhaps been a tree grown from the core of an apple, eaten by a young German waiting by his machine gun in 1944 – a blond-haired, blue-eyed, homesick lad maybe? He'd eaten the apple and flung the core from his trench where leaf-mulch, rain and sun had done the rest.

When he had finished clearing the undergrowth, Francesco made his way down the steep path and along the dirt road to where he'd parked his car on the edge of the deserted village.

Storm clouds were looming to the east but he reckoned he had half an hour before rain fell. He would treat himself to a few extra minutes in Montebotolino before returning to the happy chaos of his family. Some folk found it a ghostly place. It was dubbed 'the village up in Paradise' by a local author and he tended to agree. However he was torn between wanting it to remain secret and coming to life once again. He liked the idea of the village being restored to how it once must have been when his great-grandparents had been alive. Montebotolino had been famous for its carpenters and he imagined the sounds of hammers and sawing echoing from the stone houses. Now all he could hear were the last summer cicadas and the leaves rustling in oak trees as he made his way along the grassy paths. And it was peaceful.

He wandered away from the little piazza with its metal cross erected in 1925 still standing proudly in the centre, and along a steep ridge leading to the church of San Tommaso with its *campanile.* It had once served as a defensive tower but now housed church bells. The neighbouring house was owned by the Curia and it was crumbling away. The roof had tumbled inwards and what was left of the walls was now propped up with metal beams.

On an ancient, twisted apple tree, a laden harvest of red fruit stood out against the old stones of the bread oven beside a house that Anna's father had rented. Like several others this had a bar and padlock guarding its door, for thieves were frequently tempted to this isolated spot, foraging for anything old they could lay their hands on. Even rusty rings secured to outside walls, once used to tether animals, were considered saleable. Not even the Curia's house was considered sacred, Francesco thought, as he picked up a discarded pack of cigarettes. He couldn't understand tourists who came to the countryside seeking beauty and tranquility, yet who selfishly left litter before returning to the city.

His grandmother Marisa's house was for sale, along with another couple of houses in the village. The new property tax on second homes was flooding the market with dwellings selling for ridiculously low prices. Francesco would have loved to pass down Marisa's house to Alba as a special eighteenth birthday present, to keep it in the family. But the place was falling apart. It would be a money pit and he and Anna needed any extra income for their children's education. He undid the padlock on the front door and pushed it open. The house was riddled with damp and woodworm and the floor of the upper storey had rotted away. Somebody wealthy needed to fall in love with his grandmother's wreck of a building and restore it to its former state.

But was Marisa his real grandmother? Or was she Luisella Starnucci, nee Sciotti? He didn't know anything about Luisella but Nonna Marisa had been a legend. Everybody had something to recount to him about her. Like how gifted she had been at curing people's ailments with her herbs and potions and how very kind she was. How she would give away her beautiful embroidered pieces if anybody admired them. So much so, that there had been nothing to pass onto Anna who loved anything vintage and hand made.

And did it matter anyway? He'd heard say that knowledge of the past was important for freeing the future, but how could it be possible to know everything about the past? How many stories had been forgotten over the years? How many secrets or skeletons in the cupboard were lost in time because people were ashamed or felt their past was unimportant.

One look at the metal grey sky told him that heavy rain would soon be falling and he hurried away. As he turned left out of the garden area in front of Marisa's old house, he caught a movement at the top window. A shadow, or a trick of light? Or merely a piece of loose plastic taped across the broken pane?

For a moment he leant against his car, watching storm clouds gather over the valley. The plateau of Sasso Simone loomed through grey mist, marking the boundary between Tuscany and Le Marche, looking for all the world like an enormous helicopter landing pad. All that now remained of Cosimo dei Medici's fifteenth century fortress city up there were a few stones marking boundaries and parts of a road. What traces would remain of his own family home, Francesco wondered. Would Il Mulino and La Stalla crumble away like the fortress? And what of his family, made up of Italian and English cultures, that might never have been created if Anna hadn't arrived in Tuscany ten years earlier. What would remain of their stories once they were gone? He'd helped her discover who her real father was - not Norman the British POW - but Danilo, from this very village of Montebotolino. And now the same doubt over identity had crept into the history on his side of the family and Luisella might or might not have been his real grandmother. But there was no point in dwelling on might and maybe or chasing after the missing pieces of ourselves. People could argue for evermore between nurture or nature but we are what we make of ourselves, he concluded, and we can only do our best.

He scanned the mountains covered with untamed woodland, a few patches of flower-dotted meadow breaking up the blanket of green. The river Marecchia flowed like a silver artery in the valley down below, fresh and clear. And a saying of Anna's sprung into his mind. She'd told him it was from one of her favourite poems, as she'd recited it to him in their early days, one sticky afternoon when they'd picnicked by the river. Parts of it he'd never forgotten. Life was like "a bubble on the stream…an hour-glass on the run, a mist retreating from the morning sun."

'Which is why we have to make the most of it', she'd said, and so they'd made love there and then on the bank under a willow and laughed afterwards as they removed grass from each other's sweaty skin, Anna complaining ants had bitten her on her backside.

Chuckling self-consciously at his unusually philosophical thoughts, Francesco climbed back into his old car and drove down the mountain to his family, in time for afternoon tea.

Afternoon tea. English-style. In Tuscany.

Epilogue
Marisa - 1965

It was during the winter of 1957 that my Giuseppe developed a nasty chest cough.

At night I knew he was trying not to wake me. He'd pull the quilt up over his head to muffle the sound, but the metal bed ends would shake and clatter against the wall with each racking cough and I couldn't asleep anyway.

I tried several treatments on him: inhalants from rosemary and sage and juniper berries washed, boiled and filtered to brew liquids that I gave him twice a day. At first they soothed his cough. But one morning his pillow was speckled with blood.

I knew then there was nothing more I could do for him, except ease his symptoms.

Dario had a good job. At that time he worked down in Pieve Santo Stefano for the Forestry Corps and he insisted on paying for his father to visit a specialist in Arezzo. The X-rays showed shadows on both lungs.

We didn't tell him about the prognosis. Maybe it was selfish but I thought if I told him, he would go too quickly. I wanted him with me for as long as I could have him.

On a balmy afternoon, at the dying end of summer 1958, he asked me to come and help him in his *orto*. That was strange in itelf, because as a rule he loved to escape to his vegetable patch and work alone.

'I'm going to dig around my thoughts,' he would tell me and off he would go. He'd spend hours hoeing weeds, pruning his vines, digging chicken manure into the poor soil. He'd built a bench by the hedge from old oak floorboards, and he'd planted a fig tree beside it for fruit and shade. Oh yes – and an apple tree with Dario when he was very little. They'd sown a pip from a special type of apple – I forget the name now, but Giuseppe bought it from the fair down at Ranco. 'I might not live to sit in the shade of this,' he said, 'but maybe Dario's children will.'

And he was right – years later little Francesco loved to play beneath its branches, whilst baby Teresa slept in her basket, bless them both.

There was a wild plum tree too, which he'd transplanted to the Montebotolino side of the *orto* fence. It's not there now. It survived him by only two years. An early frost killed it.

'Come and help me gather plums,' he said. 'Then you can make jam and we'll be set up for winter.'

We arranged an old sheet under the branches which were so laden they almost touched the grass. *Thud, thud, thud* went the plums as he shook the tree. Some of the fruit rolled away and I turned to collect them for my basket. I heard one more thud and when I turned, I saw he was on the ground.

If I hadn't been there that afternoon he would have lain outside for two hours or more. Most likely he would have died frightened and cold, and alone.

As it was, he never set foot in his *orto* again. He was paralysed down his left side and he couldn't speak. I had to feed him, bathe him and dress him.

I'm glad I had him for those three precious remaining weeks. Like a mother tends to her baby, I did everything for him that a man should be able to do for himself. But he wasn't a baby – he was my husband. And even though he could no longer speak, he would gaze at me with those beautiful eyes of his. His eyes spoke for him. I saw tenderness there.

And I knew he loved me.

BIBLIOGRAPHY

Mi rivedo ragazzo – Florido Fanfani

Di Guerra si muore – Maria Grazia Linares

Testimonianze di ruralità montana – Maria Teresa Tocci & Alberto Santucci

I Percorsi della transumanza in Toscana – Paolo Marcaccini & Lidia Calzolai

Per non dimenticarli – Egidio Mascioli

Il Paese sul Paradiso – Marta Bonaccini

"Il bisogno aguzzo" – Associazione centro documentazione storica civilta contadina "Dino Dini".
and
"Su, Bellarosa...su, Pastorella!" – (La fatica e la speranza dei contadini) - Centro di documentazione storica della civiltà contadina "Dina Dini", Pieve Santo Stefano (AR).

The children's project at the Scuola di Badia Tedalda. (AR).

Religiosità e mondo rurale in Toscana by Matteo Baragli, Comune di Caprese Michelangelo (Museo della città del territorio) Edizioni Kappa

Il tramonto del sistema mezzadrile in Casentino – by Giovanna Daneusig

Maremma com'era by Renzo Vatti and Morbello Vergari

What is life? – by John Clare 1793 – 1864.

ABOUT THE AUTHOR

Angela Petch lives half the year in Tuscany and the other six months in Sussex. An incurable people-watcher, she believes there are still many untold stories waiting to be shared. So she is quite unashamed about striking up conversation with strangers whenever she travels. A prize-winning author, "Now and Then in Tuscany" is her second novel, a sequel to "Tuscan Roots", available on Kindle and in paperback on Amazon. Search with: myBook.to/TuscR

Thank you for reading my book. I'd love it if you could spare a moment to leave a brief review on www.amazon.co.uk or Goodreads. It is so helpful to authors.

You can also find me on Twitter@Angela_Petch
www.facebook.com/AngelaJaneClarePetch

Learn more about holiday accommodation that inspired the book's locations.
www.ilmulinorofelle.com

I look forward to hearing from you.

Researching the route of the *transumanza*: the Via Maremmana.

Made in the USA
Monee, IL
30 April 2020